The Art of the Kiss

Holly Schindler

The Art of the Kiss

Copyright © 2019 by Holly Schindler

Published by InToto Books

Cover images by LordRunar, courtesy of iStock

Fonts: SuperFly Brush Font by Sam Parrett, Deputy Serif by Black-Bird Foundry, Typewriter font by vetre.antanaviciute, Palash - Serif Font by CorgiAstronaut, Karl Geoff by Mas Anis, Contender Vintage Font by Viaction Type.Co, Shockwave by Dirtyline Studio, Milano Sky by Lef, Underland Script by Wacaksara Co., Coats by Piñata, all courtesy of Creative Market

Praise for The Art of the Kiss

"Conveyed in narrative snapshots, the scenes of a small town romance fill the pages of this album-novel...Obsessed with the past and searching for meaning, every word is like a piece in a juxtaposed puzzle. Conversational, yet edited with considerable care, the book is like a beautifully wrapped box of chocolate—old-fashioned and sweet."
- *The BookLife Prize*

"Schindler's storytelling in 'The Art of the Kiss' is slowly and carefully built, brick by brick and memory by memory until it creates a life as a whole. It examines life at its core, relationships at their best and often their worst, tugging at heartstrings and giving way to deep thoughts of the new, the old, and the now."
- *The Lakeland Times*

Acclaim for Holly Schindler's Previous Work

★ Breathtakingly, gut-wrenchingly authentic—
Booklist starred review

★ Exquisitely imagined—
Publishers Weekly starred review

Awards

IPPY Awards Gold Medal

Foreword INDIES Book of the Year
Silver Medal

This Story

This is the story of a man. And a woman.
And a rut.

Unwelcome and unexpected, maybe. Sneaky and slow forming. But there it was, a rut just the same. By the time this man and this woman finally recognized the rut's existence, it had already been gouged so deeply into the earth that neither one quite knew how to climb out.

When had it started? The same way a rut starts for anyone. At the exact moment this man and this woman had succumbed to a comfortable rhythm: the swinging back door of their days, the routine comings and goings, the divvying up of the morning sink and knowing whose turn it was to pick up the lemon for the tea, and at the end of the day, a shared meal and scraped dishes and the flicker of the blue TV light through the living room.

Ruts, when they form, always begin at the exact moment you have found your satisfaction.

So it went with Michael and Sharon, who had been digging their rut for a good fifty years.

At least, until one sweet June day, when they found it disturbed by a force not unlike a Midwest tornado.

Of course it was good that the rut had been disturbed. Of course kicked-up dust eventually settles. But before that could happen, for a while, Michael and Sharon were surrounded by chaos. Dirt flew in their eyelashes. Everything stung.

This is the story of Michael. And Sharon. It is the story of their beginning. And it is the story of the time they began again. They each have their own side to tell: Michael, who saw life as the most magical of all the fairy tales, and Sharon, who viewed the world pragmatically, in black and white.

The rut had no perspective of its own.

Ruts never do.

But they can change the perspective of the people who happen to be standing in them.

That's the insidious power of a rut.

Michael

Once upon a time, in a town called Fairyland—

Hey, wait a minute. Don't roll your eyes one sentence in. Don't start backing up, saying the opening line of my story sounds like the setup for a bad joke told on amateur night at a comedy club.

Give your skeptical side a breather, just for a little while. Come along with me, into a tale that takes place in a small Missouri town named Fairyland.

Perhaps the founder was addle-brained. Maybe he let his eight-year-old name the town. Then again, maybe, even then, he had a gut feeling. An inkling that something…what's the word?—*bewitching*—would wind up taking place inside the city limits.

All I know is, in the town of Fairyland, I lived a real-life fairy tale.

Now you're rolling your eyes. *Yeah, right*, you're thinking. Me, some old guy with white hair and trifocals and a creaky knee. You think a guy like me doesn't look like fairy tale material. Certainly not Prince Charming.

To that, I have to say you're completely, totally wrong.

In the town of Fairyland, I won my one true love.

And in the town of Fairyland, I touched magic.

Now there you go, assuming my tale is going to involve a one-size-fits-all kind of magic. The sort that spews purple sparkles out of a wand.

The story I have to tell is not a bunch of two-dimensional coloring book garbage.

Sometimes, though, objects really can be magical. I've held a magical object myself. A camera. The old kind. With film. A 1967 Nikon F.

You're leaving me again. You're drifting away. I can feel it.

Don't. Stay with me. It's the truth. Magic exists in this world.

Try this. I think it's one thing, even here when we have only just met and skepticism is at its zenith, that we can both agree on:

What the old tales of our childhood got right—more than anything else—is that the most powerful item in the world isn't a spell or a potion. Not a poison apple or a godmother or a spinning wheel that can make gold. It's not even the camera that wound up changing the course of two lives—mine and my wife's.

The most magical, most transformative thing?

It's a kiss.

In the storybooks, kisses can turn frogs into heartthrobs and wake comatose princesses. Kisses show people for who they are, deep down, underneath the glass slippers and the stepsister warts and the royal family titles. A kiss can shine a regular searchlight on the truest love, the love that was always meant to be.

When it's real, a kiss has the ability to change everything.

Especially in a town called Fairyland.

Did I get you that time? Are you listening? Intrigued? Good.

Where was I? Ah, yes:

Once upon a time, in the town of Fairyland, I learned that fairy tales are real. I saw for myself everything a real kiss can do.

Excerpt from
The Fairyland Times
June 6, 1974

A record-breaking traffic jam brought the entirety of Fairyland to a stop shortly after noon on Saturday. While rumors originally circulated that an automobile accident had been the cause, it was soon discovered by Fairyland police that the jam was started by a photograph.

Sharon Minyard, owner of Minyard's Photography, located off the downtown square, said, "I still can't believe it happened. We've been getting more visitors lately, every day a few more. And then suddenly, on Saturday, it exploded."

It isn't the first time Minyard's photograph, *The Art of the Kiss*, received such positive attention. Three years ago, Minyard submitted her photo—a black and white of a kiss shared with her now-husband, Michael Minyard—to the International Alliance of Professional Photographers, for their annual competition. The photograph took the top prize, winning Mrs. Minyard thirty-thousand dollars in award money, and allowing her to put a down payment on her own photography studio and shop, where you can sit for a portrait, take a class taught by the photographer herself, or buy the latest in photography equipment.

"Of course I had to hang the photo in the shop," Minyard said. "It's the reason I even have the shop in the first place. But I had no idea it would elicit this kind of response."

Since Minyard's opening last month, admiration for her photo has been immediate and swift-moving. Describing the print as "timeless," "elegant," or "like something out of an old movie," Fairyland residents touched by the piece have since brought neighbors, friends, and family members to view the image for themselves. Interest gained momentum until last Saturday, when enough Fairyland-ians arrived in front of the Minyard studio at once to cause a traffic jam. One that continued to keep traffic either at a standstill or crawl for roughly two hours.

Minyard herself acknowledged that the subject matter was no doubt a big part of why she won the prestigious photography award. "Too many images we see today are so dark. The news is so dark. It's nice to get a breather from all that every once in a while."

Her customers, however, insist it's far more. Carol Bernard, a college freshman back in Fairyland for the duration of her summer break, mirrored the sentiment of all who came to view the image, stating, "When I see her photo, I know that it's possible. True love exists. The fairy tale can be real for everyone."

Michael

I suppose I was puttering. Isn't that what we say old retired men do? Men who have been married fifty years and have creaky knees and wear trifocals?

Puttering. And rummaging around our apartment with a big cardboard box marked "Donations - Citywide Rummage Sale." Whistling. While Sharon was downstairs in the shop. I popped open our hall closet door, the one with all the junk.

I honestly didn't expect anything amazing to happen. I was cleaning the place out. That's all. It was Saturday morning. A morning known for sleeping in and pancakes and not shaving. Perhaps the slowest, most uneventful morning of the week.

So it goes with magic. It never really does show up with advanced warning. It never politely rings the doorbell before busting in and demanding change.

Anyway, there I was, swinging open the door, only to find magic staring me right in the face. Stored away in a box, on the top shelf. With the old VHS tapes and the empty fish bowl. Like somehow, Sharon was done with it. Like magic could ever get used up or out of date.

I grabbed the old camera, wondering how it had drifted in there with all the other items doing nothing but waiting for their turn to finally be thrown away.

I found myself believing, in that moment, that it was the answer to the problems that had crept into our life. The solution to getting out of the not-quite-horrific but definitely-not-completely-splendid place we'd found ourselves, half a century into our time together as a couple.

"Sharon!" I shouted, bounding down the stairs, my donation box in my hand. "Where are you? Do you hear me?" I was going so fast, my tennis shoes were making the squeaky sounds you usually hear on a basketball court.

The shop was empty, as I'd expected it to be. Empty just as it had been, for the most part, for years. We'd experienced a mass exodus in excruciatingly slow motion. Victims of modern digitalization. In all honesty, I hadn't fully noticed how horribly quiet the shop really was until after my retirement from the paper.

Seemed like it just kept getting deader from there.

Sharon, who had been something of a celebrity in the era when that really meant something—before people were famous simply for being famous, when the limelight only found you because you could pitch a baseball or sing or write books or take stunning photos—had, in more recent times, become a footnote in the history of Fairyland. Kind of a smudged footnote at that. Nobody really remembered Sharon, not anymore.

Truth be told, the studio-slash-store that had once been the source of so much pride for both of us had become a sad relic. Unseen or ignored—what was the difference? It stung the same. In a complete reversal of roles, we were now supporting the store. Living on social security and managing to keep the lights on only because we'd long ago purchased the small building outright and collected rent from our neighbors. Over the years, we'd played landlord to a hairdresser, a florist, an insurance salesman, a tattoo parlor. A few cafés. A bookstore, once.

No matter who hung "Open" signs next door, they never did seem to generate any foot traffic for the camera shop. Nobody even came by looking for directions to the lake anymore. Everybody used their phones for that.

And Sharon? She worked, but not in the same way. She kind of puttered herself. Took digital photos and stored them on her computer under the lock of a password. Or she propped her elbows on the counter, wading through random daydreams, one after another, and staring through the front window, wistfully watching the world pass by. The same world that had once lavished her with love, then so cruelly turned its shoulder, leaving her behind.

I'd come to think of her situation as being confined to an old-age coma. The Brothers Grimm would have surely called it a spell. And the horrible part of it was that she'd done it to herself. No wicked queen, no poison apples.

It absolutely broke my heart. All those days, all those hours she was racking up behind the counter doing nothing. I'd offer to relieve her, and she'd just wind up going out for a walk. I couldn't believe it. A talent like Sharon's withering and dying on the vine.

But it was all about to change. I knew it.

"Look what I found," I announced breathlessly, clattering her old camera case against the glass-topped display counter.

My sleepwalking beauty stared down at it. The tiniest of changes flickered across her face. *Come on, Sharon,* I thought. *Wake up.*

"It's okay to donate this one, right?" I asked, pushing the camera case a little closer. Nudging her. Even though I didn't want her to donate it—and knew, in all honesty, she never would. I wasn't actually asking her to donate it. I was asking, instead, that she remember.

Sharon flinched. She flicked the latches, exposing the old Nikon.

It didn't look special at all, there in the unforgiving fluorescent lights. It did look like junk. All those scratches and gashes. That large dent on the left-hand side.

Sharon and I both knew better. In fact, I was part of putting the magic there. Decades ago.

Come on, Sharon, we can tap into that magic again. I know we can. Believe it.

Sharon

Once upon a time, my foot.

Look, Michael's telling you his side of the story, describing our lives from his point of view. That's fine. He's got this whole lovely metaphorical thing going. Which is definitely worth a listen and all that. Really. I'm not an unromantic person.

But I told him the day we met I wasn't a fairy tale kind of girl. That's still the case. I don't do pink frilly anything, and to this day, my houseplants are mostly dead.

Really—what're you supposed to do with the things? Either I don't water enough, or I drown them. What's the balance? Why's it all a secret?

Stupid plants.

I don't have time to go around babying a bunch of weak green shoots. Fragile flowers that droop because the sun isn't hitting them at the exact right angle.

No, I definitely don't have time for that.

Or the interest, frankly.

I'm a girl who listened to the fights on the radio with my dad. I'm a girl who was just fine without a man around when Michael stuck his foot in the mostly-closed door of my life.

But if this story's getting told, it's not getting told without me. And I can tell you right now, that day he came clomping down the stairs, screaming my name, I figured whatever he was yelling about was something innocuous—I don't know, dryer lint.

I closed the laptop and pushed it aside, like I always did when he started chatting and interrupting my thoughts.

But then he had to go and push that old camera under my nose. Let me tell you, I got hot fast—Dad used to say I could go from zero to livid in two seconds flat. He'd once said I could have been a world champion boxer myself.

Sure. Boxer. One jab to my lip, and he'd have been in the ring, going at the opponent bareknuckled.

He just liked the fact that I was tough.

Unlike houseplants. (Really. What's the point?)

But that camera had once been the most important physical object of my entire life. (Well, that and my wedding ring, anyway.) If a girl ever had reason to get sentimental about something, it'd be that old Nikon.

Still. Magic?

I never thought so.

You want to know what magic really is? It's a synonym for *inexplicable. Lucky.*

There's no real magic in the world. Not literally. Fairy tales are a bunch of childhood nonsense.

And I hadn't been a child in eons.

"I mean, you're not using it, right? So—maybe somebody else should." Michael rattled the donation box again, already filled with a few of our own expendable household contraptions: an electric pencil sharpener, a blender in chic 1978 avocado green. Someone else would love the macramé owl. Someone else would step into the skins we'd shed.

It should have been easy. I mean, it's not like electronic gadgets have souls. They don't have feelings or make plans or become part of our cheering squad. Which, of course, is why they seem interchangeable. Why it's easy to update or flat-out discard our gizmos. Why it's with less than a shrug that we can trash an oven that's cooked a decade of Thanksgiving turkeys. Why you don't give so much as a second thought to slapping a $1 garage sale sticker on the kitchen telephone where your little boy—no, no, *young man*—had once worked up the courage to call a girl for the first time. Why it seems reasonable to recycle the record player that had played the first love song you'd ever danced to with your husband.

You keep the memories. You discard the out-of-date devices.

Usually, anyway.

"Someone else might have a use for it," Michael said, pointing at the Nikon.

"*I* might use it again," I blurted.

A knee-jerk reaction, really. I put the camera back in the felt-lined case and squeezed it onto a shelf packed with two padded camera bags full of various lenses, a light meter, and an old folded tripod.

I didn't look at Michael. I couldn't have stood the smug look that was surely flashing on his face. I wasn't sure what his goal had been. What he hoped to accomplish.

All I knew right then, at that moment, was that I felt in my gut that the old camera—dented and scratched and definitely the worse for wear—wasn't done yet.

Neither was I.

From the Studio Walls

Bottom Step
1

Eight-by-ten, black and white. The photo of her dad hangs where Sharon would be sure to bump into it, whether she was stepping out from behind the front counter or rushing to greet a new group of students in the back.

By now, it's been up long enough that a thin haze of dust has adhered itself to the top of the frame like skin. Like something that can't come off, not without some pain attached to it.

Markers of time are often like that.

But the picture itself was little more than a fluke. Taken as a joke, really. A candid shot, snapped on day one of her new business, that photography studio in the basement of her childhood home. A portrait snapped in the same way little Sharon—the one still in pigtails and anklets—had once stuck her tongue out at her father.

Back when she was little, the stuck-out tongue was a term of affection. Being raised by a single dad meant you learned to express what was in your heart in a different way. A way most mothers would have considered unladylike at best.

Not that Sharon even knew, growing up, that their life was different. Her mother had died young in a horrible wreck before Sharon had said a single word of English to her—not so much as a "hello." Sharon only knew her father and their own ways.

But there he is, as he's been for decades, frozen in time, one in a sea of framed photos all over Sharon's shop, her studio. There he is—in that picture, decades younger than Sharon is now—forever sitting on the bottom step of the basement stairs. Can of Pabst in his hand, pepper-gray, curly hair shooting out from the crown of his head like springs from a busted gadget.

Caught in a half-grin, his belief in Sharon shines bright in his eyes. Sharon tells herself, even now, there's a hint of admiration glowing in his eyes too.

Day one. The beginning of it all.

A beginning that had only come to be after a lifetime of Sharon listening to her father's *buck up*s and *you can't quit now*s. A life of *you're smarter than the rest of them*s and *make them listen*s.

A beginning her father had insisted on.

"You can do this, Sharon," he'd told her over dinner at their favorite Chinese place, less than two hours after her college graduation. "Any numbskull can get some crummy job. So what? You can make a real go of it."

Day one. A studio in her father's basement. Her father smiling at her, so pleased that she had agreed to go after it. Hunt her dream down, chase it, track it.

Day one.

It remains one of Sharon's favorite images on her studio wall.

And perhaps the most important.

MARCH 25, 1967

Maybe, Sharon was already thinking as she stood in the parking lot, tattoos were visual proof of bravery.

Not that she was brave at all. No matter what her dad tried to say. He was her dad; it was his job to pick out nice adjectives and pin them to her shoulder. In reality, she was having a hard time making herself go inside the parlor.

It was supposed to be easier to take her photos at home than in Columbia, the university town where it still felt like everyone was watching her. Judging her. Gearing up to run her off their property. She needed to put together a portfolio for her photography course. The same class she'd signed up for with a shrug and a "Why not?" The extracurricular course that had felt so surprisingly familiar and comfortable, right from the start.

Except for the permissions thing. That still felt weird.

Who was she to ask permission? Like she was some sort of professional. Really. They were going to see through that the minute she brought it up. Mostly, at twenty-one years old, she felt like an overgrown kid.

But then again, part of her tried to reason, why wouldn't she be intimidated by the tattoo parlor? Wouldn't anyone in her right mind feel that way? The place was rough—it even looked rough for somebody who'd grown up listening to the fights on the radio. And to add to her uneasiness, it was located on the corner of the same block that had long had the reputation for being the rowdiest in Fairyland.

It was kind of funny, actually, the idea of Fairyland having any streets at all that were seedy. Oh, sure, the place was big enough that you never did literally know everyone; it was big enough that you had police cars and actual crime and unemployment and hardship. But all those things kind of seemed like an affront to the town itself. In a town named Fairyland, it often seemed that even the trash piled on the curbs, waiting for pickup, should have twinkled.

Sharon tried to imagine it: magic trash. Somehow, the idea wasn't enough to bring a smile to her face.

She shook her head, silently scolding herself for her foot-dragging.

"Fine," Sharon grumbled, clutching her camera and stomping into the tattoo parlor in the same way that people ran to the end of a diving board and launched themselves off the edge, all at once, straight into the water.

The inside was no less rough than the outside. In fact, it might have been worse. Not grimy, not grungy. But it was the kind of place that implied it had seen some of the worst parts of human nature. Cracked leather chairs. Guys with similar cracked leather faces. Brutal-looking guns filled with needles. The entire shop frowned at her mere presence. Not the men inside it. The *shop* frowned.

The owner—thick, sun-weathered skin, gray-streaked goatee, cigarette between his fingers—chuckled at the sight of her.

Sharon straightened her back, tossed her long black hair behind her shoulder, and marched closer to him.

Another man—even taller and beefier than her father—was getting ready to lower himself into a chair. He eyed her with curiosity (and perhaps a touch of amusement) as he continued to unbutton his shirt.

The place reeked of testosterone and pain, not unlike the boxing gym her dad had dragged her to once. Sharon had all but forgotten the awful experience, but it came roaring back in the most unwelcome way. It had been one thing to listen to the fights, she remembered, and another entirely to actually see men hitting each other. It was bloody and brutal and mean.

That was exactly how the tattoo parlor felt: bloody and brutal and mean. Making it even worse was the fact that Sharon had no father to hide behind.

But what was she going to do? Run away?

Still trying to get her mouth to work, Sharon let her eyes bounce among the designs hanging on the walls. She didn't want to see the shirtless man.

The old metal chair creaked as he sat, grabbing her attention.

She stole a quick look, finding that he already had a tattoo in progress on his left arm. A giant leopard.

And if his tattoo was in progress, didn't that mean the leopard was being completed in spurts? That the pain was so bad, it could only be sustained for so long? That at some point, it all became unbearable?

The idea made Sharon's scalp feel tight. It was suddenly too cold in the parlor. She shivered.

"You come for the show?" the man in the chair asked, clearly perturbed by the way she was gawking at him.

"I—I—"

Her face was getting hot. *Oh, come on,* Sharon chastised herself, *you're not blushing, are you?*

Sharon turned toward the owner. Or he might have been an artist. Who knew? But he, too, was scowling, cigarette sticking straight out between his lips.

A new feeling came to Sharon. It engulfed her awkwardness, her embarrassment at being too young and inexperienced. The feeling, simply, was resentment. *Permission.* She took offense to having to ask and to everything the word implied about the imbalance of power between her and this man who might or might not grant it to her.

Maybe it was the way she'd been raised, her father insisting she barrel her way into a situation like any man would.

Standing there in the tattoo parlor, eyeing the men staring back at her, she knew that the outside world did not view her as her dad did. She was young, yes, which really did mean these men automatically thought she had no right to wear any hint of authority. And she was pretty, which meant she could not also be smart. She was a woman, which meant she could not also be good.

She could see it in their faces.

The men grew amused. They wore crooked, knowing smiles.

She gestured toward her camera, the one her father had bought her, the one he'd insisted on when she'd mentioned the class. "I've got a feeling about this," her dad had told her when he'd given her the Nikon. The best he could find. Far better than Sharon had imagined he'd purchase when he offered.

"I'm Sharon Grayson," she announced, her voice buzzing against the parlor walls. "A photographer." The first time she'd ever introduced herself that way.

The men chuckled. But it wasn't just laughter. It was dismissive. Their chuckles said, "Photographer, eh? Sure, sweetie."

Sharon's lip began to curl. She hated being sweethearted. Even if it was only in her imagination.

The owner—or artist, Sharon still didn't know for sure—took

a drag on his cigarette that made all the wrinkles on his face deepen. There were stories in that face begging to be told—chapters and chapters of them.

The kind of stories Sharon wanted to capture on film.

So she tamped down her growing anger, held up her camera, and announced, "I was hoping you'd let me take a few shots. A tattoo in progress."

He cocked his head to the side, asking, "What for?" His tone suggested she'd brought her camera to his shop the same way little kids sneaked cameras into carnival freak shows.

As Sharon started to explain that wasn't what she'd had in mind at all, he mumbled, "Ain't really the kind of place for a girl."

That did it.

"I'm a *photographer*," Sharon corrected. "I already told you that. I go in search of the best photos. Period."

And because he still wasn't convinced, Sharon smacked the man in the chair with the back of her hand. "Move over," she said. And pointed toward the small feather design on the wall.

Heart ready to burst, she announced, "Put it right there," pointing to the inside of her wrist.

The men nodded slightly, with appreciation, and it felt to her that even the shop stopped frowning. She was no longer an observer. She was one of them.

And if they were all one and the same, she wouldn't depict them as freak-show stars.

In the split second before the tattoo gun bit into her flesh, Sharon promised herself she'd never be a mere observer. She'd always fight to be seen.

She was never going to be invisible.

PHOTOGRAPHY FACT

Sharon Minyard's
Portrait Class

1979

I'll start this class with the most important concept you can ever learn about portraiture. The concept I want you to take with you all the way through our time together. This entire class. A concept I hope you'll carry with you as you exit my door and head out into the world to take your own portraits on your own time. It doesn't matter if you plan to take portraits professionally or just want to take better pictures of your friends and family.

Listen. Repeat this to yourselves:

Whatever makes a good portrait for a man should make a good portrait for a woman.

Sounds reasonable, you're thinking. Maybe you even feel a little let down. Maybe, you think, I built that up, acted like I was about to unleash some great life changing revelation, and all I gave you was a no-brainer.

It's not, though.

What makes a good portrait for a man should make a good portrait for a woman.

And yet, that's not really the case, is it? A woman is invariably posed to best showcase her beauty. Bare shoulders, pretty round face. A man is posed to present himself as strong. Intelligent. A person of his own making.

That's what the print media would have you believe, anyway. Every single time you flip through their pages.

Portraiture, so often, is about making someone appear attractive. And so, to achieve that end, what do we rely on? Stereotypes. Clichés. Oversimplifications. Women need to be soft. Men need to be strong.

I didn't want to photograph stereotypes. Neither should you. It's why I vowed, early on, never to differentiate between the sexes in the portraits I took. Male or female, the goal was to bring out the extraordinary in every face, in every shoot.

Every single human being is, in their own way, unique.

The thing is, when you stop trying to make your subject attractive, and just focus on finding it, that extraordinary, unique, standalone quality—whatever it happens to be for that person— when you capture it on film, your subject *becomes* attractive. A vision. Stare-worthy. More so than if you had set out with this goal in mind.

Funny how that happens.

This Story

*O*ur story continues with a girl. And a dream that is digging its heels in the ground, refusing to come true.

This girl—the one chasing her dream—will become the disruptor in Michael and Sharon's world. The fully-formed F5 tornado. The rut eraser.

Of course, Michael's decision to bring that camera downstairs was a big part of it. It helped put everything in motion.

But the camera would have stayed on their studio shelf, where Sharon put it, never to be removed from its case, had Heather and the busted fragments of her dream not showed up on the Minyard doorstep.

Don't expect Heather to tell you much of this story.

Michael and Sharon will. They'll put ideas in her head and words in her mouth that may or may not have ever really been there. Because they each view Heather, this great disruptor, through the filter of their own eyes.

But don't for a second think this is somehow a devious exercise. Don't think that either one of them is using Heather as a way to bend the truth—or flat-out lie to you.

We all fill in the blanks. Maybe not in such elaborate ways as Michael and Sharon are about to. But when a friend is short with you, don't you tell yourself it is because they are in the midst of a divorce—trouble at home? Or when a spouse is upset, that it has to do with trouble at work?

We couldn't be the source of anyone's trouble. Absolutely not.

Doesn't that sound familiar?

Don't we put together scenarios in our heads—perhaps in part as a kind of self-preservation—that explain the behavior or wants or ideas or dreams of the people in our lives? Don't we invent a running narrative for all the people we deal with on a regular basis?

So do Michael and Sharon. They have created especially elaborate scenarios about Heather.

As we begin, Michael the old storyteller will set the stage, introduce the characters. Explain how he sees the pieces all fitting together.

Sharon, less reliant on verbal description, will tell us about a single scene that's been stuck in her head. One she feels perfectly sums up a big part of Heather's story. One that really got her thinking about the story she's shared with Michael for half a century. A scene that doesn't require what she might call "all the long-winded fuss."

And yes, their versions of Heather's story are blends of fact and fiction. Sharon and Michael have filled in the missing details by digging into their own hearts, projecting their feelings onto her.

In a way, that's the beauty of their stories—they'll tell more about themselves than they ever will about Heather.

Of course they will. They're hungry for their voices to be heard.

Excerpt from
The Fairyland Times
Classifieds
March 4, 2018

ALL YOUR PHOTOGRAPHY NEEDS: Weddings, Senior Portraits, Engagement Pictures, Family Pictures, Special Events, Social Media Marketing, Publicity Photos. Contact Heather Scott, owner of Photo Phrenzy.

Michael

That Saturday morning in early June when I brought Sharon's camera down to her—the same morning when we unearthed magic and the dirt started to swirl around our rut—was also the same morning we both got sucked into what can only be referred to as a modern-day Cinderella story. One that is both recognizable and unlike anything you've ever heard before.

What's a Cinderella story without a poor, pitiful waif? A downtrodden soul? A bedraggled castaway?

Rest assured, we have one in the gentle and agreeable Heather Scott.

Our Heather was an orphan. To be fair, you'd probably say that at thirty-four, she was laughably far too old to be an orphan, but I'm going to put my foot down and insist we hearken back here to fairy tale language. Heather—an orphan, a bedraggled soul, an only child raised by a single mother who'd died of cancer five years earlier—did, by this point, live alone in a tiny little hole of an apartment at the bottom of two flights of creaky stairs in an old redbrick building. The windows leaked, the complimentary washer and dryer in the shed out back worked every other Tuesday, and the fridge was held together with bungee cords. The wooden floors gave her splinters when she walked barefoot. The heater in the center of the apartment (which she unaffectionately referred to as The Creature) clanked and coughed frighteningly throughout the night. The Creature was controlled by a wayward pilot light which was perpetually going out, and each time poor Heather relit it, the cantankerous thing hacked up some sort of black soot, spraying it all over her face and hands.

Yes, just like the first Cinderella, whose rotten stepsisters tormented her, turning her into nothing more than a kitchen maid forced to sleep on the hearth and soil herself with the day's ashes, our own Heather also frequently found herself, throughout the cooler months, covered in soot coughed up by The Creature.

"You really need to switch to a lower-tar cigarette," she once tried to joke as she replaced the tarnished cover plate. But as usual, The Creature only seemed relieved to have gotten the junk off its chest. It did not think she was funny, nor did it feel bad for totally wrecking yet another T-shirt.

She couldn't have come to this tale with a better set of fairy tale credentials.

Heather was also attempting to succeed as a professional photographer at the exact point in time when the rest of the world had decided photographers were as useful as a sixth toe. Camera and business card in hand, she was forever pitching herself, offering to document birthday parties or marriage proposals—but had snagged embarrassingly few takers. What did they need her for? Everyone had become something of a digital photography expert. And she could forget about weddings or headshots or some kind of commercial gig. Without a decent portfolio of previous work to submit, who would ever hire her, pitiful little needy waif that she was?

Another woman might have been pushier. Brazen, even. But

as Heather's mother withered away, she'd made her only child promise, over and over again, to lead with kindness once she'd gone.

"Good things will happen to you when you are good to others," her mother had declared, stretched out upon her deathbed, too weak by then to so much as squeeze Heather's hand.

(Oh, stop grumbling. A dash of melodrama can be good for the soul.)

And so our Heather had conducted herself in a somewhat milder manner, refusing to oversell herself. Hyperbole and making promises she wasn't sure she could deliver wasn't exactly what her mother'd had in mind, now was it?

She left her business cards at gas station counters and stuck them to bulletin boards inside local cafés and libraries. So many of them, she sometimes felt like Gretel scattering breadcrumbs behind her to mark her trails. She returned regularly, walking down the breadcrumb-marked paths, following up, checking back, meekly asking about possible work. People would smile at her, act glad she'd reminded them. They promised to call. Why, they'd probably need a photographer soon. Very soon, in fact.

Yes, they said, they would call.

But they never did.

Heather sold the occasional stock photo of rustic Missouri landscapes (winding dirt roads, unused railroad tracks, fields of Queen Anne's lace, and rusted barbed wire fences) while working two part-time jobs, one sacking groceries and the other corralling kids at a Build-A-Bear. She'd taken a class picture at a preschool, a job that had required more patience than talent—and led to absolutely nothing. Not a single additional job acquired through word-of-mouth. She was drowning in bills and debts despite her efforts. After several years of getting nowhere, her situation in life had begun to feel not like a starting point, a bottom rung on a ladder, but permanent. As if she'd been encased in a concrete vault with no escape hatch.

As the meanest little boy in the neighborhood—whom she'd once stupidly let in out of the rain when he'd forgotten his own house key—liked to tell her (taunt her was more like it), she and The Creature were destined to be together forever and ever and ever. *He* would never be old and still stuck in their crummy neighborhood, ha, ha, ha.

Good things will happen to you when you are good to others. Yeah, well, she *had* been nice. To everyone. Even Darth Billy, as she had come to refer to the mean little taunting neighbor. And where had it gotten her? When was that luck going to kick in, anyway?

Finally, finally, maybe it had.

The husband of Heather's best friend had dropped her name at a stuffy cocktail party where names must have been spewing everywhere like water from fire hoses for hers to come up. But it had, in fact, led to a "gig," as her ex-boyfriend would have described it. Official photographer for a family reunion. Booked and pre-paid, the whole shebang. And the guy—Liu, that was the client's last name—owned a marketing and advertising firm. *Looking to expand his business*, that was the way Tom, Amanda's husband, had described Liu. So sure, to start with, it was nothing more than a Saturday afternoon shoot in a park. But handled right, Heather dreamed, it could lead to something big.

She'd preened herself to look the part (or what she imaged looked the part), lightening her hair for the occasion using a fifteen-dollar home highlighting kit and scrounging through her favorite thrift store for a simple khaki knee-length skirt, which she paired with a fitted pink T-shirt and a pair of pink flats that didn't appear to have been worn once. She'd packed her gear up and carried it to her car.

Unsurprisingly, Heather drove a ten-year-old Cobalt with

flaking purple paint, a rusted bumper, a "Photo Phrenzy" sign in her back window, three hundred and twenty thousand miles on the odometer, and various internal ailments, including a faulty transmission and cirrhosis of the intake manifold.

She cranked the ignition. In response, the Cobalt shrugged.

"Didn't you hear me?" Heather asked, slamming her foot into the gas pedal and cranking the ignition again.

Still, not a single wheeze or sputter. The lights on the dash flashed briefly, as if to acknowledge that yes, what passed for her transportation had in fact heard her plea. But that didn't change its response.

Heather's eyes swelled as alarm lit up her entire body. "What am I supposed to do now?" she asked the car…and the empty parking lot…a nearby bird cocking his head at her as if questioning whether she was in her right mind.

Sensing trouble, Darth Billy steered his bicycle in circles in the lot behind her. "Vroom, vroom!" he shouted. And then he dissolved into the kind of laughter usually reserved for wicked step-family-members and arch-enemies.

Michael

Ah, yes. Arch-enemies. Of course, a Cinderella story is nothing without a villain or two. A heaping handful of those cruel, nasty, wicked stepsisters, perhaps. Scoundrels and mischief-makers bent on wreaking havoc.

Maybe Heather didn't see herself as a real-life modern-day Cinderella. But everybody recognizes they have enemies. And on that lovely June day, when her Cobalt decided to officially succumb to its assortment of maladies, Heather really did believe that the one and only villain in her own life was none other than Darth Billy.

Little did she know, as she dialed up her emergency contact (who also happened to be her oldest and dearest friend), she'd called the individual who was in the process of becoming her absolute worst nemesis.

A few blocks away, Amanda's phone went off in the front passenger seat of her Escalade. "Sweet Child o' Mine," the ringtone she'd assigned to Heather.

"Call, Mommy," her son alerted her from the backseat of the Escalade. And then he sang along with the opening guitar riff (or tried to, anyway—it always wound up sounding a little like a police siren coming from him).

Amanda's attention shot up to the rearview. Rather than her little boy, she saw the crow's feet splintering out from the corners of her brown eyes, below her threaded eyebrows.

"I'm driving, baby," Amanda told her son. A nice excuse. In all honesty, she plain didn't want to talk to Heather.

Aiden swung his feet about in his car seat. Amanda's heart swelled. She loved her son—and his older twin sisters, Eva and Olivia. She loved their silliness and their discovery of the world and their freshness and their energy and their cuddliness. She even, on occasion, loved their tears because they were something she could soothe away.

The ringtone started playing again, the guitar riff sounding almost sinister to Amanda.

Aiden sang. She watched in the rearview as his eyes popped and his face twisted with joy. He waved his arms to the beat. He raised a hand, balled his fingers into a fist, and tugged down.

Amanda smiled. In her family's closest circle, Aiden was renowned for the tugging. As a baby, he'd tugged on long hair and necklaces, cords that cinched hoodies tight. Once he'd started walking, he'd tugged window curtains and throws from the couch and his sister's favorite princess wand from her hand. He was always making fists in the air above his head and wrenching them down, like he thought he could tug something utterly delightful straight out of heaven.

If Amanda could tug something from heaven, what would it be?

The mere question made her aware, suddenly and sharply, of a painful hole deep inside her. Out of nowhere, several weeks ago, she'd discovered it: a black, festering hole. Maybe it had been there for a while, and she hadn't noticed it. But after more than a solid month of poking at it and hoping it would clear up on its own, it now had her as worried as she would have been if she'd found a hard lump in her breast.

Her cell sang out again. The hole throbbed.

At a stoplight, Amanda turned the phone off and opened the glove compartment. Before she could toss the phone inside, fistfuls of business cards tumbled into the floorboard.

They all belonged to Heather.

"Oops, Mommy!" Aiden shouted, dissolving into giggles.

Amanda struggled to scoop them up, her cheeks flaming. Why was she so embarrassed? Aiden couldn't even read.

Sometimes, she supposed, a person could be embarrassed by her own actions without anyone knowing what she'd done.

She welcomed the embarrassment. It showed that her conscience hadn't packed its bags and left town on the 7:30 Greyhound.

For weeks (none-too-coincidentally, about as long as she'd been aware of the awful sore spot in her chest), Amanda had started seeing Heather's Photo Phrenzy business cards. Oh, they'd been hanging long before then. But that was the point Amanda really started to notice. And they were everywhere. On the bulletin board at the public library and the counters of the gas station where she filled her Cadillac and the butcher where she bought her lamb chops. Until finally, one day, she'd cracked. In the vestibule of the restaurant where her family ate their Sunday brunches, of all places.

Aiden had begun crying inconsolably for some incredibly toddler-ish reason (the boysenberry syrup got drizzled on his plate and he didn't like it because it was purple, or he'd wanted two slices of bacon instead of one, or he'd been denied the ability to take off his socks). She was rocking him in a vestibule where the rest of the diners wouldn't be bothered, while her own French toast and

34

eggs were growing cold, and there it was, yet again: one of Heather's cards. Stuck to the bulletin board between a customers-only coat rack and a display of thick Sunday papers.

Amanda stared, the awful hole inside of her throbbing and pulsing. On the opposite side of the vestibule's glass wall, next to her plate of congealing French toast, Amanda's family was scarfing down their own breakfasts. She swallowed hard, her saliva like the burn of a martini.

Everything in that moment hurt. And Amanda had no real idea why.

But she did know the longer she stared at the card, the worse the ache and the burn got inside her. Her face hardened, and Amanda snatched Heather's business card, shoved it deep into the pocket of her church slacks. For a moment, the pain subsided, replaced by a rush of satisfaction.

She'd immediately gone back to hushing and rocking and consoling Aiden.

It could have ended there, of course.

But it hadn't.

Instead, Amanda had stolen the cards every single time she'd encountered them: at the gym, at her salon. She tugged them out from under thumbtacks, scooped whole stacks of them from check-out counters. She couldn't explain why she kept at it. But once she'd gotten started, she hadn't been able to stop.

She hadn't been able to see Heather, either. Not once since she'd started stealing her business cards. She was sabotaging her friend. How could she look her in the face?

Such a funny word, really: *sabotage*. Somehow far too serious to describe what Amanda was doing—taking down some silly little cards. But also, at times, the perfect word to describe what was in her heart.

The car behind her honked. "Beep, beep!" Aiden echoed.

Amanda slammed as many cards as possible back into her glove compartment, and hit the gas.

Why does Heather keep calling? Amanda asked herself. *I haven't returned a single one of her messages in eons.* Then again, the two had been friends for decades. Why would Heather think Amanda was anything but busy?

Amanda pulled into a parking lot. Her hands clenched into fists as she listened to the voicemail: Heather's desperate plea for a ride.

Amanda drummed the steering wheel, trying to sort out what to do.

"Hey, baby?" she finally asked, her eye in the rearview again. "You know what I'm thinking?"

"What!"

"Since your sisters are having an adventure with their friends today, you and I ought to have an adventure too."

"Yeah!" he screeched.

"You want to go on an adventure with me? It has to be our secret."

"Seeec-wet!" he repeated, kicking his feet.

"If you let me make one quick stop, we might even wind up going to the park. You want to play in the park?"

"Paaaayyyyee!"

Amanda sighed. She knew Aiden had no idea what he was really agreeing to—*park*, he might have understood that one. But "adventure" and "secret"? He'd only been responding to the enthusiasm in her own voice.

No matter. She picked up the rest of Heather's cards, feeling a brief thrill when her fingertips brushed against them, almost like they were souvenirs of her kill. She tossed them into her purse just before she pulled back out into traffic, glaring through the windshield as she headed in the direction of Heather's apartment.

Michael

You knew it was coming. In a story that features magic, a Fairyland setting, and a Cinderella-style waif, you had to suspect I'd say it sooner or later: Meet our Prince Charming. In Heather's world, this specific Prince Charming was most commonly referred to as Ryan. He was, in fact, her ex-boyfriend. And when Amanda hadn't immediately picked up, Heather'd panicked and called him, spewing all sorts of frantic explanations and a single simple request: a ride to her shoot. (The bus would take too long, and a cab or an Uber was plain too expensive, and, and, and…) One ride, she promised, and then he'd never hear from her again.

To be completely honest, Heather wasn't sure if calling an ex-boyfriend to beg for a ride thirty-two hours after he dumped her was truly the most pathetic thing a girl could do.

But it was pretty close.

She waved as he pulled to a stop near her curb. From a distance, she swore she could already see his bright green eyes. Only two percent of people even had green eyes. But that was how Heather had always thought of Ryan: as a rarity. More attractive than most (in the most classic, manly way), smarter than most, a polite door-opener and what her own mother would have called a "regular sweetheart." Showing up to take her out in dress pants and a button-down shirt in an era when men were tattooed and sloppy, out on dates in jeans and ratty sneakers. So few of them walked girls to their front doors anymore—at least, not if they suspected they wouldn't be invited in themselves.

A guy coming to rescue his ex would also certainly be called a rarity.

But what else could he have been? After all, he was *Prince Charming*.

Seeing him again gave her the same excited dip in her stomach that usually accompanied rounding the top curve of a roller coaster.

Ryan killed the engine, and she knew she needed to get a move on, waddle along beneath all her photography bags—the ones that had been in the Cobalt's trunk, now slung over both shoulders and cradled in her arms.

But for a moment, it was kind of nice to drink him in. It was nice to remember the first time Ryan had ever been to Heather's building—which was also the exact same day they'd met.

Sharon

I'll admit it. I'm a sucker for the stories of how couples get together.

Try this one on: Heather and Ryan first crossed paths at a stoplight. Like something straight out of a rom-com. Heather's car idled in the lane neighboring Ryan's, her blond hair swirling in a crisp (but not yet cold) autumn breeze, her face hidden by enormous sunglasses. There she was, lip-syncing to a song playing in her car, the crummy old Cobalt coughing and sputtering and shuddering and threatening to die.

Ryan realized, goosebumps trailing down his arms, that it was his song she was lip-syncing. That was his voice spilling out of her rolled-down windows.

He'd honked to get her attention. But he honked at the exact moment the light turned green, and Heather'd simply assumed the honk was somebody telling her to hurry up, come on, get going, *hit the gas, honey*. She'd flinched and lurched into the intersection.

Ryan had always had somewhat lucky starts, probably due to his good looks. Doors opened for him all over the place. And he was

40

lucky that very afternoon because no other car had been behind her. So Ryan had veered into her lane and trailed her. All the way to an apartment building even crummier looking than the Cobalt.

"I bumped into it online," she'd confessed when he asked her about the song. "I liked it, so I downloaded it. My best friend—Amanda—she was all the time making me listen to her favorite small-label stuff while we were growing up. Somewhere along the way, I guess she got me hooked on the independent unsigned acts. Diamonds in the rough. The raw and unpolished."

They laughed. They exchanged names. They realized that they had both grown up in Fairyland. That Heather had even heard Ryan's band play during a high school talent show. Which meant she had, without realizing it, been a fan for decades already. Before she could stop herself, she was inviting him into her apartment. Opening yet another door. Introducing him to The Creature. Telling him of her own dreams and the lackluster career she was fighting to keep alive.

They'd ordered a pizza. But they had so much to say to each other, the pepperoni with extra cheese was cold and congealed by the time they got around to eating. The pleasant evening began to slide toward becoming a somewhat chilly October night. So they scooted closer to each other beneath the glow emanating from The Creature. In their lighthearted fight over the last slice, he kissed her.

It's the kiss, of course. *That's* the image that sticks in my mind. But not for the reason Heather wanted it to stick when she told me about it. Not because it was lovely and romantic.

Because I'd been around. And because by the time Heather told me the story of how she and Ryan had met, they were not some gooey new couple. They were exes. Because I knew that when their lips met for the first time, Heather was thinking all about how they understood each other. They were two people whose dreams weren't necessarily translating into giant piles of money. And yet, they chased them anyway. They were two people who did not believe that growing up should be about giving up your passion.

With Ryan's lips on Heather's for the very first time, Heather knew she'd met a man who felt just like she did. So what if so many people out there in the "real world" considered her foolish? This man—this handsome, delightful, green-eyed rarity—believed the same thing she did.

And Ryan? What did he feel as they kissed for the first time? Quite simply, that he had found a girl who admired him. A true fan.

And so, that night, they fell. She for the man who understood, who got it, who wasn't giving up. He for the fan who already, a handful of hours after exchanging their names, adored him.

They fell for who they wanted each other to be.

Not that either of them knew it. You never do, when you're in the middle of a scene that's still playing out.

The thing is, if Heather wanted to know where everything between her and her beloved went wrong, if she wanted to find out where, exactly, it started to unravel, she could have traced her steps all the way to this very scene.

The moment she and Ryan fell apart was actually the moment they got together.

Because they fell for such different reasons.

It was almost like the two of them were in two completely separate love stories, right from the very start.

Michael

The day they met was pretty much a tiny little speck in the rearview mirror as Ryan sat in his car, parked along the curb outside of Heather's building. Was it on Ryan's mind? Of course.

No sense getting sappy about it now, Ryan told himself. After all, he and Heather were over.

He popped the door. The handle slid a bit against his touch, which surprised him. It meant he was sweating.

Perhaps you think sweat seems unbecoming for a Prince Charming. What did a Prince Charming have to sweat about? He was a prince, complete with a chiseled jawline and a vintage white Mustang (ahem, you know, the white horse). The fairest girl in all the land should have been his for the picking.

But this khakis-wearing prince, the "regular sweetheart" Heather's mother would have undoubtedly approved of, wasn't finding it to be true. Yes, like all Prince Charmings, Ryan felt he had everything in his life all figured out—except for the love part. There he was, an independent musician who played gigs all weekend long and taught guitar lessons at Slade Music, a local instrument shop. He made extra cash on the side in Slade's small recording studio, mixing radio jingles and even a few songs here and there, mostly for demos. Finances were tight, but he was fulfilled. And yet, the love thing had eluded him.

Ryan often felt his true problem lay in the fact that sometimes, Prince Charmings were nothing more than nice guys. And it's well known amongst us storytellers what kind of luck nice guys usually have with women. It's well known where they mostly finish in life's long race.

Ryan slipped out from behind the wheel, hands out, wordlessly offering to take the load off Heather's shoulders. As soon as she reached for the strap of one of her bags, her hair fell in soft daffodil-colored waves, sending out a plume of the special-occasion floral scent she'd splashed on the nape of her neck. The scent was, as they might say in an old pulp romance, intoxicating. Ryan instantly regretted answering her call.

His reaction was totally out of whack, especially considering the girl was a catch this particular Prince Charming had cast aside. Two days ago, he'd been certain a worthier princess was out there wishing upon the night's first star that he would get off his duff already and find her. Right then, Heather didn't feel like someone he'd told goodbye. She didn't feel like an ex.

Love was like that, Ryan found himself thinking—despite his best efforts not to be so sentimental. Love was stubborn; it was a blemish on a coffee table that could never be lifted. You could put a magazine or a decorator doodad over it. You could not see it for months at a time. You could even forget about the candle that had been knocked over, scorching the wood. But inevitably, you'd be doing some everyday chore—something like dusting—and you'd lift the doodad, and there it was, the burn mark every bit as dark as ever.

Maybe what he felt for Heather was still there. Stubborn.

Not permanent, though, right? he asked himself. *Surely these feelings can't be permanent.*

He did his best to ignore whatever these emotions were that had bubbled up to the surface uninvited. (It didn't have to be love, of course, his overactive brain assured him. It could be loneliness. Grief. A twinge of grief always accompanied someone leaving your life, no matter the circumstances.) But so far, any efforts to explain away his rapid pulse and red cheeks were futile.

Why didn't he come clean, tell her he'd made a mistake?

Not so fast, he reminded himself. *Maybe there was no mistake. Lonely—that's still a possibility.* Maybe he needed time. She'd popped back up before he'd had a chance to fill the hole she was leaving behind.

"I can't tell you enough how I appreciate this," Heather rattled. "I tried Amanda before I called you. Three times," she insisted, even though she'd already told him as much on the phone.

He grunted a kind of strangled *you're welcome* as he started to place her gear in the trunk. But he was surprised to find he'd forgotten to remove his amp and microphones after his last band practice. He usually took far greater care with his equipment. It was too important to leave in his car, parked on the street in front of his building. Three of his neighbors' cars had been broken into so far that month. The breakup with Heather had taken his thoughts hostage. He hadn't been himself.

He attempted to move his things out of the way to make space, wishing all over again that he hadn't agreed to drive her.

"You sure my gear will be safe back here?" Heather asked. "It's going to roll around. Any chance your stuff'll tip?"

"It's good," Ryan assured her. His voice cracked. Had she noticed?

He cleared his throat. "Where is this gig, anyway?" How could he have agreed without asking? For all he knew, it could be in Poughkeepsie, or Juno, or Siberia.

Heather's sudden sheepish look didn't help.

"It's in Fairyland, right?"

She bit her bottom lip. "It's out of town."

"How out of town?" Ryan asked. When she paused, he pressed, "It is still in Missouri, isn't it?"

She shrugged, nodded. They didn't have to leave the state, at least.

"How far?"

"It's in Goldeneye. About an hour—or so—away," she croaked.

Darth Billy zoomed by on his bike, making loud, obnoxious kissy noises.

Excerpt from

The Fairyland Times

Michael Minyard's
"Observations from the Tower" Column

March 24, 1967

Construction vehicles parked outside the long-empty 362 E. Commercial Street address have readers asking what's happening with the old property.

Buyer Murio Vargas says he has big plans for the building. "A bar. Real old-school. Stage for local bands to play. But I don't want to tear the inside out completely. I don't want to gut the place."

At the still-young age of twenty-nine, Vargas has already had plenty of experience with the liquor industry, having worked with his family's distribution company in some capacity for more than a decade. "Done it all—worked in the offices, even drove a truck for a while. Really like to get off the road. Put down roots," Vargas said.

Of course, as *Fairyland Times* readers have been quick to point out in my travels through town, the Commercial Street property has something of a dark past. For decades, the building was the town's mortuary. A few of the older residents recited some of the superstitions from their childhood. Rhymes and warnings, beliefs that bumping into the door by accident meant you—or a family member—would be the next body carried in through the entrance, for instance.

"Place still gives me the shivers," remarked Fred Russell, seventy-five, as he stood on the square where the Commercial Street address was in full view.

Vargas did not see this history as a detriment, however. Instead, as he led this reporter through the interior, he was quick—almost proud—to point out that the original wooden platforms still remained attached to the walls, complete with holes "for draining the body fluids. At least, that's what they tell me. I'm used to wild stories surrounding bars, and when we open, that'll be the wildest story yet."

Vargas indicated the platforms would not be removed from the building, explaining, "Why would I erase the past? It is what it is. Besides, buildings are special. This one sure is. Heck, you look at a building long enough, you start to realize places really do have about as much character as the people who step through their front door."

Of course, in a town called Fairyland, it's easy to see the old building as a Sleeping Beauty, and to view Vargas as a Prince Charming of sorts, waking it up from a long slumber.

When this reporter pointed that out, Vargas simply laughed. "Maybe so, maybe so," he agreed. "This building's history oughtta get the crowds in to start with. People will come out of curiosity. But I hope it'll be the music and the good times and good drinks that keep the crowds coming back for years." Running his hand along one of the old mortuary platforms, he added, "Talk about raising something up from the dead, though, eh?"

APRIL 28, 1967

Sharon knew that her tattoo, now a month old, should no longer be itching. But as she sat in her photography class, that's exactly what it felt like it was doing: buzzing and twitching and itching. When she glanced down at the small feather, she halfway expected the edges to appear pink and irritated all over again.

They weren't, though.

It was probably just her nerves. All around her, portfolios were being flopped down on the tiny little desktops that filled her college classroom. Her professor droned on as he handed back their graded final assignments. Something about common themes he'd seen in the work. Sharon couldn't be sure. It was hard to hear him with her blood pounding through her ears.

He paused at her desk. Her turn.

Sharon raised her eyes from her tattoo to stare up at Professor Franklin. His brown mustache wiggled a bit, like he was about to say something directly to her.

He seemed to think better of it. He plopped her portfolio

down and pressed forward, picking up what he'd been telling the class, returning the portfolio to the student seated in front of her.

She opened the small plastic booklet, flipping through the pieces she'd chosen, all taken in Fairyland, the result of an idea that had finally awakened her from a deep sleep as her deadline neared.

The unfinished leopard tattoo. Murio Vargas standing in the building he'd just purchased, waving his arms about, explaining to her how planned to reinvent the old mortuary. A gardener planting seeds just outside the public library. Her father chopping vegetables in the kitchen for their dinner. A living room wall her neighbor was in the midst of covering with floral paper. A rusted car body on a tow truck being pulled into a mechanic's shop.

Works in Progress. That was the title and the subject matter of her portfolio.

Across the back pocket, where she'd placed all the permission forms she'd painstakingly had signed by everyone featured in the collection—her father and the men in the tattoo parlor and the neighbor and the owners of the businesses along the square—the prof had scrawled a giant "A." He had also added: "Sharon, these photographs might be about works in progress, but they most certainly were not taken by a work in progress. Great work. Brilliant insight."

Her chest swelled. She'd done it.

Her tattoo flashed up at her once again as she closed her portfolio. For the rest of her life, anytime she needed it, there it'd be—her tattoo, reminding her that her dad had been right all along, and she really did have it: Guts.

And if Professor Franklin was right, a little bit of talent too.

Michael

I know exactly what you're thinking. I promised you a Cinderella story. *So what happened to the waif?* you're surely asking. *Did she get a fairy godmother? Did she make it to her shoot? And what about Amanda? What sort of adventure did she have with Aiden? Was it something awful, since she was becoming Heather's enemy?*

All good questions. The morning of the shoot, while Ryan was helping Heather put all her gear in his trunk, Amanda was coasting to a stop beneath a nearby overgrown sycamore, its limbs concealing her fortunately gunmetal (shade-colored) Escalade.

She ran her fingers through her auburn hair—roughly, out of frustration—chastising herself for not returning Heather's voicemail immediately, telling her not to worry, she was on her way.

Why hadn't she bothered to return her call? Because she had assumed no one else would come save her? While she was at it, why hadn't she told Aiden where they were going? He utterly loved Heather. More, even, than the park. Had she not quite made up her mind about helping? Had she liked the idea of leaving Heather to twist in the wind a little while, making her sweat and worry?

But why? Heather was her best friend. Why would she want her to feel that way? And why was she annoyed now that Ryan was already here?

Amanda wasn't sure. All she knew was that she needed to shush Aiden before he could see Heather and call out to her, his piercing little-boy voice shooting straight through Amanda's rolled-up windows.

"It's a game," she told Aiden. "We can't let Heather know we're here." And put her fingers to her lips like she did in the library.

Aiden giggled, making fists and tugging.

Amanda frowned watching Ryan put Heather's gear in his trunk.

What was he doing? Hadn't he and Heather broken up? Hadn't that been the subject of one of Heather's avalanche of unanswered voicemails?

A strange surge of pain radiated from the festering black hole inside of her. (What *was* that hole? Why was it refusing to heal? Why was it only getting worse?)

When Ryan pulled from the lot, she lifted her foot from the brake enough to start gliding down the street. She kept herself a good three car-lengths back.

Good grief, was she stalking them now? Why? What did this accomplish? What was she planning to do?

Amanda slipped behind a pair of sunglasses so that Heather wouldn't recognize her in the rearview. Which seemed ridiculous. It wasn't like Heather couldn't have recognized the car.

Forget ridiculous. It was more than goofy. Frankly, it was kind of twisted.

Ryan and Heather pulled into a gas station parking lot.

Amanda followed, steering quickly to the far side, behind a

truck pulling a boat.

Had they seen her? She wasn't sure. They were talking and didn't appear to notice her. Did she want them to see her? Why was she hiding?

Finally, Ryan got out, reached for a nozzle at the nearest pump. Heather popped her own door to circle around to the trunk. She removed her camera and walked toward the nearby sidewalk.

Why?

Amanda stepped from her Escalade and freed Aiden from his car seat.

Together, she and her son headed for Ryan's car.

What are you doing? Amanda asked herself.

Ryan glanced over his shoulder and waved.

Amanda clutched her stomach, feeling like she'd been punched. Less than a year ago, around the same time Heather had announced she'd wanted to introduce her new love to her best friend, they'd all gone out to dinner together. Amanda'd chosen the ritziest joint in town, worn her swankiest cocktail dress and her chandelier-iest earrings. She'd gotten tickled at how Ryan and Heather had looked like a couple of out-of-place kids from appetizer to dessert, neither one of them ever managing to get comfortable with the starched linen tablecloth and their dress-up clothes and the wine list. So tickled, in fact, that at one point, somewhere between the consommé and the poached salmon, she'd excused herself to the ladies' room and had doubled over the sink in a round of belly laughter.

When she'd finally returned, Tom was playing the Good Husband role, carrying on the conversation in her absence, asking Ryan what he did for a living. Amanda bit her lip, ready to have to stifle more laughter. It was going to be something absurd. Like he'd say he was an "entrepreneur," which of course meant he had been unemployed since tossing his high school mortarboard hat into the air.

54

Or he was going to be a big famous actor, right there in Fairyland! Something decidedly juvenile.

But, no. Ryan was a musician, Heather had announced, smiling at him, her hand on his arm. A musician, recording engineer, and a guitar teacher over at Slade Music.

"You'll never believe this," Heather told Amanda. "We saw him play. In high school! And we loved his band. But we went to different schools..."

Amanda curled her fingers around her salad fork, every bit as tightly as her jeans had once circled her early-twenty-something thighs. She was the one who'd really loved music growing up. The one who'd been obsessed, the one with the towers of vinyl, the one who'd known the lyrics to every song on the radio, the one standing in mile-long lines (once in the rain and once in a blistering heat that had resulted in a second-degree sunburn) for concert tickets. It was her addiction—Amanda's—and Heather had simply been dragged along for the ride. Shortly after Amanda's "I do"s, she'd given up her albums to make space in the master bedroom for an armoire to hold her husband's business shirts and a separate rack for her own heels.

She listened to music on her phone now, mostly as she pounded the treadmill at the gym. She hated digital music. She still had her concert T-shirts, though. Tom had started to tease her a few years ago, asking, "When're you going to toss those things?" Initially, she'd teased him back, saying things like, "I noticed a few grays on you the other day. You'd better be glad I'm not one to toss old stuff." But she'd gotten a little worried about it, and just to be safe, she'd haphazardly stuffed them all in a black plastic bag in the attic. She'd figured the lawn-and-leaf bag (her husband's own storage container of choice) filled with unfolded, wadded items would lead Tom to believe it was something he had himself put in storage, something he hadn't been able to part with. The shirts would be safe.

Amanda was thinking of the shirts as she approached Ryan, the musician who had come to Heather's rescue.

It made the hole inside her sting all over again. Come to think of it, she'd felt a strange burning sensation in her chest the night they'd all had dinner together. Had that been the start of the festering hole inside of her? Had it really opened up that long ago? Now, the wound was old enough to be infected and painful?

But what had given her the wound in the first place? She still didn't know for sure.

"I got her message," Amanda explained with a shrug. Her mouth shook a little beneath the weight of her smile. "I got to her place just as you were pulling out. I can drive her to her shoot. If you need to be somewhere else. Or if it's awkward for you—since—you know—the breakup."

A nice save. But did she mean it? Why did she offer? To make up for the awful things she'd been thinking about Heather? To make up for the business cards stuffed in her glove compartment, her spur-of-the-moment sabotages?

Surely that had to be it. Didn't it? So why didn't it feel right?

"It's kind of a long drive," Ryan muttered, eyeing Aiden. "It's okay. I've got it."

Before Amanda could figure out what to say next, Aiden spotted Heather, calling her name and racing toward her as fast as his toddler legs would carry him.

"She seemed pretty nervous about the gig, so I suggested she warm up, take a few practice shots…" Ryan rambled in Amanda's ear.

Heather didn't hear Aiden calling her name. She was too busy lining up a shot of an old store across the street. Whatever the business was, it was housed in one of Fairyland's turn-of-the-century buildings, the two-story stone kind, with living quarters upstairs. A giant striped cloth awning rippled over the entrance in the June breeze. Amanda frowned. The awning was too big. It did nothing but conceal the name on the plate-glass window. Come to think of it, Heather's camera strap was also doing plenty of swaying and fluttering. In her apparent rush to take Ryan up on his practice shots suggestion, she'd failed to drape that strap around the back of her neck.

Intent on getting to one of his all-time favorite people, Aiden increased his speed, adding a few unsteady but ecstatic skips along the way.

"Traffic—" Ryan warned, but Amanda knew that wouldn't be a problem. Aiden would never run into the street. He'd never run farther than Heather. Sweet Heather, who listened to Aiden's nonsensical stories and colored with him on Amanda's living room floor and played cars, all while making jokes about how nice it was to get away from Darth Billy. She frequently told Aiden he would never grow up to be mean like that. No, Aiden would be a cool guy, a good guy. A smiling Aiden would lap up Heather's compliments while Amanda gritted her teeth because it was getting to be lunchtime, and Aiden would need his peanut butter sandwich. There they'd be, Heather the Neat Visitor and Amanda the Peanut Butter Sandwich Getter.

"Heper!" Aiden called.

Heather turned, offering him one of her best *hey, fella glad to see you* smiles.

He raised his hands into the air. "Heper!"

Heather held her camera with one hand as she waved back, her strap moving hypnotically.

She leaned forward, reaching for Aiden.

Aiden reached back. And found something to grab onto—the camera strap.

He tugged.

The camera tipped, tumbled.

And shattered.

Heather let out a sharp, piercing yelp of pure anguish. Before she could stop herself, Amanda smiled.

Michael

"No, no," Heather pleaded. "Do something." Who was she talking to? Certainly not Aiden, who had recoiled at her scream and headed back for the safety of his mother's arms. And it certainly couldn't be the asphalt at her feet. It wasn't like asphalt had ever been known for its ability to rescue—well—anything. Asphalt wasn't exactly great at rewinding time or unsmashing shards of glass and plastic.

Pavement couldn't cushion a fall, couldn't soothe the bruises caused by a sudden unexpected catastrophe. And it couldn't straighten its back, level out a steep hill, either. Which meant the busted parts of her camera didn't stop rolling.

Poor, distraught, horrified Heather began chasing her fractured pieces into traffic, not caring about oncoming cars. In that moment, she'd turned into a reckless child chasing her runaway ball. As though gathering up the camera fragments would make some sort of difference. As though the Nikon DSLR could ever be made whole again.

Somewhere behind her, Amanda's voice warbled, "Heather!

I'm so sorry!"

Heather carried the shards to the opposite side of the street. She plopped onto a wooden bench under a store awning, sweating and panting and distraught.

She tried to power on what little remained of the camera.

It let out a pitiful squeaky noise like a bird with a broken wing. The lens was cracked. Buttons were missing from the crushed and dented back.

It was over, over.

"Kaput," Heather moaned.

She gasped, trying to catch her breath. Her mind swirled, her thoughts becoming a tornado. What emotion should she grab onto? What did she feel more than any other? Disappointment? Sadness? Frustration? Anger?

Anger.

Heather fumed.

At least, she fumed for a slice of a second, until a wail hit the air. Across the street, Aiden sobbed in his mother's arms. Amanda cooed and Ryan stroked his head, attempting to comfort him. He cried in his vocal little-kid way that had every bit as much to do with flat-out screaming as it did with real tears.

Well, that did it. She couldn't be mad. Not when Aiden was that upset. It wasn't like toddlers went around plotting to ruin the world. They just didn't know what they were doing.

Regardless, Heather's life was now a complete and total wreck, in as many shattered scraps as her camera. Her reputation had rolled down the street along with it. She would miss her photo shoot, and no one would ever trust her enough to hire her again.

It would all come crashing down. She'd have to settle for a full-time job. The kind of mind-numbing soul-sucking permanent job that meant she'd done it, she'd caved, and Photo Phrenzy would never again be her business, only a hobby no one would ever take seriously.

Oh, what a terrible word. *Hobby.*

Heather would wonder, for the rest of her life, how close she'd been. Mere minutes away from finally getting her dud of a career off the ground, becoming a recognized, professional photographer?

She'd blown it.

Yes, *she*. Heather. It wasn't all Aiden's fault. In fact, very little of it was actually his fault. She should have taken a thousandth of a second to toss that strap behind her neck.

As her mind reeled, a knock exploded behind her shoulder.

Startled, Heather swiveled toward a plate-glass window.

An older woman inside the shop was making some sort of strange hand-swirling motion at her.

Did she not want Heather on her bench? Was she telling her to go away?

No. That wasn't a *shoo* motion she was making with her hands. It was going the opposite direction. *Come in, come in*, that's what she was saying.

Heather leaned back to get a look at the name painted on the glass.

Minyard's Photography.

Sharon pressed her face closer to the window, having seen the entire disaster play out on the street. She motioned again, urging Heather to get off the bench and step inside the shop.

JUNE 11, 1969

When Missouri weather permitted, the square was Michael's favorite place to have lunch. He enjoyed eating where he could see Fairyland's comings and goings. People with their kids in strollers or dogs on leashes. Men in suits with an hour to grab a bite. Shoppers weighed down by bags nodding greetings at each other. Window washers waving their squeegees about. Even the occasional frustrated cop or two giving a few parking tickets. The harried expressions, the clock monitoring, the rush.

Always, if he was patient about watching a person long enough, he'd see it: a look of total relief. It might be no longer than an exhale. But it was inevitable, there on the square during the lunch hour—the moment of a sigh. The lighting of a cigarette. The first bite into one of the tamales sold in a cart on the corner. Plopping down on one of the benches surrounding the square, soaking up a minute away from the office.

Yes, Michael could count on it: the sweet look of a brief moment of peace.

After a while, it was almost a guessing game. He'd focus on

one face, one individual, and try to predict what would bring their little slice of comfort. How they'd find their breather, their break.

He'd gotten quite good at it.

This particular day, instead of relief—or even the promise of relief—he saw an unwavering look of intense concentration. It sharpened one woman's face, refusing to lessen or let up. When a breeze caught her long black hair, she simply brushed the locks out of her eyes, her focus unbroken.

A photographer. She had to be, with her unfolding of a tripod, her repeated checking of what had to be an exposure meter...

This woman was working. In the midst of the square's hustle and bustle. In what traditionally amounted to the pursuit of a little slice of noontime ease.

Murio stepped from his namesake bar to prop a sign in his window advertising sandwich specials. Seeing the woman, Murio waved.

She waved back.

And still, no relief. Not pouring from her, anyway.

Instead, she went right back to her setup next to the curb on the opposite side of the street from Murio's.

A car approached, honked at her once for having edged too far into his lane. The driver rolled his window down and shouted at her. Some kind of halfway-flirtatious hello.

But the young woman—even from a distance, Michael could tell she was, in fact, quite lovely—didn't move. Or flinch. Or hurry up. She took her photo. And then another.

Only when she had finished did she take a step backward.

A woman who stopped traffic. A woman who couldn't be pushed aside.

Michael grinned. He liked that.

He wanted to talk to her, but also didn't want to interrupt. He watched, waiting patiently for a pause. Some indication she might be open to a hello. But when she finished, she simply folded her tripod and took off before he had a chance.

Michael promised himself that if he ever saw her face-to-face, he'd be sure to find out all about her.

Excerpt from
Wikipedia

Sharon Grayson Minyard (born September 12, 1946) is an American photographer and businesswoman. Minyard was especially prolific from the 1970s-1990s, garnering several international awards. She is best known for her strikingly realistic black and white photographs of midwestern small-town life and its people, most of which were taken in her lifelong home of Fairyland, Missouri. She has been heralded for the uncanny depth and respect present in her realistic portraiture. Her work has been showcased in photography exhibits nationwide. In her two most active decades, Minyard was frequently cited as one of the most influential photographers of her generation.

Sharon

I wasn't thinking about Michael anymore. I wasn't thinking about his donation box or how he'd brought down the old Nikon. Not when I saw that poor girl out there on the bench. The one who'd just broken her own camera. I wasn't thinking about my empty store or time gone by. I needed the girl to come inside, come closer. I swear, it was like looking at me.

I felt it even before I knew for sure what was going on. Trust me—you do tend to get a twinge of nostalgia when, out of nowhere, you're suddenly staring at the ghost of your younger self. That was why I knocked on the plate-glass window in the first place. I never did that. Any other time, I'd have assumed the girl on the bench was taking a breather and wouldn't step through our door if I shouted anything less than, "Cash register's open. Help yourself!"

With each movement, the rattled young woman entering the store dropped another black plastic shard or screw. She began dropping words too. No, tossing them. Telling a strange, garbled story. Something about needing help. Fast. Which was also odd. Even in its heyday, nobody had ever raced into Minyard's on the verge of a meltdown.

The lens tumbled onto the floor.

We both squatted to pick it up.

As our fingers tangled clumsily, I gave this stranger an up-close once-over. The new highlights. The well-put-together outfit that had also clearly seen the inside of a washing machine more than once or twice. The tag on the girl's equipment bag—slung over one of her shoulders—that read, "Heather Scott."

"You looking for a replacement, Heather Scott?" I held up the busted lens.

Heather hesitated. "I—I—"

Together, we headed toward the front counter. Camera pieces thunked against the glass top.

Heather sniffed. "I can't believe…it happened so fast. I have a shoot—an honest, real, paid-in-advance job. My purse is in the car across the street. But I doubt I have enough. Can I charge a new camera on a couple of different credit cards? Is there anything left that I could trade in? Do you ever reuse parts? Are there even any functioning parts here? I mean, this can't be fixed. Can it? Do you fix cameras like this? You don't, do you?" The girl played a round of hopscotch as she jumped from one problem to another. But then again, I knew from experience panic usually made you do that.

"You're a professional photographer?" I asked.

"Not really. Sort of. Almost. I'm trying."

I almost laughed out loud. Because I'd lived it. All of it. It engulfed me—that constant tired feeling, the long nights, the low-grade pulsing ache that stemmed from questions I could not turn off: *Can I do this? Will it ever work? Will anyone ever believe I really am as good—no, better—than other photographers if I don't have credentials? How do I get credentials if no one will hire me? How can I prove myself if no one gives me a shot?*

I knew what it was to look at a dream and see broken pieces. It all came back to me as Heather stared at the fragments of her camera there on my counter.

It was hard. It was scary. But it could also be thrilling. The unknown is thrilling, isn't it?

And then, as I was trying to claw my way out from underneath my own unexpected journey into the past, Heather's eyes started pinballing between the frames covering my walls.

From the Studio Walls
The Art of the Kiss

Some works are impossible to title, but not that one. *The Art of the Kiss.* Those words sprang to Sharon's mind the moment the image emerged in her darkroom.

Over the years, some people had looked at her masterpiece—two faces in black and white—and insisted the couple weren't kissing *yet.* Said the two were less than a breath away. They saw anticipation, the kind of longing that can make your every cell burst open like cherry tomatoes left too long on the vine. Others argued this interpretation was completely wrong; clearly, their lips were already touching. Barely. But touching nonetheless. That kiss was happening. They would whisper the word emotionally sometimes, like it was three different sentences: *Hap. En. Ing.*

Regardless, everyone agreed the kiss—whether it was already taking place or about to happen—was no mere peck. It was the kind of kiss that hit with the force of a hurricane, and could only come after years of searching and heartache and plucking *loves me, loves me not* petals from forget-me-nots. A kiss that melted the outside world. Stars aligning. One for the storybooks.

Isn't that the kind of love everybody longs for? Isn't it the grand fantasy? And there, in black and white, Sharon's picture offered proof positive that the search wasn't futile. *Look here*, that image shouted. *It exists. It's real.*

As the photo's fame grew, people came to Sharon's studio for no other reason than to see that very picture, their eyes growing hazy with dreams. If they hadn't yet found love for themselves, Sharon's photo assured them it was right to keep looking. And if they'd already found it, the photo reminded them of the joy it brought them—the first meeting, first kiss. As their memories bobbed up to the surface, those onlookers often repeated, "We've been so lucky, so lucky."

The Art of the Kiss, Sharon came to realize, was as much about the viewer as it was about the subject.

And that was exactly why the image was so powerful.

Sharon

The thing was, I'd kept the entire studio perpetually covered in my best work, each photo matted and framed. I thought the glass gave the walls a glossy look, almost like the store had been covered in mosaic tiles, the kind that together create a giant cohesive picture. A mural.

In a way, it *was* a mural. Together, the images told my story. Where I'd been, what I'd seen, how I'd felt looking at the world through my lens. Portraits. Landscapes. A few close-ups of inanimate objects, new ways of seeing so many everyday items. Even the editorial work I'd gotten over the years. A *Time* magazine cover of children in a classroom for an issue on the state of American schools. My husband. My customers. A Dodge Dart packed tight with frames going to an out-of-state exhibit.

A wordless biography. A photographer's life.

That first day with Heather, her eyes bounced past it all—including the image of Dad I was always so fond of—and stopped where everyone's eyes had always stopped. On the old black and white hanging near the ceiling. My magnum opus. *The Art of the Kiss.*

I found myself grimacing. If only, I caught myself thinking, she'd looked at it with a critical eye—then moved on to study my other work. Like a photographer should.

"My boyfriend broke up with me because of a photo I took," Heather blurted in a half-sob. Her tone suggested, *One more rotten thing in the pile of rotten things that keep on happening to me.*

I froze, not sure how to respond. If I even should respond. Sometimes, people don't want advice. Or consoling. They want to vent.

"Some dumb selfie," Heather went on. "Ryan missing my lips, kissing me on the cheek, and me looking at my phone. He said it summed everything up between us. Him trying to kiss me, me look-ing someplace else. Like I *was* someplace else." Her face drooped, and she sucked in a deep breath before murmuring, "'Look how I get to you.' That's what he said. All sarcastic. Like my phone turned me on more than him. But I guess—I kind of do keep choosing pictures over him.

"And I don't even know if my pictures are any good or not. What if I'm choosing *bad* pictures over him? It's one thing if you're talented and choose to pursue your passion over a relationship. I mean, at least you could justify it. But what if I'm not, and I didn't fight for my boyfriend, and in the end, I don't have a career or Ryan either?"

She plopped her elbows on the counter and cradled her head in her hands. "I wish I could twist the lens on my life and put every-thing into focus."

I was a statue. Completely mute. Not that it mattered. Not to Heather.

She raised her head, her eyes going straight back for my old image. "*That* picture," she sighed. "I don't know if I could ever take something like that. It doesn't even look like a picture. It looks like a painting. Like real artwork, you know? Because it's so full of emotion. Those two aren't strangers," Heather whispered. "They're—everything to each other."

Heather didn't realize that it was me up there in that photo. Me and Michael. Not that Heather really should have recognized me, really. The Sharon on the wall had long black hair, '60s-era eyeliner, a youthful face. The Sharon behind the counter possessed none of those things. I had a crown of white hair and a collection of wrinkles. I was not what anyone would describe as young. I hadn't been for quite some time.

"It hurts when somebody you love tells you the love you've given back isn't good enough. Like what you've offered is broken or faulty or something. I mean, is love some kind of artistic thing? Like drawing or singing? Some people do it really well, and other people not so much? That can't be right, can it? Isn't love love? It's not something you're supposed to critique, is it? Some love isn't better than other love, is it?"

Heather flinched, blushing slightly. "Sorry," she muttered. "He—I guess—it's a long story, but my boyfriend's on my mind because right now, we're kind of stuck together. Which is my doing too. I mean. My car wouldn't start. He agreed—since I was going to be a goner without him—to drive me to the shoot. Before I broke my camera. A day alone in a car with your ex."

"Sounds interesting," I managed to croak.

"Makes giving a root canal to an alligator seem like a pretty swell time, comparatively speaking."

I let out a little burst of laughter and started to come out from behind the counter, almost ready to grab her into a hug before I could stop myself. What is it about an offhanded joke that makes you feel you've shared something private with another person? As though you've become friends, somehow.

"It's not like me to babble on this way. I never do that. It's not—" Heather put her hands to her cheeks in a *What have I done?* pose. "I'm sorry. I'm wasting your time. I should cancel my shoot. I shouldn't make my client wait for me."

Okay, really. How many times does this ever happen to any of us, in life? There I was, the exact right person to step in and help this poor girl.

Maybe, if it had been the two of us, just me and Heather, I would have rescued her in the obvious way. I would have grabbed my charged-up DSLR and told her since it was already used but functioning, it was on the house.

But then I heard it: A slight rustling from the stairs.

I knew we weren't alone. Michael was watching me. And Heather.

Why was he eavesdropping? And another thing—a question that had been bugging me relentlessly, at least until Heather'd shown up: Why'd he bring that old camera down to me in the first place? It almost felt like he was trying to prod me into some kind of action. Goad me.

Into what? Working? I had been all along. Attempting to change with the times. Didn't he pay enough attention to me to realize it?

What did he want from me?

All I knew, right then, was that it felt like he was telling me I wasn't enough. Before I could stop myself, I was telling Heather, "Wait right there," and bolting at top speed away from the front counter, racing across the shop toward my shelf with the extra lenses.

There it was. The Nikon. Our Nikon.

The magic camera. I knew that was what Michael thought of it.

Magic.

74

Years ago, the word had rung in my head in kind of a quaint way. Right then, I couldn't turn the questions off. Why magic? Why would Michael ever think that? If I had to have magic to succeed, that would have to mean I had no power of my own, wouldn't it? Had my hard work not accounted for much in his mind?

How could it have, if he thought I'd found success because of some dumb camera?

Magic. At that point, the word was ringing in my head in a darker, almost sarcastic way.

I didn't know anything about Heather. The girl could have been a hack. A regular no-talent. She'd already rambled on about a picture she'd taken on her phone. Did that mean she considered self-ies with Instagram filters fine art?

Had Heather broken her own camera in a moment of clumsiness, or out of frustration? Would she break my Nikon? Break it out of ineptitude? Or irritation? Or—worse yet—instead of breaking it, would she decide she hated the ancient thing, and trash it? Dump it off at an electronics recycling location, collect a few dollars to put toward a new digital camera? The girl had no ties to me. A return was not guaranteed.

Then again, did I want her to return it? Now that she—and all these new questions—had arrived, did I actually want to get rid of it? Would it be a relief?

I reached for the handle on the case and stopped. I could see myself reflected in the white metal of one of the latches. Blurry and distorted and out of proportion. The black feather tattoo on the inside of my wrist, which had long ago faded to blue, almost looked bigger than my head.

I snorted a chuckle in the way people do when they're trying to say something that really isn't funny at all. The blue tattoo, the white hair…I looked like a woman fading away.

Like an old photograph.

He was still there, I knew. On the stairs. Would I hurt him if I actually went through with what was on my mind? It was drastic. Wasn't it? Giving away this enormous part of our lives together?

What did I want him to see?

Again, my eyes settled on my tattoo, the one that had for decades been reminding me how tough and gutsy I could be.

Gutsy enough, even, to give magic away.

"I have just the thing," I blurted, before giving myself a chance to second-guess it. I grabbed the case and raced back toward the counter, toward the poor girl who needed my help.

"I hope it's cheap," Heather moaned.

"It's free," I offered cheerfully.

The expression on Heather's face turned accusatory, like she figured I was out to scam her.

"Best camera in the entire store," I insisted. I clicked the silver latches open and exposed the 1967 Nikon.

"It's used. And it's…Is that a film camera?" Heather asked, disappointment saturating her tone.

"Yes. I've still got some film in stock, believe it or not—"

"Don't bother," Heather groaned. "I can't use it. Not for a professional shoot. I barely remember those old junky summer vacation film cameras Mom and I had when I was a kid."

That was probably true. And it hit me all over again how much time had passed. How different the world was. I didn't want to set the girl up to fail. I honestly believed the camera had life left in it. I'd built an entire career on photos taken with that Nikon, and I was certain this girl could too—if she gave herself and the camera a chance.

But I was also filled with so many other wishes. Mostly that Michael would snap out of whatever funk he'd settled into and see me as I was. Not a bunch of dumb fairy tale promises that never come true for anybody, anyway. Me.

"Maybe there's a chance I could get by using my phone," Heather mumbled.

"No way," I insisted, leaning over the counter. "I'll show you how to use it. I know all the tricks to make this particular camera work." And because I wanted Michael to realize how ludicrous it was to believe that fairy tales were out there walking around on the sidewalks, because I was certain the best way to yank him away from his silly thoughts was to hear them repeated out loud, I said, "If you get in a bind, this camera will show you everything. All you have to do is ask it for help.

"This camera," I added, loud enough for Michael to hear every word, "is magic."

Michael

Once upon a time, in Fairyland, magic lived and breathed.

And then it was given away.

Just like that. Like it was nothing that mattered anymore.

I gripped the stairs to keep from falling. Sharon might as well have given me away.

I stood silently as she walked to the storefront window, propped her hands on her hips, and watched Heather carry our camera away, her figure growing smaller before disappearing altogether.

Behind her shoulder, I could see my own hazy reflection in the plate glass.

Mirror, mirror on the wall, what's the fairest thing of all?

Not this, I caught myself thinking. Not giving your personal magic away to an absolute stranger. Most definitely, not that.

JUNE 14, 1969

I t was a random thing, really, the way Sharon and Michael met on that early summer day in 1969.

At least, it would always seem random to Sharon.

To Michael, it seemed more providential. Inevitable.

It happened in the jazz section of Bleeker's Records. Of course it did. If it involved Sharon, it would have to involve the jazz section.

She bumped Michael—but then again, Sharon had bumped a lot of people that Saturday. The stack of albums in her arms was heavy enough to make her elbows bow out to the sides awkwardly.

"Sorry," she'd said. Actually, it was something more along the lines of "Awahhh-y," since she was talking around the pen in her mouth. She'd been tallying up the grand sum total of what she was buying. At $2.99 a crack for an album, it tended to add up fast. And her available cash supply had been steadily dwindling.

Her eyes fluttered slightly wider, then narrowed into a squint as she sized him up, quickly deciding he was the epitome of a stuffed shirt. *Really*, her grunt said. *Who goes to a record store on a Saturday afternoon wearing a tie?*

He even had on horn-rimmed glasses. He had the look of Clark Kent, with no superpowers to back it up.

"Got quite the collection there," Michael observed, not wanting to let her slip away.

"Uh-huh." Still around the pen. More like, "Ulhsh-hah."

She raised an eyebrow, wordlessly asking him to step aside. The records were getting heavy, and she was trying to point toward the Thelonious Monk portion of the "M"s.

"Planning a party?" he asked.

"Ululh-uh."

That was a no to Michael and to the party bit both. Michael knew it was. But he slid a giant chunk of her albums out of her grasp anyway. She could hold the rest with one hand. Which meant she could use her free hand to slide the pen out of her mouth.

"Music to relax my clients," she explained.

"Yeah? What kind of clients?"

She flinched—or maybe grimaced. Asking herself, *This guy isn't looking for a full-blown conversation, is he?*

Michael wasn't her type. Clearly. They couldn't be more different, Michael in his business suit and Sharon in her linen bell-bottoms, her long flowing black hair and her black eyeliner looking more well-suited for the pages of *Rolling Stone*.

Michael, it turned out, was intrigued enough for the both of them.

"Photography," she finally offered.

"No kidding?" he asked, even though he was already fully aware of what she did for a living. Even though he remembered seeing her taking shots outside of Murio's. He couldn't let her wiggle away. Not yet.

She shrugged. "To distract them. You know. Like waving a teddy bear in front of a toddler's face. Anything to get them to forget their picture is being taken. Get them to relax and smile naturally."

"And jazz does that," Michael challenged. "I didn't know Fairyland had so many fans."

"Look," she sighed, "you seem like a nice guy. So I'm going to tell you there's no need to flirt with me. Because there's a whole story going on here you don't know about. And I guarantee you, the minute you find out all the gory details, you aren't going to be interested at all anymore."

To emphasize her point, she made a big show of hiking her purse higher on her shoulder—and flashing the inside of her wrist in the process. Michael's eyes landed on the small feather tattoo. It was an odd thing for a woman to have a tattoo—an odd thing for anyone other than a sailor to have a tattoo in Fairyland in 1969, actually.

Sharon had no doubt encountered plenty of people who had allowed a few drops of ink to help form their opinion regarding what kind of woman she was. Clearly, Michael thought, she was waiting for him to frown or cringe or show some sign of judgment.

But really, it only intrigued him more.

"So what, exactly, is this big story of yours?" he asked. Then quickly apologized, "Sorry—I'm used to asking questions. Digging for information. I'm a journalist."

Sharon grumbled, nodding at the tie, "Big interview this morning?"

"Opening of the new Piggly Wiggly."

"Ah. Hard-hitting investigative reporting."

Michael grinned. Despite her best efforts, he was yet to be annoyed in the slightest. "You might have seen my column. 'Observations from the Tower'—"

"Oh, yeah. It's got a whaddayacallit—a cartoon-looking castle turret—at the top of it, near the title. Instead of your own picture."

"You've enjoyed it, then."

"No."

"You've read it, though."

"No. Well. Occasionally. Especially when you focus on new businesses. Potential new clients, you know. But the rest of the time, I usually skip it. Nothing personal. I don't believe in fairy tales."

"You don't—"

"Nah. Don't like 'em. *Really* dislike the name of this city. I know you're probably playing off it in your column. But Fairyland. It sounds…" She finished her sentence by shuddering.

"Who doesn't like fairy tales? Not even for fun? Not Cinderella?"

"Oh, maybe that one. In the old Grimms' version, Cinderella cuts part of her feet off to prove that glass slipper couldn't possibly be hers. That was kind of cool. Almost like a horror story."

"That's not the way it goes," he argued. "The *stepsisters* cut parts of their feet off because they were trying to prove the slipper does fit. Because they wanted to be princesses."

"Oh." Sharon's face twisted into the same expression she might have worn sniffing a carton of soured milk. "My version makes better sense."

"Does it," Michael said through a crooked smile. This girl was getting more interesting by the second. "Michael Minyard." He shifted the weight of the albums and extended his hand. It seemed the right way to greet her. With a handshake.

"Sharon Grayson."

"*Midnight Cowboy*'s playing at the—" he started, before their handshake had even ended.

"I told you," Sharon interrupted, "it's not me. The girl you're looking for. I'm not her. Here's the story: My houseplants are dead. I live with my father. I started my own photography business in his basement. I'm putting in insanely long days right now. Mostly twelve to sixteen hours. I develop my work in my own darkroom well into the night. I don't go out for long two-martini lunches, and I don't watch TV in the evenings. Every once in a while, Dad sits on the bottom step of the basement while I work. He drinks beer and talks to me while we listen to the fights on the radio. I don't read 'Hints from Heloise.' As far as your paper goes, I'm mostly into political stories, but I do also check the comings and goings of the local chapter of the Rotary Club for possible business contacts. I do not do great laundry, I am not a whiz at folding bottom sheets, and I have never learned to cook."

"I see," Michael said, still unable to stop smiling.

They stared at each other, an uncomfortable pause opening up.

"I guess I'd better—" Sharon said, nodding toward the checkout counter. She held her hands out to take the records back, but Michael insisted on carrying them.

Sharon sighed with annoyance, but said nothing, deciding it was easier to go along with it.

When the cashier handed Sharon her change, she lunged for the stack, but Michael beat her to it.

Sharon raced ahead, opening the door for Michael.

They walked across the lot, to her 1962 Dodge Dart.

"Listen," he said after placing the albums in her front passenger seat, "I need a headshot. For my column in the paper."

"Do you, now."

"And I was thinking maybe you—"

"You don't have staff photographers at the newspaper who can handle something like that?" she challenged.

"You want the job?"

She did. Michael could tell.

But she shrugged, as if she could take it or leave it. "Only if I get photo credit," she said smoothly.

"Every week?"

"Every week."

This time around, Michael's smile wasn't merely appreciative. He was doing it again. Being flirtatious.

She offered the same I-could-take-it-or-leave-it shrug.

That time, Michael was certain, she meant it.

~From Michael's Notebook~
June the something-th, 1969

Sunday—I think. Might be Monday by now. It's awfully late.

I've never been a journal keeper. Or a confessional writer. But then, out of the blue, I met a woman.

She is beautiful.

And hardheaded. And smart. And tenacious to the point of being stubborn.

She's opinionated and seems to present a kind of gruff exterior that reminds me of a junkyard dog.

And yet, she is beautiful.

Not beautiful *despite* what some might call questionable attributes.

She is beautiful because of them.

~From Michael's Notebook~
2015

Friday. I think. Hard to keep track sometimes. Especially here, three full years into retirement.

I'm still not really much of a journal writer, often going months between entries. But even with all those pauses, those flat-out stops and starts, I realize I have collected enough written-in journals through the decades to wrap the globe a time or two.

Lately, all my entries dance around this phrase, one I've written before:

I met a woman.

And now, we've been together for more years than we were ever apart.

Excitement never lasts. I know that. It leaves us all thirsty for more. Maybe in not such an obvious way as excitement left me and Sharon, the stream of admirers and customers filing straight out the studio doors, never to return.

It was a thrill ride, being with Sharon during the height of her own fame, renown, admiration, interest. It felt like being on a rocket that kept climbing. Boosters exploding.

Mostly, these days, it feels like we've made our trip, we've danced with the stars, and now we're rusting in the junkyard.

Michael

Mere minutes after Heather left with our camera, I was pacing our apartment with a fury I hadn't known for years. I paused a time or two to give my donation box a frustrated kick.

Who was I mad at? Me. I was the one to blame. Why did I have to unearth the camera? Why couldn't I leave well enough alone? We were comfortable—weren't we? Me and Sharon?

Something bad had just happened. I'd watched it unfold. Something out-of-the-blue that had upset my attempt to break Sharon out of her spell. Something that had to be repaired.

I ran a hand through my white hair, pacing. Pacing.

I hadn't wanted to upset her. I just wanted her to come back to us. I wanted her to remember when things had been so good. So exhilarating. We could get back there. I still believed it. Didn't she?

On the second or third trip around the living room, my eyes landed on one of my notebooks.

The same notebooks I'd scribbled in incessantly over the years. Decades of them. The scribbling, somewhat predictably, had exploded since my retirement from the paper. I had piles of notebooks by that point, all filled with my longhand observations of life. Ideas. Snatches of poems. Jokes. Anything that had passed through my mind and down my arm. Anything my fingers had insisted needed to be scrawled onto a page.

If only she could hear me, I thought, the sounds of Sharon's favorite jazz station floating up from the studio below.

I grabbed my latest notebook, and with a distant, muffled saxophone in my ears, I raced out the back exit, toward the square.

"You need something?"

Booming. That's the only decent word to describe the guy's voice. His words rippled and echoed across the slabs of concrete that made up the town square.

The man who'd spoken to me was huge. Imposing. Thirty years my junior. And perturbed.

Surely he was the DJ for KTXY—Fairyland's lone jazz station. One of Fairyland's few radio stations, period—the other two played country songs or classic rock. Anything else we happened to be able to tune in broadcast from nearby bigger towns. I told myself I was lucky that Sharon's chosen station was just a few blocks away. Walking distance.

Maybe. Maybe I was lucky. The way the DJ glared at me made it clear he hadn't come outside to be friendly. He'd simply had enough of me staring wistfully through the plate glass and into his space, watching as he spoke into his microphone.

He didn't know about this place. He couldn't have. He surely didn't know that years ago, the location of this very radio station was Bleeker's Records. He couldn't have known that a lifelong love affair started right inside. My love affair. He couldn't have known that when I looked through the glass, I saw the ghosts of us. Me and Sharon.

I knew, though.

And I knew immediately how he was seeing me. The same way the rest of the world had begun seeing me, right about the time the grays settled in. He saw an old man. Somewhere along the way, my value had lessened. Old people have about as much worth as used Styrofoam containers. Something that's served its purpose, and now that the sesame chicken takeout has been gobbled down, needs to be disposed of.

That's how the DJ was staring at me. Like he was thinking, *Must be some way to ditch this guy.*

"I was hoping for a few minutes of air time," I said before he could quite figure out how to shake me.

The DJ chuckled. No way did I look like the kind of guy with anything of value to say.

Nervous, I pushed my glasses up higher on my nose. I glanced through the door he was propping open, eyes bouncing across the microphones and computers and all those crazy light bars moving up and down. I figured they had to be some sort of sound measures—whatever they're called—marking the rise and fall of volume. A semi-familiar Dave Brubeck piece played softly. I didn't have much time to get all my convincing done. Probably until this particular song ended, and the DJ needed to set up the next one.

"For what, sir?"

"To read," I explained.

He grimaced.

"Spiral bound notebook," I said, holding up my bright red college ruled. "Best laptop going." And grinned, fingers crossed.

The guy grunted.

"I used to be a writer for the local newspaper. Had my own column for decades: 'Observations from the Tower.' Like I was watching all of Fairyland from up high, right? Where I could see everything. I've never stopped writing—"

"You ought to start a podcast." He was starting to look like a wall. Something I was never going to get through.

"No, see—I want my wife to listen to me. Really hear me. And she's not going to go trolling through a bunch of podcasts. She thinks they're laughable. But she regularly tunes in to your station. She loves jazz. I know for a fact she's listening now."

"Look, Mr.—"

"Have you ever lived in a city?" I asked. "A big one?"

The guy sighed. He could have knocked down trees with the force in that sigh. He had no idea what we were negotiating. What was hanging in the balance. *Only my whole world.*

"I went to college in one. Totally different sounds, especially after growing up in a place far smaller than Fairyland. Never thought I'd get to sleep with all the horns and the shouts and the engines and the dogs and the slamming doors and the—"

The guy started to suck in another breath for a new sigh. The kind that could send me flying like dandelion seed. So I got right to the point. "Then I went home for Christmas. And—"

"Lemme guess. You couldn't get to sleep without the sounds of the city."

I never knew that impenetrable walls could get bored so quickly. "You've heard this one."

He started back through the open door.

"The thing is," I shouted, "my voice has become like those horns and shouts. My wife's stopped hearing it. She sleeps right through it. I've faded into the background. Got to change things up to get her attention."

"What for?"

I couldn't exactly tell him the truth, could I? What was the truth? That my wife had fallen into a spell of her own making, and given our magic away.

My mind latched onto the phrase: *she's given our magic away.* Maybe there was a way I could tell him that. Without giving him the details that would make him think I was senile.

"I need her to miss us," I explained. "I need drama. Without drama, what's left? Isn't a dose of drama the key to a good story? I'm afraid our drama's been replaced by the day-to-day. The routine."

I turned my face away from the open door and toward the hazy plate glass, the spot where my memories came to life once again. I saw Bleeker's, saw the aisles of vinyl and Sharon with that pen in her mouth and me sliding her records from her arms. I saw us then. And when I looked at the glass from a different angle, I saw me now, hovering on top of it all. My own reflection, which seemed faint, nearly unrecognizable. An old man staring into the past, at the time when he'd still been able to go after magic.

Mirror, mirror on the wall. Who's the fairest...

"Maybe love isn't fair," I blurted, taking my eyes away from the glass. "Maybe it's not anything you should have ever counted on. Maybe it doesn't necessarily get more valuable with time. Maybe, in the end, it's cruel. But I don't want to think that's true. Do you?"

The wall unfolded his arms. That last bit got to him. I could tell.

"Two minutes," he consented, holding up the same number of fingers for emphasis. "Then you're out. Okay? Two minutes. If it's bad, I can tell my boss you wandered in while I was in the restroom."

Two minutes. Sounded like heaven.

On Air

*M*irror, mirror, on the wall—who's the *fairest of them all?*

How many times have we heard—then repeated—those very words? We recited them as children. Mindlessly. Chanted them as we played-pretend through summertime games, diving deep into imagination's waters.

Stories are powerful things, I've come to realize. Because stories—our make-believe play—well, that's how we come up with our own personal vision of the world. What the world is, what it can be. What *we* can be. How we can navigate its highest highs and deepest disappointments.

In our heads, our lives are fairy tales. We each cast ourselves as the prince or the princess, and the road blocks in our lives we deem evil. We are good, our opponents are bad, and we move forward knowing that a golden sunset is awaiting our chariot and a kindly fairy godmother is somehow guiding the way when times get especially tough.

We believe. Because we have been taught to believe—not by what we have personally witnessed, not by any factual accounts, but by stories.

Yes, "Magic mirror on the wall. Who's the fairest of them all?" We're certain the mirror will say, without hesitation, "Why, *you* are the fairest in the land!" No one else comes close.

None of us could possibly believe we're actually the wicked queen—or a fire-breathing dragon.

You know, sometimes, I wonder about that old magic mirror in Snow White's tale. It had obviously been sharing its daily ritual with that black-hearted queen for quite some time. Had the queen once been extraordinarily beautiful? Is that why it praised her for being the "fairest"? Or instead, had the magic mirror seen past her superficial question and into her deep-down need for continuous praise, and decided a little fib—a white lie, a little bit of ego-stroking—might do her some good…until it got out of hand? While I'm at it, why would a magic mirror be confined to trivial requests about a woman's appearance? Or, for that matter, to giving the same rote answer over and over?

Had the queen changed over time? Had she grown cruel? Had the mirror witnessed her descent? Had her increasing cruelty made the mirror begin to see her as ugly? Was that why the mirror began to name young Snow White the fairest?

Or had something else happened—something that at first glance would appear benign, but in reality, was far more dangerous than anything, *anything* else?

Consider, if you will, the possibility that after days and months—even decades—of staring into the same face and saying the same exact words over and over, the magic mirror began to long for another face to gaze upon. Any face. It wasn't so much that the mirror saw the queen any differently. It was that the mirror began to hunger

94

for another turn of events. Perhaps the mirror—so magical, so powerful—succumbed to the most human quality of all. The mirror, in short, grew bored.

Yes, boredom. The most evil, most wicked, least recognized danger of all.

Was Snow White *truly* the fairest? Or did she show her face at a particularly low point in the mirror's existence? Did the mirror latch onto her, repeat her name, because it needed to destroy the mind-numbing routine?

And haven't we all done something similar?

We all grow blind to the startlingly beautiful things that surround us. The light dancing on the nearby lake. The antique chair in the corner of the living room. We forget it's there. Because it's part of our everyday. Humdrum. Ho-hum. Boring.

Hi-ho, hi-ho, and it's off to work we go! Only, we drive the same route at the same time on the same days. We sit in the same chair. We sleep in the same bed. We eat on the same plates. Day-to-day existence and schedules and deadlines are not the sparkling stuff of fairy tales.

At least, we don't think it is. But the answer from the old mirror, I'd argue, might very well be proof that day-to-day boredom can, in fact, seep into fairy tales. It's far more destructive than any wicked queen or evil stepsister with a rotten plan.

Yes, boredom finds us all, my friends.

But here's the worst part of it: What happens when the things we become bored with are not physical objects? What if we become bored by a feeling, an emotion? What if—just what if—the thing that bores us most is love? What if the very thing that had once aroused our every sense, dilated our eyes, raised the hairs on our arms, made the world brighter and more vibrant and fragrant…Oh, when love is new, doesn't the world smell fresh and clean, like it does after a summer rain?

Forgive me. I ramble. I'm an old man. It's what we do.

But it doesn't erase my question: What if we become bored—by love? What if the thing that once excited us more than anything can pale, lose its power? Fade to oblivion?

Now, you're listening. You've stopped whatever it is you were doing a moment ago—peeling an apple or running on the treadmill—because you know you're...

Guilty.

You've felt it. We all have. It's not merely that the heat of passion has cooled. We know that happens. We all recognize it. We expect it. What I'm talking about is worse, and you know you've felt it.

We have all been bored by love.

Love of a person.

Or maybe it was simply love of a place. Love of home.

Or love of an activity, a pursuit that had once made you feel whole—more like *you* than anything else.

And what if...stay with me, here...what *if* this being bored by love stems from something deeper, something far closer? What if the truth—the horrible, rotten, completely unvarnished truth—is we get bored by the day-in, day-out of *us*?

We seek escape. We seek refuge. We blame others. We blame obstacles. But in all stark, bare reality, we are bored with ourselves.

Our passion dulls. It grows tarnish. Because, as I said, we are bored with ourselves. More than we are bored with our surroundings. Our careers. Our spouses. We are bored with ourselves. Just like that magic mirror, we are sick to death of finding the same face in our reflection day after day after day after day.

"Mirror, mirror, on the wall. Who's the fairest of them all?"

If only we were shinier, flashier, more exciting. If only.

"Mirror, mirror, on the wall. *What's* the fairest thing of all?"

To learn that love is fragile? That it grows old? That it dries out, it cracks and breaks? It bores us? That we bore ourselves?

We bore ourselves—and that means everything, *everything* involved with us gets boring.

Love gets boring. Because we are bored with ourselves.

Don't let your love get dusty. Don't take it for granted. Even if you swear you haven't seen it in a while—it's not because it's not there anymore. Love *can't* be that fragile, can it? Didn't the fairy tales promise us more?

What do you need to do to keep your love shiny?

To make sure it stays anything but humdrum?

What is it that you love? What would you be willing to do to keep it?

Sharon

I actually said it out loud, right there in the middle of the shop: "Who do you think you're fooling?" Did Michael think some microphone would make him unrecognizable? Was he trying to disguise himself? He hadn't introduced himself. He hadn't used his name. But wasn't all that fairy tale junk a dead giveaway? His old newspaper column'd once had a castle turret at the top of it, for the love of all things *in a land far, far away...*

Of course, in our story, the "fairyland" wasn't far away at all.

In our story, everything was uncomfortably close.

I cranked the volume on the radio and leaned in to listen.

I wondered if giving away the camera had actually had a bigger impact on him than I'd anticipated. Was that what this was about? Was it why Michael had gone to the radio station—*my* favorite radio station, the one that played jazz? Because of the camera? Because of the girl who'd stopped by? Heather Something. Right then, I couldn't even remember her last name, especially not with Michael's voice coming through the speakers.

How did he even get on air, anyway? Who let him?

I listened, my heart hammering in the way it only can when you're furious. It doesn't just beat. It throbs, creating aftershocks all through your veins.

He was bored with our life? Oh, yeah, I heard what he said. *Bored with ourselves.* But he also said bored with everything he touched. With love. With his life. With me. Right? Bored with me.

He longed for the old days, when people flocked to our store. When my *Art of the Kiss* had literally caused a traffic jam, so many people all trying to see our image for themselves. Like I was a rock star.

Was I not as special if I didn't have the same audience? Not worth as much if the world wasn't beating down my door?

What if, more than he loved me, he loved the promise of who I could be? Had it been more about the excitement that had surrounded me back then? The excitement, not me as a person?

Maybe I couldn't remember Heather's last name. But I could remember what she'd said. *Isn't love love? It's not something you're supposed to critique, is it? Some love isn't better than other love, is it?* My love wasn't good anymore because I wasn't the same person? My love didn't feel as flashy, as special?

That was preposterous. I tried to tell myself that. But he'd said it. *Bored.* He'd used that very word.

How long had he been bored? A week? Ten years? Longer? Had he been bored during the long days that had made up our busiest seasons, bored with the work we'd both put into the studio? It had fueled me. I'd considered it all something we'd made together. I'd loved that he had always been there, helping with advertising and fixing customers' cameras, often working with me well into the night after having put in a full day at the paper. Doing the cooking in the evening when I was busy downstairs trying to wrap things up, usher the last few students or clients or shoppers from the store.

He'd always had a knack for fixing things. All those busted cameras he'd repaired. All those ideas he'd had for pulling us out of semi-sluggish times.

We'd been in it together. Hadn't we?

Or had he always felt something different?

Most of all, I wondered why he didn't talk to me. *Really*, I grumbled to myself repeatedly. *He tells all of Fairyland instead of looking me in the eye?*

Why did he think he needed to go to such extremes?

Anger kicked up all these thoughts over and over again, sending them to swirl through the air, then turn right back around and smack me in the face again.

Right then, I had no idea how to make sense of any of it. The picture was blurred and the most important pieces were outside my line of sight. I only knew that Michael was upset. All because of what? Giving away some camera? Or had that simply been the breaking point?

Don't get me wrong. I didn't watch the Nikon walk out of our door without a pang of regret. Goodbyes are never easy.

Bored. Every time I thought of the word, I made a fist.

I told myself I needed to calm down.

Mostly, I needed to wait for Michael to get home.

Excerpt from
The Fairyland Times
Entertainment Section
April 10, 1969

Grand Opening Tonight! Murio's Bar and Grill - Southeast corner of our downtown square. Dance to live music every Thursday through Saturday nights. Mention this notice and receive half off one cocktail of your choice. Offer good this Friday and Saturday, Happy Hour to closing.

MAY 30, 1969

Sharon stood on the sidewalk, cover charge in hand.

"Place used to be a *mortuary*," the bouncer told the girls in front of her.

The girls sucked in deep breaths, put their hands on their chests. Let their eyes swell. Muttered something that displayed their general shock or revulsion.

Sharon sighed, threw her weight onto one leg. This was stupid. And besides, she felt strange here all by herself. Really strange. She needed these girls to get a move on before she talked herself out of it.

She'd been thinking of coming for weeks. No. Months. Murio had been inviting her, "You gotta come see the place at night."

But good girls did not go to bars. Not alone, anyway. They went, as Sharon always had, with a date. A woman in a bar on her own was a different breed.

Still. Her Fairyland pictures were awfully tame lately. Her work needed some bite. Even her early pictures of the tattoo parlor'd had that.

She'd waited until her dad's poker night. Kissed him on his cheek when the cigar smoke was thick in the kitchen and he was holding a full house. "Back soon," was all she'd said when he tried to ask where she was off to.

"Any creepy stories?" one of the girls asked.

"Oh, the things I could tell you," the bouncer said, puffing his chest out. The motion accentuated the fact that the top three buttons of his shirt were undone.

"You ever have any problems," he told the girls as he opened the door for them, "you come find me."

Sharon stepped forward. The bouncer grinned, preparing to start in again with his story.

But he stopped as soon as he got a good look at Sharon's *don't mess with me* expression.

He straightened his back, took her money, and offered a polite, "Have a nice night."

The entire bar throbbed with a pulse, a tug, an undertow. Packed full of people, full of music, and full of another feeling, one that instantly infected Sharon, even though she couldn't quite identify it, not at first.

What she did notice, as she began to snap her photos, was that the colors men had chosen for their shirts were far brighter. Girls' skirts featured far shorter hemlines. Hair was bigger, makeup darker. Everyone here had turned themselves into neon signs. Hard to miss. Flamboyant. Gaudy.

She fell in love instantly with the pageantry of it all, the way everyone had made themselves up in order to venture out after sunset. She had never seen this side of Fairyland, not through her photographer's eye. A girl on a date did not look outward, did not take in her surroundings. Now, here, alone, she saw it all.

And because she saw it, she was finally able to put into words the feeling that had engulfed her upon entering. Each and every person, it seemed, was engaged in a quest to find that illusive something missing from their lives: love, adventure, perhaps a taste of wildness.

The room thumped and roared and whipped itself into a near-frenzy. It was raucous, joyous. Even as she relished capturing it on film, even as she enjoyed the look of the bar and the electric buzz in the air, underneath it all, Sharon detected a few distinct notes of sadness in the scene.

Sharon fell into the rhythm of work, forgetting herself until she bumped into someone. "Sorry," she muttered as she started to swerve around him.

But the man put a hand on her arm, stopped her from taking another step forward.

"Buy you a drink?" he asked.

Sharon frowned. She was working. Couldn't he see that?

Clearly, he didn't. That knowing grin on his face said he was seeing a woman alone in a bar and nothing else. Which meant he wasn't seeing *her*, Sharon. He was only seeing his own ideas, seeing who he expected her to be.

This was just what she was afraid of. It was exactly why Sharon had been dragging her feet about visiting Murio's after dark.

He wasn't the only one, either. She could see it all through the crowd, all those men turning every so often so look at her. All of them wearing that same awful knowing grin.

When they didn't know anything. Not about her.

Sharon excused herself, bumping and weaving her way to the bathroom.

In the mirror, she found the same old Sharon. Same long hair, curled slightly at the ends. The same eyeliner, same lipstick. She had not presented herself any differently than she would have stepping out to the grocery store at noon.

And yet, because night had fallen, and because of where she happened to be standing, everything about her was being interpreted in a completely different way.

She shook her head, clenched her jaw. Wiped her lipstick away with a paper towel. Pulled her hair back, securing it with an elastic band she found inside her camera case.

She stepped back into the bar. She needed to shake off the encounter that had unnerved her. She needed to forget what had been in those strangers' eyes. She needed to get back to work.

Through the viewfinder, she searched for a new subject.

There it is, she thought, *right in the middle of the dance floor.*

From the Studio Walls

Murio's.
1969

The crowd at Murio's had peeled back from a woman in a sequined top. She twirled and turned in the middle of the dance floor, pausing to lift her long skirt slightly and hold it to the side, mimicking the stance of a matador waving his cape and provoking an angry bull to charge.

I dare you to come at me with the worst of your assumptions, the woman's stance challenged the crowd in Murio's. The same assumptions that said any woman in a bar must be seeking male companionship. That said a woman who wanted to dance needed a partner. And if a person didn't behave as they were supposed to, why, there must be something wrong with them.

Was the woman drunk? Up to no good?

Absolutely not. The music was vibrating through every pore.

Pummeling her. Demanding she express what had settled into the deepest parts of her heart. Insisting that sometimes, a woman needed to talk with something other than words. Sometimes, a woman needed to dance.

There she was, alone, stomping a roomful of assumptions into tiny, unrecognizable bits. Why should she wait for someone to ask her? Why couldn't she just dance?

Sharon snapped her photo, unable to ignore the upturned face, the smirk. A woman daring to defy expectations and rules and standards and patterns. Needing no partner. Seeking no approval.

Asking only for space. To dance for herself.

Sharon

I hated waiting for answers. About anything. Especially *why*?

Michael returned late in the day. I wouldn't have even known he was back if I hadn't smelled dinner wafting downstairs. He'd no doubt used the back entrance, which was weird. Sneaky. Almost, even, a little cowardly.

Why can't you talk to me? The question buzzed inside me like the radio does when I've turned it up too loud.

The meat Michael was searing gave the shop the smell of an outdoor barbecue, of a picnic. Like the Fourth of July. I had a soft spot for the Fourth, actually.

Enough of a soft spot that the smell started to untie all the knots just under my skin. I was drifting backward, into memories that felt so incredibly fresh. Vivid pictures seared forever on the photographic paper of my mind. (How's that for a metaphor, Michael?)

Ah, but really, how could those memories not feel fresh? Our younger selves are never very far away—not even versions of ourselves that are fifty years gone.

JULY 4, 1969

"What's the matter?" Sharon asked when she discovered Michael standing on her front porch. Or, really, her father's front porch.

His face tumbled. "Matter?"

"Was something wrong with the headshot? Did your newspaper decide not to use it?"

"It appeared at the top of last week's column. Right there next to my byline. With photo credit, as promised. Didn't you see it?"

Of course she had. She'd torn through the pages looking for it first thing, before reading the headlines. Her dad had even started a scrapbook. Pasted Michael's column on page one.

The remaining blank scrapbook pages, the ones that needed filling, made him happy. So much for Sharon to accomplish.

Those blank pages—and all her father's expectations—had given Sharon something of a stomachache, frankly. Funny how blank pages could be heavier and harder to breathe under than a pile of bricks.

Still. None of that answered what Michael was doing on the

porch. Was Sharon supposed to thank him? Why? They'd had a business agreement. *Agreement*, Sharon's preferred word. She didn't like the tone of the word *promised* he had so casually slung out. Like he'd done her some sort of favor.

They'd had a business transaction. If the paper was going to continue to run the picture she'd taken, their transaction was completed. Over. Finished.

Wasn't it?

Besides, it was a holiday. Why would he show up unannounced on a holiday?

He was making Sharon awfully nervous. She shifted her weight from side to side. She reminded herself she was no fidgeter. But no matter how she scolded herself, she could not stop.

Maybe she was tired. She'd become obsessed lately with taking nightlife photos. Which meant she'd been spending what felt like half her nights in Murio's, chasing down what she'd considered her own brand of storytelling, and the other half developing her images in the darkroom.

Sleep was a luxury she couldn't afford.

But Michael already knew all this. He'd seen her not-so-incredibly-grand photography studio. He'd already found out (by drilling her with reporter-esque questions while she'd attempted to pose him) that her dad, the retired mechanic, was collecting his pension *and* working part-time to maintain the buses for the public school system, all to help fund his daughter's floundering small business.

Michael knew Sharon was little more than a novice in her field. She was no Edward Steichen or Man Ray. No one of any regard in the photography world. She hadn't even gotten as far in her chosen profession as he had. Michael had gone after what he wanted, and had made a point to show Sharon he was already doing it, even though they were practically the same age. He certainly hadn't needed truckloads of time to get his life off the ground. There he was, appearing in print each week, and making enough money to take care of himself. He'd no doubt opened a savings account—the height, Sharon thought, of all things sensible and mature.

Why would Michael be standing on the porch now? To rub in his supposed superiority?

Michael offered a crooked, sheepish grin. "Wanted to stop by and thank you. For your work. And to—well. I suppose I wanted to know if you were up for a Fourth of July excursion."

Clearly Sharon was up for a Fourth of July excursion. She was dressed in a red, white, and blue chevron patterned sleeveless sundress, which she'd paired with a giant white floppy wide-brimmed straw hat and a navy blue cardigan, tied around her waist, in case the air should turn a little cool after dark. She was holding a picnic basket. Nobody in town looked more primed for a Fourth of July excursion than she did right then.

But Sharon also had her camera case with her. "I've got some work to do—" she started, in an attempt to rid herself of him. Hearing the thundering footsteps behind her, she raised her picnic basket and quickly added, "Dad and I were on our way to the park for a kind of all-day outing. You know, an afternoon in the sun, then the big fireworks display later on. And I'll be photographing the crowd." *Why didn't you tell him you had a date?* she asked herself, fuming silently. The lie would have been the easiest way to get rid of him.

She opened her mouth to add as much, but she was already too late. Her father—all 6'4", three hundred and twenty brawny pounds of him—was pushing through the door, and he was slapping Michael's shoulder and inviting him to pile right into his truck and join the two of them.

Of course he would do that. It was her dad's way. Everyone was always invited. The mailman drank lemonade on their porch every summer, the neighbors slept on their couch when their own bathroom flooded, and Sharon's college friends had always kept toothbrushes in their medicine cabinet.

They *still* kept toothbrushes in the medicine cabinet, in case they happened to be passing through town—on a business trip, maybe. They still had a place to stay, should they ever need it.

She felt a bubble of hope float higher inside her. Maybe a trip with her father wasn't something Michael had in mind.

But he smiled, nodding in quick agreement.

And so, picnic basket secured in the truck bed, the three of them crowded onto the bench seat. The men chatted while Sharon did a quick prayer (or hundred) for rain.

As soon as they hit the park, Sharon shoved the picnic basket at her father, saying, "Gotta see about getting some good crowd shots before it gets too dark."

That was all it took. She was off then, maneuvering through the happy-to-be-outside, celebrating bodies—adults swallowing giant plastic forkfuls of potato salad, kids chasing each other, dogs barking, babies wailing, one girl twirling, showing off the streamers she'd tied to the ends of her braids.

She'd officially ditched Michael. She should have known it would be so easy. Should have suspected her dad would hook him into listening to another one of his long-winded stories, this one about the time a five-year-old Sharon had mistaken hot sauce for ketchup when dressing up her own Fourth of July hot dog. "Doesn't like the stuff to this day!" she heard his distant voice bellow for what had to have been the ten thousandth time.

Now she really could get to work.

She scanned the crowd as she pulled the Nikon from its case, wondering where to start. Hard to get her head wrapped around this scene. It was just so different from the nightlife photos she'd been taking at Murio's lately.

She hoisted the strap she'd attached to the camera case over her shoulder, trying to decide what feeling she wanted to highlight in this scene—what she wanted her shots to depict here in the daylight. Wholesomeness? Family life? Happiness. Or contentment, at least. Funny—the bar scene was all about searching for everything you felt your life was lacking. It was about filling those aching holes. But a Fourth of July picnic was about sitting back and enjoying what you did have—family, friends, laughter, time. Lots and lots of time. Fourth of Julys felt as if the day had been lengthened to accommodate the festivities.

Sharon started walking, weaving through a sea of blankets and shade trees and Tupperware containers, the billowing smoke from camping grills, women in sun-blocking hats, men in plaid Bermuda shorts. As she moved, she became aware someone was following along behind her. A pretty tall someone, judging by the size of the shadow in the grass. Moving every single time Sharon moved.

She didn't know who it was, only that it clearly wasn't Michael. He would have said something—he wouldn't have simply trailed her. He was too chatty for that.

Was this guy really following, or was Sharon being unusually paranoid? Had Michael's appearance at her father's door made her prickly and distrustful when there was no need to be? As a test, she turned sharply, toward one of the food vendors set up for the folks with no picnic baskets—and the folks who wanted another frozen lemonade to go along with their mother's special German potato salad.

The shadow followed.

Sharon slipped into a long line at the concession stand.

So did he.

She ached to run, but was afraid of looking unreasonably suspicious—that kind of thing, she knew, could come across as accusatory. Besides, her dad had taught her long ago not to run from a stray dog. Dogs raced after you, caught you, and attacked.

Anybody who trailed along after a woman in the middle of Fourth of July picnic was exactly that—a real dog. And, unfortunately, a brave one.

Better to wait and let whatever was going on play itself out.

She stayed in line, slowly snaking toward the ordering window. Her eyes scanned the menu posted on a sandwich board. Bypassing the corn dogs and lemonade, she asked for a single slice of watermelon instead.

Once she'd exchanged her coins for a large pink slice, she raced away, her camera in one hand and the watermelon in the other, darting between a group of kids with water guns.

He came too. Without bothering to order any food for himself. He couldn't have ordered. He hadn't had enough time.

Sharon's flushed face felt hotter even than one of the nearby bombarded-by-summer-sun chrome bumpers parked along the edge of the park. She scowled. Little did the strange man behind her know, she'd collected a few protective tricks while out photographing Fairyland after dark. Scare tactics. She swiveled, throwing the watermelon as hard as she could. It all happened so quickly, the man didn't have a chance to dart out of the way, pretend he'd never been following her at all.

"Ow," he groaned as the watermelon rind struck his shoulder. "What gives, Sharon?"

"Peter," she sighed with relief.

Of course. Peter.

As a favor to her dad, he'd been traipsing after her lately, in a decidedly not-so-out-of-sight manner. Everywhere she went during her night shoots.

He was a cop, after all. By day, anyway. The son of one of her dad's old mechanic friends. It made her dad feel better to know someone was watching out for Sharon as she wandered among what he referred to, in an anxious kind of grumble, as "that dang bunch of barflies."

Even though he considered her tough. When it came right down to it, there was still a difference. Girl tough was never quite the same.

At least, to hear the men in her life tell it.

Even her father.

"Peter, knock it off."

"It's my job."

"No, actually—"

"My unofficial job," he corrected, nodding once toward the opposite side of the field. Toward Sharon's dad, who sat alone on their blanket.

Alone? That couldn't be right. And yet, it was. Michael was no longer at her father's side. Catching her eye, her dad raised a hand to wave.

She waved back limply. And quickly began to scan the crowd. Where had Michael gone?

She wasn't sure, but suspected that he was probably standing close enough to watch her.

Which was a little creepy, honestly.

Peter was looking even more muscle-bound than usual, thanks to his somewhat slim-fitting baseball T-shirt featuring the name of his precinct's team. It occurred to Sharon that she might be able to use him to her advantage. Maybe, if she leaned closer to him, Michael would get the wrong idea about the two of them and give up.

Sharon didn't have time for Michael. Not that he wasn't kind of sweet. She didn't have time for any man, frankly. She had other concerns, not the least of which included a floundering business that required near-constant CPR.

Besides, Michael had already learned that though she was, in fact, moving forward, bit by bit, she was still not what anyone other than her father would have called impressive. She was no one with the accolades that meant she deserved to be looked up to. She was no one that commanded attention and respect. And yet, he was trailing after her anyway? That could only mean one thing: he thought she would easily give it up. What girl *wouldn't* gladly choose a respectable marriage over a flailing photography career? Photography wasn't for Sharon, anyway. She had the wrong length of hair and the wrong shape of hips. Wasn't that it? Wasn't photography a man's game?

Sharon didn't think so. And she had neither the time nor the inclination to prove it to Michael.

She needed to get rid of him, once and for all. She leaned toward Peter, attempting to appear infatuated. No—absolutely *absorbed*.

Peter squinted. "You look beat," he observed.

Not exactly the response she'd been hoping for.

She wasn't trying to win Peter over, either, but with his words hanging between them, she wondered: She'd been out the night before—did it show? Had her eyeliner smudged? Were her eyes bloodshot? Did her hair smell like an ashtray?

If Peter hadn't been aware that Sharon was into nightlife photo shoots, had he not known her and her father, would he have made all the same assumptions about her spending her nights in a bar?

Woman of ill repute. She might have laughed when the archaic phrase popped into her head, had it not also been a real possibility.

"You know what you need?" Peter asked.

Sharon tilted her head and offered what she believed to be an alluring closed-mouth smile. This was going to work. He'd offer her

a drink. Maybe a bite to eat. Something that would seem decidedly couple-y, and send Mr. Short-Sleeved-Dress-Shirt-on-the-Fourth
packing for good.

(*Really*, she caught herself thinking. *Who wears dress shirts
to picnics? Talk about straitlaced.*)

"What's that?" Sharon asked, leaning on one leg. Closer and
closer to Peter.

"You need to get married," he barked, turned, and headed
into the crowd without giving her a chance for a comeback.

"Trouble in paradise?"

Sharon jumped. Michael stood less than a foot away. Grin-
ning. Holding a cup of lemonade toward her.

Had he been there the whole time?

"No paradise," she admitted.

"I guessed as much."

"Did you."

"Sure."

"You taking notes for one of your big assignments?" She
pointed at the tiny notebook poking out of the top of his shirt pocket
before accepting the lemonade with her free hand.

As she waited for him to respond, she took a sip. It tasted so
good. Surprisingly cool, a relief from the July heat, and more sweet
than tart, just the way she liked it.

He shrugged. "I don't mind the lesser assignments. I don't
even think they're lesser."

"You don't."

"Life—contrary to what you hear on the nightly news—isn't
an unending stream of tragedies."

"And what *is* life, professor?" *Why am I teasing?* she asked herself. He'd get the wrong idea if she wasn't careful.

"Oh, laundry and dirty dishes." He grinned again, but his

tone indicated he wasn't teasing back—he meant it. "Polishing your shoes," he added. "Studying facts for a history test. And slowly, after a towering pile of days, a stack of calendars stretching up to the sky, you become a different person. Who you were meant to be all along. You're a journalist—or a photographer—instead of a student. You're driving a Chevy instead of pushing a toy car across your mother's living room rug."

Sharon didn't like the way his words resonated. She didn't like the way her hands were sweating and her legs weakening—yuck. Like she was the doe-eyed girl in some corny pop song.

She didn't listen to pop songs. Too predictable. It was one of the reasons she liked jazz.

But she certainly hadn't expected Mr. Dress Shirt to say something so emotional, so sentimental. She'd largely ignored his fairy tale talk at Bleeker's, chalking him up to being one of those all-business types. Now, his words were hitting her like the rhythm and tones of the songs she preferred. Sharon liked surprises. This one was even sweeter than the lemonade.

She cleared her throat and observed, simply, "So you prefer human interest stories."

"The high school basketball team and the annual fall quilting bee. The piles of days that make people who they are."

"Interesting," she murmured. She certainly didn't want to appear intrigued. She was trying desperately to think of a way to untangle herself from him, but all she could come up with was waving at her father again, who had been joined by two of his retired buddies.

"I like the way you can count on it," Michael went on, his voice growing increasingly sincere. "The dewiness of June mornings, the way it sparkles in the soft sunlight. The way daffodils are always the first to bloom each spring—sometimes even before the snow's stopped falling for good—and inevitably give way to tulips. The cool

118

relief of the first autumn breeze that always arrives after a long scorching August, right on time, like a train sliding into a station.

"Most of all, I like being part of it. I like knowing that soon, like every year, the mayor will partner with the current high school track star for the three-legged race, and everybody will eat their weight in watermelon, and the women of the First Baptist will sing every patriotic song known to man while the fireworks go off tonight. Odds are, they'll sing 'America the Beautiful' three times."

Sharon liked what Michael said, despite her very best efforts not to. She reminded herself that she preferred things outside the norm, and Michael was talking about the opposite—about patterns and things you could count on to never change.

Then again, a man talking like this was anything but normal. Wasn't it? Peter surely never would have ever waxed poetic about the autumn breeze and daffodils. Neither would her dad, come to think of it. Before Sharon could stop herself, she found herself wanting another taste of Michael's words. More, even, than she wanted the lemonade.

As her mind spun and she fought to latch onto something to say back, she became aware that in the distance, voices were crying out, "Watch out!" And, "Duck!"

Who were they yelling at? Sharon glanced up as a wayward softball careened toward her, quickly growing larger as it also grew closer.

Dangerously close.

Her entire body tensed. She needed to move, but it was already too late.

Just as it had been too late for Peter to avoid being splattered with her watermelon.

The softball thunked against her camera, knocking it to the ground.

Busted.

Sharon

The stench of firecrackers grew stronger—harsh, gunpowdery—filling my nose. Making my eyes water.

That's how real that old scene was. I was smelling it. It was all so vibrant: the sunlight and the crowds and the scents. The details of that dusty old memory were back, popping like fireworks around me. I could feel the fresh horror all over again as I recalled the sight of my shattered camera. Everything I'd planned and hoped for had centered around that Nikon. Just as Heather had attached her dreams to her own camera. Two lives, two separate accidents—mirror images.

Mirror, mirror, on the wall, I thought, Michael's radio words coming back to me.

Only, as I blinked myself fully into the present and the memories receded, the firecracker stench continued to grow stronger.

What was that smell? Michael certainly hadn't been shooting bottle rockets in our living room.

I raced into the kitchen, finding it thick with smoke.

Michael

"What happened?" Sharon yelled while I flapped a dishtowel against a blazing burner.

"Grease fire—must have dripped when I basted the brisket." My voice was a little more frantic than I wanted it to be.

Sharon grabbed the baking soda, dumped it on the flame, and covered the burner with a nearby skillet lid.

With the fire suffocated, we stared at each other, panting and relieved. A brief moment of intense fear, followed by the *everything's okay* rush that arrives once danger has been eradicated, had semi-exhausted us both. Simultaneously, we wound up crumpling to the tile floor. Staring into each other's eyes, we started to laugh.

But our laughter dried up as quickly as it had begun.

Memories hung in the air between us, as acrid as the lingering smoke. Now, staring at her, I was hearing the words I'd uttered on the radio.

She had to have heard them too.

Wasn't she going to say something about it?

While I was at it, was she going to mention giving away her

camera? The one that had broken half a century ago? The one that I'd brought back from the dead?

JULY 6, 1969

Some heroines simply do not sit around waiting to be rescued. Instead, they hit the Yellow Pages when disaster strikes.

When Sharon plopped the phone book on the kitchen table during that Fourth of July weekend long ago, her father didn't so much as glance up from his breakfast plate.

She squinted at him. Didn't he recognize a girl thwarting disaster?

"What're you looking up?" he asked, running a piece of toast through his egg yolks.

"Camera shops."

He snorted. "It's a holiday weekend. And Sunday. Dream on."

"Somebody's got to be working in their shop. Playing catch-up on paperwork or putting up a new display while they're not open. If I let it ring long enough, somebody's got to answer."

"And if they don't?"

"I'll just go down the street banging on doors. If I have to drive fifty miles, so be it."

"If it was so pressing, why didn't you start yesterday?"

"It was still a holiday weekend yesterday." Sharon stuck her chin out defensively.

"Think I'd wait a few days if I were you," her father advised, slurping his coffee. Sharon noticed he was still wearing the white undershirt he'd slept in.

"Wait for what? A miracle? If it was fixable, he would have brought it back yesterday. Or called or something. Why'd I ever let him take it to begin with? What was I thinking? I was *hoping* I wouldn't have to spend the next decade or so trying to pay off a new camera, that's what. No way is Michael Minyard bringing that camera back in one piece. You didn't see it as close up as I did. It was shattered."

"I've got a feeling about him," her father said, and returned to his morning paper.

Sharon frowned, wanting to ask for more details. And deciding, in the end, to shake it off.

Only, she couldn't. Her father never sugarcoated anything. And he had never, not once in her entire life, ever lied to her.

He slathered a piece of toast with marmalade and handed it to her. "Eat up. Takes a lot of energy to listen to phones ringing and never being answered."

Sharon grabbed the toast and snatched the phone off the hook, the curly cord stretching between the kitchen wall and the table. She'd barely gotten halfway through dialing the first number when their doorbell rang.

"Bet that's Michael now," her father said.

"Please," Sharon muttered. "It's a neighbor. Somebody didn't get their paper delivered and they want to borrow ours, or they're looking for the cat that ran off during all the fireworks commotion and hasn't been seen since." She hung the phone up and carried her toast to the front door.

"I bet on the cat," she called out, throwing the door open.

But no—no worried neighbor. Her smile faded.

There he was. Michael. On the porch. Pushing her camera case toward her.

"Oh," she said, not noticing the sticky jam she was getting on the case as she accepted it. "I know. It's unfixable. Don't worry—"

"No, it's done," he said. He had that look like he could hardly hold back the laughter bubbling up inside him.

"Done?"

"Fixed."

She frowned. "How—"

"Why don't we go try it out in the studio?"

"There's no way—"

From the kitchen, her father shouted, "Don't leave Michael on the porch all day, Shar."

She flinched. "I guess—one shot—wouldn't hurt. But I'm warning you, these things are sensitive. There's no way. Even if it technically takes a picture, I'll still see all the differences during development. It was nice of you to try, but—"

"Would you like some coffee, Michael?" her father asked, carrying a steaming cup into the living room.

"Hey, thanks," he said, reaching out to accept his offer. The coffee was fresh and the ceramic sides of their cups were thin. Michael grimaced, fingers burning as he wrapped his hand around the cup. He gripped the handle quickly, shaking the pink, nearly-scorched fingers of the other hand.

Sharon wore a look on her face that said she was more than a little annoyed by the whole back and forth. Yes, her father was the type to loop everyone in, extend invitations. But the over-eagerness, the nauseatingly sweet tone her father used...it was a little much, even

126

for him. Almost like her father had decided to treat this guy like some sort of long-lost family member.

She clearly did not believe some half-baked fairy tale spouting journalist was capable of putting together a serious column—let alone a camera full of delicate pieces, all of which had been smashed to oblivion.

And yet, both Michael and her father could tell by the interested look on her face that she was dying to give it a go.

Michael was on her heels as Sharon headed downstairs.

She flicked on the lights and popped open her case. She ran her fingers around the camera, surely feeling the new ridges and scratches that weren't there before.

Sharon placed the camera on her tripod, her eyebrows all slammed together in a *can't be* sort of way, while her lips mouthed a silent *please please please still work* kind of prayer.

She attached her shutter release cable and turned. "You want to sit—" she started, motioning toward the stool where she'd taken Michael's headshot. He'd already pulled the simple blue smudgy background down from a large overhead roller—the kind that had once allowed maps to be pulled down in front of the chalkboards in their own high school classrooms. Instead of sitting on the stool to pose, as he had for his column headshot, he was holding one of the nightlife photos she had spread across a table. But he wasn't simply looking at it. He was inspecting.

Sharon's face twisted into a look of sheer mortification—like Michael'd opened a page of her diary.

"You think I stink," Sharon said, snatching the photo from his hand.

"No, I don't."

"I'm not a little kid. You can tell to me straight."

"I think these are an amazing starting point. But I also know

127

you're about to far surpass all this."

"And why is that?"

"Because I am a sorcerer."

"A sorcerer," she repeated sarcastically. Clark Kent was trying to convince her he really did have superpowers. "In Fairyland. Do you have any idea how ridiculous that sounds?"

Michael offered her a crooked grin. "You know what rarely ever changes? Fairy tales. For the most part, they're the same."

"A story told is a story told. Why would it change?" Sharon responded, still fingering the cable.

"Oh, no," Michael corrected. "A story told becomes a story repeated. And all good fish tales usually grow with each telling. Become wilder, more unbelievable. I'm a story man, remember? I know these things. And sure, there were a few variations in fairy tales, especially when the tales were new. But fairy tales during more modern times? Not so much. We must really love those stories, because we don't change them. We simply repeat them verbatim, over and over.

"Right now, right here, I'm telling you that what we are living in is a fairy tale and I am a Fairyland sorcerer, and these photos," he paused to point at her latest images, "don't matter, because I have changed your camera. It is, madam, like all fairy tale gadgets—the wheel upon which gold is spun. It is the beautiful carriage that will now carry you forward. It is Cinderella's glass slipper, returned by the prince, that fits. Magic awaits you with this camera."

"And why, dear sir, did you do such a thing? Why have I become the chosen one?" Sharon asked, deciding to play along. Figuring, at this point, that his story was merely an excuse. Her camera, suspicion told her, was actually still broken. This tale was simply a way to soften the news that the camera could never be fixed.

Michael didn't answer immediately. He crossed to her record player and dropped the needle on the vinyl. Jazz notes filled the basement as he gathered her in his arms.

They danced, but not clumsily. They swayed together like they'd done this before. Like they somehow understood how their partner moved, no stumbling period needed to get to know each other.

"Want to hear how I fixed it?" he murmured in her ear.

Sharon stiffened and started to pull away. "What is this? You showing me you can fix me?"

"Fix?" Michael looked an odd mix of wounded and offended and sorry. "There's nothing to fix here, Sharon. Not with you. There never was."

He took her up in his arms again, and continued, "I fixed the *camera* by thinking of you, the princess who doesn't need me. I know you don't. I happen to think we'd be good together. You and me. Amazing."

Before she could stop herself, Sharon was letting go, giving herself permission to become part of Michael's fantasy world. For that brief moment, it was true, all of it—the camera was magical and the world sparkled. A man accepted her and didn't want to fix her. She could be Michael's and be her own woman separate from him. She could dance here with him and all by herself in the middle of Murio's, any old time the mood struck. She could be supported without giving up being strong. She believed that Michael saw her as tough, and not just girl tough. That he would never send a Peter to protect her as her dad had lovingly done. Michael had spent who-knew how many hours fixing her camera; he had uncovered parts on a holiday weekend. And she believed it was not out of pity but because he had been overcome with genuine affection for her. Already, after only a few brief meetings. She believed that the world belonged to the two of them. And that they could make rules to fit them, not the other way around. She believed fairy tales really did come true.

They grew ever closer as they danced, taking tiny steps, never venturing far from the Nikon. "You and me," Michael repeated. "My abilities and yours. All tangled up now in that single camera." The song surrounding them swelled, hitting a crescendo. Michael's face lowered toward hers. "Take a picture of us," he whispered. "You'll see it. Everything we can be."

Sharon closed her eyes. The sense of melting into Michael brought such shock that Sharon squeezed her hand—the one holding the camera's shutter plunger. The one that would have taken their picture, if only that camera still worked.

Only, it *did* take their picture. At the moment their faces met—or maybe in that slice of a second before their lips touched.

Hard to tell for sure. All Sharon knew was that she had heard the snap, sensed the flash against her closed eyelids.

How? Sharon's shocked face seemed to ask, pulling away from Michael.

It shouldn't have. No more than fairy tales should ever come true.

And yet…

Sharon scrambled to crack open her camera, pull out the film.

Michael

It sounds nuts. I know it does. As crazy as a story taking place in Fairyland. That camera should have been useless after the Independence Day fiasco. But it wasn't.

It was magic. My hands had made it so. After that accident, I'd turned an ordinary, everyday object into the kind of powerful tool that could make dreams come true. Abracadabra.

Her dreams and mine both. And that *kiss*. Wow.

But what had happened in the years since? After a million goodnight and hello kisses? Million. Such a lazy number. We lean on it when what we're really saying is "too many to count." This woman, the same I had once hungered to get close enough to speak to, had, by that point, kissed me so many times that I could rely on that lazy number. Million. An unfathomable amount.

Had the fire between us been reduced, at that point, to mere embers? Little orange specks in the midst of ashes. Cinders, that was a better word, the preferable word. Because that meant there was still something left that could reignite at any time. Combustible material. Yes, combustible was so much better than contentment. Contentment was fine for small snatches of time—for picnics and vacations and little moments in-between adventures and new chapters. But what if contentment was all that remained?

I crossed my fingers for cinders.

But I was also painfully aware that my latest notebook was open on the kitchen table. Right where she could find it. I'd been putting it there, day after day, for the past several months. And she had never picked it up to read it. Not like she used to.

Still, we sat, silently staring at each other, our memories covered in cold ash, two players in a real, ongoing Cinderella story.

But what role did I play in it? Prince Charming? Or a villain? Was that possibly the reason for her detachment? Somewhere along the way, she'd started seeing me as her arch-enemy?

I could no longer read her thoughts. Not anymore. I had no way of knowing if that Fourth of July weekend ever crept into her head. If she thought of it with affection. Or if the mere idea of it weighed on her with regret or what-ifs or images of a life unvisited, decisions that could have been made another way.

A planet-sized chasm had opened between us.

I was terrified the clock had already struck midnight.

AUGUST 2, 1969

Sharon and Michael stood on the sidewalk, listening to the bouncer tell the story of Murio's. A new bouncer, one that Sharon hadn't yet seen. But the same story:

"Used to be a *mortuary*."

The small cluster of young women gasped.

"The tables they used to lay the bodies on to drain them are still inside."

One girl turned her eyes—lids loaded with blue eyeshadow—toward the front of the bar. "Maybe we should go somewhere else."

"Don't you worry," the bouncer told her protectively. "You ladies have any problems, you come straight to me."

He nodded once at the girls, implying that they would not have his own personal protection at one of the bars off the highway.

Yes, they were safe here. On the Fairyland town square. Under his watch.

Michael glanced at Sharon, who rolled her eyes.

Michael swallowed a laugh as he handed over their cover

charge.

They slipped inside, immediately drifting off in two different directions—Sharon into the crowd and Michael toward the bar.

He ordered a vodka tonic, which he placed next to his notebook, and twisted his barstool to face the crowd. They'd chosen Murio's for the first of what Michael hoped would be many working dates.

He leaned back, already smiling as Sharon prowled the edge of the crowd.

"So."

Michael flinched as the single syllable hit his eardrum like a hammer.

He glanced up, finding himself next to a man twice the size of the bouncer outside. With an unapologetic *gotcha* look on his face. "You and Sharon. Here together," he said.

He'd startled Michael, sending his thoughts scattering like birds frightened by a sudden noise. Slowly, though, as his thoughts settled again, he recognized the man.

"Peter. Right? From the Fourth?" Michael asked.

"Good memory." Peter offered his hand. "She keeps telling me that I don't have to follow her," he added, shouting directly into Michael's ear.

Michael nodded slightly. "Sounds like Sharon."

"She tells me—basically to get lost. And that she'd cover for me. Tell her dad I was still out here. Keeping an eye on her."

"So why don't you take her up on it?" Michael asked, his voice laced with a slight but ever-growing annoyance.

Peter offered a sly smile. "Been doing it long enough that she feels like my sister or something. I keep thinking, though—maybe sometime she gets lucky. And maybe I'm not needed anymore."

Michael stared Peter down. "Lucky? Lucky how? She's not

looking to pick somebody up. She's a photographer. Doesn't need anyone defending her, either. She can take care of herself just fine. I came here to be close to her while I worked on my own column." He nodded once at his notebook. "But as long as I'm here, you can take off."

Peter wheezed a laugh. "Sounds *exactly* like something Sharon would say." He slapped Michael's shoulder in an almost congratulatory way.

In an abrupt change of subject, Peter asked, "Column, huh? What's it about?"

Michael nodded, beginning to understand. "So are you reporting back to Dad that I passed the test?"

"Ah, you passed already. This was just..."

"Confirmation?"

"Maybe." Peter shrugged.

A nearby flash stole their attention. Together, they turned to watch Sharon at work.

From the Studio Walls

Murio's.
1975

Light from the disco ball created a polka-dot pattern on the faces of the young couple. Frozen in time, seen only in profile, seated at a tiny table near a wall, hands touching. A portrait of newfound desire. Of feelings they had not yet expressed out loud, but that were ready to unfurl, shamelessly, one more new bud in the spring.

The photo had been taken during the last time Sharon slipped, Nikon in hand, into Murio's.

She hadn't known it would be the last, not until she was back in her darkroom. Not until memories began to swirl, one image after another, swimming through her developing solution.

She saw her own first night at Murio's, being mistaken for a woman on the prowl. And she saw herself later on, when she'd become *The Art of the Kiss* Sharon. Fairyland's hometown celebrity. No assumptions or misinterpretations. They all knew her by then.

But it wasn't all work. And she began to see those images too. Fun nights with Michael and Peter. The three of them sharing cocktails and the latest stories ripped straight from the pages of their own lives. Saw them raise their glasses in a toast, their arms swept out in wild gestures, their mouths open in laughter.

She saw the friendly arm punches Peter gave her, their sibling-style rivalry fueled, surely, by sharing Sunday dinners at her dad's place. Peter's folks often showed, carting homemade desserts.

Of course they'd had dinner together. Everyone was always invited. Her dad's way.

Image after image. Inside Murio's, throughout the years, the faces remained ever-changing. Different groups, new crews. Didn't that mean there would always be new pictures waiting to be taken?

Sharon had once felt certain of it.

But after a while, Peter's parents moved to Florida. And Peter left to join the force in St. Louis, coming back to visit now and then. The now and then stretched farther and farther until he didn't visit at all.

Image after image, night after night. Recently, Sharon's after dark photos had begun to feel less and less satisfying.

She blinked the memories away, placing her current image of the couple beneath a disco ball in the stop bath.

Yes, she knew, the faces had changed, but the story was the same. Over and over. New couples, firsts, youth. Here, right in front of her, was photographic proof.

She had already done this. She was traveling old ground, sinking her feet into her own footprints.

Even before she'd framed this portrait of new love, she'd known that her Nightlife Period was officially over. Time to move on. How strange, she thought, that beginnings and endings were so often twisted together, like the stripes in a peppermint stick.

MAY 9, 1987

At ten years old, the last thing Charles Liu wanted to do was go to some boring old camera shop.

But then again, it was where his father was going to spend his Saturday. He intended to buy a camera for Sara Liu's twelfth birthday. Which meant that Charles didn't really have much choice in the matter. Not if he was going to spend time with him.

Charles most often saw his dad from the back. The man was perpetually racing off to catch yet another flight out of town. Charles wasn't exactly sure what his dad did at IBM—something about networks and computers—but he did know he hated his dad's job. He hated it for taking him away, and for being more important, it seemed, than Charles.

Charles had already vowed that he was going to have a big business of his own right there near the square of Fairyland. He would never go on long work trips and be away more than he was home. He was going to have a wife and three kids and a Golden Retriever, and every night, his whole family would be all around him, like the plastic balls in those bins he and his friends liked to jump into at their favorite pizzeria. The one with the video games and the superfast go-kart track.

But in the meantime, he was going to spend Saturday with his dad, even if that meant he was going to get stuck at some crummy old camera shop.

Inside, Minyard's was packed. Which seemed a little weird, since it was more than seven whole months until Christmas. In December, his mother made it a point to take Charles and his sisters to the mall, give them money to buy presents for each other. The toy stores would be crazy, swarming with people who sometimes fought over Transformers and talking Cabbage Patch dolls. Charles would grab the presents for his sisters and race toward the front counter while leaning forward with one arm draped protectively over his head, attempting to make sure he didn't get whacked with anybody's angry purse.

Minyard's kind of reminded Charles of that, as he inched his way around people much taller than him.

He stuck close to his dad, a little afraid that they might get separated.

At the edge of the crowd, his dad tried to steer Charles toward a "Kids' Cameras" display.

Only, the aisle was jammed. And no one had any interest in moving. They were staring up, like they were in some kind of hypnotic trance.

Charles quickly realized it wasn't a trance at all—they were simply staring at a picture that hung up high, near the ceiling.

A kissing picture. Charles shuddered. The fire in his cheeks grew hotter when his own dad stopped to look at it…and even worse, when he tilted his head a bit and his eyes took on a twinkle.

One of the onlookers—a man about Charles's dad's age—called out to a woman behind the counter. He called her Sharon.

Told her how much he liked her picture.

Everyone nodded, adding their own compliment—yes, it was so touching, beautiful…

Charles began to let go of his embarrassment. It drifted off, like a helium balloon out of his hand. It would be so nice to get that kind of attention, Charles thought, his eyes roving back up toward his father again. How wonderful it would be to make people smile.

Sharon

We heard the downstairs buzzer first thing on Sunday morning—the morning after I'd given away our camera. Somebody out on the sidewalk below, telling us they were at our door. We never got buzzed. Not anymore.

"Minyard Photography?" a female voice asked.

Michael approached the intercom, pressed the button to speak, and offered, "This is Michael."

"Michael—Minyard?"

"Yes."

"Minyard Photography?"

"This is Michael."

"Michael—Minyard!"

"Yes."

Michael and I exchanged confused glances. I stuck my head in our apartment window and glanced down at the sidewalk below, where I found the girl from the day before doing some sort of celebratory dance. Specifically, she banged her knees together three times and pumped her fist before jutting her neck forward in a chicken-style pecking motion.

"Michael Minyard!" she repeated joyfully.

"Yes. May I ask who this is?"

She must have worried she was losing him, because her words were coming faster—almost like she was chasing him with sentences. "Iknowyour signsaysclosed. ButIboughtacamerahere. Fromawoman. YesterdaywhenIwashere. Shetoldme—"

"I think you're looking for Sharon," Michael said.

"Yes! Sharon. That's her name. Sorry. I should have said that first. See, she hooked me up with this film camera…"

But I was already thundering down the steps.

This was going to be great. Because at that moment, I believed that this Heather person had returned because something had gone wrong. She was infuriated. She'd caught us at home, and now, she was going to complain (it was the one thing people were good at anymore), wailing that she couldn't make the ancient camera work, that it was a hunk of junk. That's why she was celebrating. She had me cornered. She was going to demand—I didn't know. Some sort of retribution. And while she was at it, throw the useless camera back in my face.

Not that I was glad some horror had befallen the girl at her shoot. But she was young, and everything's fixable when you're young. One messed-up shoot couldn't possibly derail her. I'd make everything okay. Offer to get in touch with her client to help smooth things over. Break out my own (albeit, out-of-date) list of contacts. Maybe someone needed a senior picture. Grandbaby's first photo shoot. Something. This first client of hers could prove to be nothing but a blip, a bump. People weren't necessarily forgiving, but they had short memories.

Yeah, that's what I was thinking then. And listen, it was all a bunch of balderdash, as my dad would have put it. I could rationalize

142

it all I wanted (and look, I really did think my old Nikon still had some life left in it), but the truth was, the day before, with Heather's broken camera in front of me and Michael on the stairs, I'd been doing something for myself. Not Heather.

I guess that's the way we wind up hurting others, isn't it? We fall victim to moments of extreme tunnel vision. We don't realize, in the exact moment that we take action, how we could potentially do damage to someone else in the process.

Anyway, on that Sunday, when Heather returned, I was doing it again: thinking of myself. I was so happy. I could stop trying to come up with a way to address what had happened the day before. The camera. The radio. I'd never have to bring it up in some awful, thorny confrontation. I was convinced Michael would hear the girl's anger and he would have to come to grips with the fact that there was absolutely nothing magical about that camera at all.

Nothing.

Magic. Please.

It was me. Don't you see that? I didn't need some dumb magic, Michael. I didn't.

I threw open the shop door.

"Sharon!" Heather cried, out of breath.

I ushered her inside, where her angry words would have a better chance of carrying all the way upstairs.

Heather said, "I had no idea where to get film developed anymore. I started with this place, since you were the one who gave it to me, and I noticed when I got here, you have developing listed on your window..."

She gestured toward the plate glass, which we'd last had fully painted in the mid-'90s. Since then, I'd been touching up the sign myself, but never did it occur to me to remove the service completely.

"Wait," I interrupted. "You need something developed? You

143

mean you actually used the camera?"

"Uh, yes?" She shot me an expression that seemed to ask, *Isn't that why you gave me the camera in the first place? To take pictures?*

"You didn't have to delay your shoot? You didn't, say, have to make your client wait while you found a big box store where you could pick up a digital camera?"

"I—no. I didn't have any money. No."

"Your—boyfriend? The one you mentioned?"

"No. I'd already put him out asking for a ride. No, I couldn't do that. I guess I could have tried my friend. Her son was the one who broke the camera in the first place—but that really wouldn't have been right, either. They already felt bad enough. Poor little Aiden." She shook her head.

Poor Aiden? Who *was* this girl? Some syrupy sweet Pollyanna?

"I know it's asking a lot, probably," Heather said. "Being Sunday and all. And I know you're closed, but would you mind? Developing? I think," she added, reaching into her purse, "I think I have enough to pay you. I went through my coat pockets last night…"

Good grief. Was she serious?

"Look, getting to see what you took is payment enough," I assured her. As proof, I immediately headed toward the darkroom in the studio's basement.

Heather followed without hesitation.

I couldn't decide if that made her a trusting soul or a fool. Our basement was one of those unfinished spaces with not a single back door or ground-level window to offer a method of escape. A concrete floor that'd be easy to hose down after a homicide or two. One way down, one way out.

My flip-flops echoed with each step as I made a beeline for the metal sink along the far wall, positioned beneath a rope clothesline that stretched across the length of our basement. Heather started gnawing on her bottom lip. I don't know, maybe jugs of developing chemicals had awakened the girl's fears. *All the better to melt your skin off, my pretty.*

I reached into the back pocket of my jeans to retrieve a pair of reading glasses. Nobody's afraid of old people with reading glasses, and the back pockets of my jeans had been embroidered with faded purple peace signs. (Fashion that had never died, not completely, that I had stumbled upon while shopping and bought in a moment of reminiscence.) Come on, though—how many sociopaths were old ladies in faded blue jeans covered in peace signs?

"Hand me that jug over there, will you?" I asked.

But Heather was hesitating. If I were her, I'd probably have started thinking this was how good girls met bad ends. Because, like her, they were broke and had no other options. That was how nice little would-be princesses wound up in the woods eating poison apples. Didn't Snow White actually have massive student loans and debt collectors coming after her? Hadn't her horse been repossessed, and wasn't that why she was hiding out in the woods with seven strangers in the first place?

I was sure I'd heard that somewhere.

Ah, but then, Michael probably would have corrected me, wouldn't he? Like he had that first day in Bleeker's? Shown me there was no place for modern cynicism in fairy tales.

I'd disagree, of course.

But Michael wasn't around. It was just the two of us girls. I offered her an *it's honestly okay* smile.

She smiled back. And slid the jug from the shelf.

I flicked on those creepy red darkroom lights—the kind that show up in old movies. I grabbed a pair of tongs and began to pour the developer into a small basin, humming softly.

"This room doesn't get a lot of use anymore," I admitted. "But I never quit making sure we'd have the right supplies. You never know who's going to walk through the door, and I couldn't exactly turn a potential customer away because my chemicals had expired, right?"

Heather placed the camera case on the ground, flicking the clasps open.

"So what'd you think of it?"

"I didn't—it wouldn't..." Heather shrugged pitifully. "The camera was tricky."

I bet it was. I did my best to hide the new smile trying to break through. "Trouble, eh?"

Heather let out a sigh of pure, unadulterated humiliation. "One. I only managed to take one picture."

And then she began to tell me her story.

Heather

I got there forty minutes late. With my ex-boyfriend. And your old film camera, which I really didn't know how to work.

The Liu reunion was easy to spot. They had on coordinated khaki skirts or shorts with navy blue tops. The littlest ones were squealing and chasing each other, getting all wrinkled and muddy. One little boy was even burying another boy in the sand near the tire swings.

Apparently, kid time worked like dog years, and forty minutes was the same as seventeen billion hours.

Charles spotted me fighting all my camera gear. I know, I know. It wasn't like I really needed it anymore. So much of it was for my old camera. But I was so nervous, I didn't really know what I was doing.

He hurried my way, frowning beneath a sadly windblown mop of black hair. I was sure it wasn't the professional picture he usually presented as owner and Chief Executive of Everything at Liu Marketing Strategies, Inc.

He started talking (ahem, *scolding* me), even while he was still

147

walking my way. His voice was a cocktail of one part annoyed boss mixed with two parts infuriated-but-trying-to-dial-it-back-because-we're-stuck-together-for-the-semester teacher, topped with a garnish of perturbed father. Every single syllable was making me curl up and shrink, like a piece of pink meat in a hot skillet.

I was frying. And all I could do was stand there and take it.

"…hoped you'd have been here to document some earlier moments…" he was snapping. "My *father* is here…Only have cell phone photos…"

In the background, high-pitched shouts of kids playing rang as taunts. The same *nanny nanny boo boo* tease that Darth Billy loved to lob at me.

Was Liu firing me?

No, he was pointing. "…at least you can take the family photo…"

I scrambled to unearth the Nikon. It was so foreign to me, it might as well have been one of those giant cameras that showed up in Civil War dramas—one of those contraptions with the black cloth hanging off the back that photographers stuck their heads into.

Ryan had crossed to the other side of the park. He'd perched himself on top of a picnic table and wormed his earbuds into his ears. Had he heard my tongue-lashing?

My face flamed at the mere possibility.

The Lius gathered near a pavilion. Most of them gathered, anyway. The younger members didn't want to come. A few teenagers were sent out to wrangle them up. But the little ones were dragging their feet, and it seemed like the wrangling was gearing up to take a while, which was okay. I really needed the extra few moments to remember the instructions you'd given me at the shop, Sharon—how to focus, how to wind the film.

I realized I should have asked you how to tell grumpy people to pose. After another ten minutes (or six and a half weeks—who could tell at that point?), I took a deep breath and tried to make a motion for the Lius to squeeze together. How many generations had Charles told me were there? Four? Five?

A little kid screech hit the air as someone on the front row tried to separate a girl from a boy standing next to her. He was the only person *not* dressed in the same khaki and blue colors. Instead, he was wearing a pair of worn-out black cotton shorts and a faded Nike T-shirt. "He's not family, sweetie," the grown-ups tried to reason. "He can wait a minute, then you can play."

But the little girl screamed again and refused to pull her arms away from her friend's neck.

Her parents gave up quickly. Maybe they wouldn't have if I'd gotten there sooner. Maybe they were already feeling pretty worse for wear themselves. But they agreed. Fine, they all sighed, your friend can stay. The two kids beamed these enormous victory smiles at me.

The rest of the Lius followed, giving me their best, most practiced smiles.

I flinched. Gulped.

Game time.

I squeezed the shutter button, but the camera refused to co-operate.

I'm not kidding. It actually felt like the camera kicked my hands away.

I frowned. And tried again.

Nothing. No click. No groan. No snap. No hint of a sign that the camera even worked.

My panic exploded. I felt like crying. Everything was slipping through my hands.

I was ruining everything.

"Uh—why don't we try it over here?" I asked, pointing. My

149

voice was soft and musical, covering the strangled feeling I was fighting. Sweat broke through my shirt, making dark splotches. I kicked off my flats—which were stupid to wear to the park, anyway. I tossed them with the rest of my gear, piled next to Ryan at the picnic table.

I tried to act like that was so much better—like the shoes had really been holding me back.

From the picnic table, Ryan kept his eyes on me, the nitwit conducting a calamity.

I was so mortified. He was such a beautiful person, there to help me even after he'd decided he didn't want me in his life anymore. All I was doing was digging myself deeper into my catastrophe. I was so lost. And your camera wasn't working.

"What's wrong with you?" I hissed at the thing, too quietly for the Lius to hear.

My eyes prickled with tears. *I can't blame the camera*, I told myself. *The real truth is I'm not good enough.*

My dream was crumbling. Even after you and Ryan had tried to rescue me. I'd never had the right to imagine a dream like that could be mine. I didn't have what it took.

I tried another shot, anyway. What else could I do? Still, your camera refused.

Refused, because I didn't know what I was doing. I was pathetic. No good. A faker.

But as I stood there silently scolding myself, I did realize how tightly—even angrily—I was holding the camera. Maybe I was being too rough. Maybe that was every bit as wrong as treating people harshly. Maybe, right then, in my sweaty desperation, as tears were forming and my ex was staring at me, grateful he'd broken things off, and a whole family was missing their opportunity to actually enjoy the perfect summer day together, I was treating the camera with cruelty.

150

Isn't that stupid? I was worried I was being mean to a camera.

But see, I'd promised my mom…I know it sounds pretty flimsy, but I'd been told if you were good to the world, the world would be good to you. And when you think there are no options left, you wind up believing in senseless rabbit foot stuff.

So I relaxed my grip on the camera in an apologetic way.

But the torture didn't end. Not yet. We kept dancing around the park, me and the Lius. One location after another, one attempt after another. Sun, shade, sun and shade, green backdrop, stone backdrop, sky backdrop. And every single time, the camera kicked against my fingers. Refusing my request.

Antsy and hot and bored, the children fidgeted and scratched and whined. They tugged their shirts out as soon as their parents tucked them in. They mussed their hair as soon as it was slicked into place. They wailed and they complained and they swung their arms and made weird sputtering noises with their lips. They dug the toes of their polished shoes into the dirt.

The adults had given them permission to play while they'd been waiting for me. And by the time I'd finally shown up, they were too far into their games to stand still and pose.

The whole thing was a giant wreck.

And then I remembered, finally, what you said. "Let the camera show you the way. Ask for its help."

So, armed with the memory of the promise I'd made to be kind, and with your own words swirling in my head, I turned my back on the Lius. I whispered to the Nikon, "I'm not asking. I'm begging. Which shows how desperate I am. I'm pleading with everything I have, which I know doesn't sound like much. But to me, it's the whole world. Today's shoot is everything. The beginning or the end. This guy's the sort to tell everyone all about me—either in a good way or a bad one. This is make-or-break time. Either everything I want for my life begins to happen right here or everything falls apart."

I sucked in a breath. And for what had to be the six thousandth time, I raised the camera to my face.

The moment I looked through the viewfinder, I gasped.

The park wasn't bathed in the severe glow of midday sun. Not anymore. Instead, as I swiveled, scenes before me grew sharper—more colorful—shifting like the bright beads inside a kaleidoscope. Had I finally twisted the right knob? Adjusted the lens in the right way?

The camera will help you, if you let it… That's what you'd said.

"Show me the right spot," I whispered to the camera.

A streak of light etched itself across the viewfinder as if to say, *This way. Follow me.* And I did. I chased it across the park until I found myself staring at an old elm tree. Underneath its limbs, the light was soft and yet not too shady. The colors were summery and delightful, and the glare of the sun promised to be out of the Lius' eyes.

I called to them, pointing at this new spot.

The weary family followed my instruction. Can you believe it? They were still with me, for some strange reason. They gathered into a strange, semi-unorganized, exhausted clump, shaking their heads as if asking wordlessly, *What next? Climb the tree?*

Without lifting my eye from the viewfinder, I motioned for everyone to smoosh a little closer together. The tiniest details cleared, coming into perfect, sharp focus. When the colors grew strong enough to pulse, I pressed the shutter button.

That time—finally—the camera granted my wish.

Sharon

Was she joking? Waiting for me to laugh? Playing with me? As Heather seemed to have, for a second, questioned my motives on the day we met, I started to wonder about hers. Had she cooked up some sort of plan? Was she up to something dastardly?

Judging by the look on her face, it seemed the girl believed it. All of it.

I knew it couldn't be true. The camera showed her the way. Come on. I'd used that camera for decades, and it wasn't like the thing had ever literally talked to me. Not like Heather had described. Whatever Heather thought had happened in the park was nothing more than the power of suggestion.

"I was so grateful to have taken one picture," Heather babbled, "it just didn't occur to me to try to take another. Not until I was in the car on the way back and it was too late."

I hummed as I worked to develop the photo, my fingers fumbling a bit in my hurry. Was I trying to reassure Heather? Or myself?

It was going to stink. It had to. Who got the just-right shot the first time around? For that to happen would have to be a work of…

Well. A work of magic.

Magic. Are you listening to yourself, Sharon? You know that's hogwash.

When I hung the picture on the line, Heather grunted with disappointment. "Not exactly award-winning, is it?" she grumbled.

Staring at it, a ripple of utter shock started at my head and trailed down to my toes.

What was this? I'd prided myself on never, not once, ever dismissing Michael and his metaphors, his poetic views. Not even during that first Fourth of July.

But I had, hadn't I? All that stuff about the camera being magical. I'd cringed and turned against it.

Now, though, I had to ask myself if he could have somehow been right.

It was ridiculous to think it, and yet, how else could I explain what was right there in front of my eyes?

She'd clearly taken a multi-generational family portrait. Every member was looking off in a different direction—some at the camera, some in the distance, some at each other. Hair in various stages of disarray. One kid dangled upside-down, knees hooked on the lower branch of a nearby tree. One of the grandmothers had her head thrown back mid-laugh. A little boy dressed differently from the rest of the family stood in the center of the front row, his arms wrapped around the neck of a little girl who was kissing him on the cheek.

"It's awful," Heather moaned. "I'm toast. Totally scorched black inedible *toast*."

"I couldn't disagree more," I said quietly, my head spinning and my pulse beating with the force of a giant's footsteps. The girl had an innate sense of timing. Intuition—the kind that couldn't be

154

taught.

Then again, *was* it innate? Or was it the camera? Was it showing her the way? Had it shown me the way too?

What's the deal with that camera, anyway? Heather's large, round eyes begged me to tell her.

I sighed and said, "Take it to your client."

"I can't take that," she groaned.

"Take it."

Michael

The phone rang, sending me scrambling up the stairs.

As much as I could scramble, anyway. I sure didn't want the girls to know I'd been eavesdropping on them again.

"This is Michael, right?" The voice on the other end of the line was deep and resonate, but unsure at the same time.

My head spun as I pushed my glasses up. I was still trying to make sense of what was going on downstairs. Had I raced up here for nothing more than some awful scammy phone call? It seemed we had become prime targets, two residents now over sixty-five, still with our old-fashioned landline.

I was about to hang up without a word when the voice on the other end started rambling, "…never seen anything like it—not even when I offer free concert tickets to the tenth caller who can answer some obscure trivia question…"

"I'm sorry—who is this again?" I gripped the receiver, ill at ease.

"Tony. From KTXY."

"The radio station. The, uh, the DJ." My head was still trying to catch up.

"You wouldn't believe the calls," Tony said.

"Calls?"

"From listeners. You jammed the lines."

A horrible sinking feeling invaded my stomach. Had they complained? Had my words come out in a confused jumble? Had I rambled too much? Didn't they all realize I hadn't been able to stop once I'd gotten started? I'd doubted, as I'd pushed myself away from the DJ's microphone, returned the headset, and stepped back out into the afternoon sun, that any of it had made any sense at all.

"Are they angry?" I asked. "Did I say something—?"

"No. And yes. What I mean is, they're not angry. But they all want to talk to you. So does my boss."

"About what, may I ask?"

"A regular spot. On air."

"Who wants to listen to me?" I wasn't sure if I was arguing or honestly wanted to know.

"They're already listening to you, Michael."

Sharon

Images in a tucked-away portfolio:

Rotten Wood in a Doorframe, 1978
&
Guts, 1978

I went through a phrase I generally like to call my Ugly Period. Took pictures of the broken, the rotten, the rusted, the splintered, the corroded.

One of my all-time favorites turned out to be a black and white of a rotten header—the horizontal beam on top of a doorframe.

Not that "favorite" is the right word, not really. These were dark images. Pictures taken while I was searching for some meaning—as though there's ever any sense to be made out of a tragedy.

158

Pictures I took in the midst of trying to feel tough again.

These weren't images I ever intended to hang. I took them for me. Developed them—said what I needed to say—and then put them away.

Finished. Done.

Before I closed the book on it all, I'll admit, I spent a good amount of time alone, just staring at the pictures. Especially the doorframe. It had this look—like the whole building around it could collapse at any moment. Sometimes, with the image in front of me, I could almost hear the sounds of splintering and cracking.

And yet, the building stood.

I guess some people, especially back then, expected women to cope with—I don't know—ice cream. Shopping sprees. Days spent under the covers. Long crying jags. As for me, I had these pictures of crumbling, decaying objects that were somehow not finished, not completely. In the midst of the worst, they seemed to invite hope. Asked to be renovated rather than razed.

Other favorites from the Ugly Period—also tucked away in the same portfolio—were of the insides of cars. All the stuff under the hood. The hoses and belts. Ernie, the mechanic at the Fairyland Garage, told me I was driving him crazy. But still I came, day after day, taking pictures of the cars that he'd dismantled. The cars he was in the process of fixing. The best of the lot, a picture of a half-taken-apart engine, its hoses and wires disconnected and laying around in what looked like a completely random order, I'd titled, simply, "Guts."

Sounds bizarre, I know. I'd spent so much time capturing living beings. Revelers inside Murio's or townspeople racing back and forth on the streets of Fairyland. Portraits. School photos. And there I was, taking shot after shot of inanimate objects.

Right then, the inanimate was solid. Safe.

And I guess, if you really want to know the truth, back then,

I thought if I kept at it, at some point, answers would finally emerge in the darkroom.

Look, if you want to get all psychological about it, the pictures I was taking were how I saw myself—broken, rusted. All my hoses unattached. Parts missing.

I'd lost a baby—one that had been planted in a spot where it could never grow. "Ectopic" sounded like a foreign word the first time I heard it spoken directly to me. "Tubal pregnancy," that was the terminology I was more familiar with. But either way, it meant the same thing. I'd lost a child. Before I'd even known about it. It also meant I'd learned I was one of the women who wouldn't go on to conceive another.

It might not have been high on my list of things to accomplish, becoming somebody's mother. But I didn't like having an opportunity taken away before I'd made up my mind one way or another about the issue. That much didn't sit well with me.

I felt like fighting, if you want to know the truth, but I didn't know who deserved a punch or a raised voice.

Maybe me.

Mostly me.

All me.

That was how I felt, anyway.

Michael wasn't demanding anything. Not for me to hurry and shake my blues, for lack of a better word. Not for life to hurry up and get back to our old normal. He wasn't even encouraging me to fall apart in his arms for a while, giving him a chance to feel strong and sturdy and needed.

I was the one making the demands on me. The one that felt like I needed to get back in shape. Back in order. Back to working condition. Put in the bolt. Reattach all those disconnected hoses. Shore myself back up.

Michael, forever the optimist, regarded my Ugly Period as necessary—but far from permanent. Those pictures *were* the same thing as me blubbering on somebody's shoulders. Falling apart for a little while.

And he knew that by letting me work through it on my own, he was actually acting as a sturdy support beam in the doorframe of our marriage.

He knew I'd get there.

Poor Ernie hoped he was right.

Michael

Letter to Sharon
left on her pillow
1978

And so it is. And so we're here.

What am I to say to you, my raven-haired love? My partner in crime? Killer of my favorite African violets? Burner of my morning toast? Eyes that make me see the world differently?

We find ourselves at an end. That's what it is: a nevermore. And perhaps this conclusion we've found is not a classic fairy tale ending.

At least, it's not the kind of ending we read with a smile. It's not the kind of ending anyone would cheer for in the movies.

A mere breath ago, it seems, we rode into the sunset. We did! You and I, together. Look at us. Here we are, in what was supposed to be the middle of our happily ever after.

162

And yet, even here, we find it. A tragedy. A finale. A never-more.

Here, post-sunset, our aching hearts are wondering why.

We'll never know—or understand.

All I know is we'll love on. One minute after another.

Because, quite simply, my dear, you and I are a twosome. A complete match. Able to cry, or mourn, and together find a way to laugh again.

I do believe in messages from the universe. And this one is telling us that we were simply destined to remain a complete twosome.

I come back to our sunset. The one you and I rode into. Remember? The moment we did, we were perfect together. You and I weren't simply good enough. We were everything.

Aren't we everything now?

Tragedy can't be allowed to convince us that somehow, that's changed. That somehow, you and I are no longer enough. That our life together is incomplete.

There is nothing to fix, Shar. There never was.

I am—and have always been—certain of the strength of us.

It is a simple thing, but here it is: I love you. I love what we have. The good and the sweet and the sad of it. Ugly pictures and dead plants. You and me curled up on our couch at the end of a long day, jazz floating through the air. *That's* what I live for.

And that, my Sharon, is indeed the guts of it all.

Michael

The afternoon following Tony's phone call, I settled into the chair in the radio station, not sure if it felt more comfortable than it had the first time around.

"Okay," Tony said, clapping his hands together once. "Got you all set here." He pushed a microphone closer to my face, handed me a set of headphones.

The lights flashed red and green all at the same time, like a confused traffic light not sure who to let through the intersection.

I frowned at the blinking red lights. Sharon hadn't been confused in the least. The way she'd instantly handed the camera over, the way she'd scrambled downstairs when our buzzer rang...She'd let Heather in. Of all people. Heather. I had unearthed that camera to remind her who we'd been to each other. Not just at the beginning— who we'd always been to each other. All that we'd weathered, everything that had happened to us. Always before, we'd emerged from disasters in the same way that camera had—battered and dented, but still capable of working, of making something beautiful.

Instead of sending my Sharon closer to me, the newly-reintroduced camera was sending her toward a person who had literally just walked in off the street. Sharon picked a stranger over me? She felt farther than ever before.

"Can't believe your wife didn't hear you the first time," Tony went on. "Judging by the calls, I'd say you've really hit a nerve with our audience."

It wasn't lip-service. I knew that. I'd already gotten a surprising number of emails forwarded to me from the station. Unintentionally, I'd hit the nerve endings of Fairyland's residents. But why hadn't my words struck Sharon's nerves like a tuning fork? Why didn't they reverberate inside her? Why wasn't she reacting to the message meant for her?

It was scary, actually.

"…everybody clamoring for you to come back," Tony continued. "Your wife's got to be the only one in town who didn't hear you."

To be honest, I was certain she had heard me. But my wife shrugging me off was too much to admit out loud—especially to Tony, who was still basically a stranger.

"I couldn't believe she missed it, either," I said, my dry mouth clacking with each word. "She rarely ever turns your station off."

"Chalk it up to first timer's bad luck. But she'll hear you now, eh?" Tony asked, nudging my shoulder. "I mean, even if she doesn't, she's surely bound to hear about it from one of our other listeners. Judging by the way they're all talking about you, I mean. Sure to pick up on the chatter somewhere."

He pointed. The "On Air" light flashed.

I stared at the black surface of the microphone.

This time around, I could imagine the entire town of Fairyland staring back at me.

On Air

Mirror, mirror, on the wall, dear listeners. Yes, it's me again. The old storyteller.

Coming to you from Fairyland—where magic is real.

Oh, you might not have guessed that was what I believed, not based on my words the last time I spoke to you. All that lamenting I did about boredom creeping into fairy tales. Maybe you thought I was the sort to dismiss any talk of magic.

But I do. I believe it's real.

It's gasping, though. It's been wounded.

That, you're surely thinking, sounds like the work of a hostile arch-enemy. Like somehow, a villain has entered our idyllic surroundings.

And you would be right.

Where can we find this scoundrel?

I must be frank with you. The worst thing about villains is that they're so well disguised.

They look like cuddly puppies or harmless little creatures who are in something of a bind themselves. They look like someone you want to befriend. They have perfect little ringlets and big innocent eyes and sometimes, to really tug at your heartstrings, they're orphans. They act sweet and talk about their dreams, and you wind up wanting to help them.

Meanwhile, they're out to wreak havoc on your life.

That's how they survive, you know. By using the most unsuspected disguises. That's why they don't have people instantly trying to crush them on sight, give them the boot out of town. Why good people don't immediately send them packing.

Come on, now, you say. Puppies and sweet little girls in a bind are vulnerable creatures. What kind of danger can a villain pose if the villain takes on such a powerless form?

Think about the villains in fairy tales. Take Cinderella, for instance. Her stepsisters and stepmother were arguably not particularly powerful creatures themselves. So what was the worst harm they could do?

Wasn't it to deny poor Cinderella a chance? Keep her from the ball? So the prince would never be able to meet her?

Had there not been a fairy godmother, they would have succeeded. Poor Cinderella would have been hidden away, out of the prince's view.

The true danger those stepsisters and their mother posed, then? Why, they were barriers to true love.

In my mind, you can't find a worse villain than that—one who plants their feet firmly, one that stands in the way of true love.

Maybe you have a different picture in your head. I'll pose the question to the people of Fairyland: What in your own life would be the worst imaginable villain? The destroyer of your success, your happiness, your love? The lines are open. Talk to me.

Michael

You bet, I had villains on my mind.

Heather had become something of a villain. At least, she'd become one to me, stealing what was left of my princess's attention.

But Heather also had a villain of her own, remember?

One that was becoming increasingly more villain-y all the time.

What *was* going on with Amanda?

Simply put, she'd been doing a bit of celebrating. Because she actually believed she'd kept Heather from her grand opportunity. Her shot at real success.

It had happened by accident, of course. The camera thing wasn't her fault. It wasn't like she'd purposefully tricked Goldilocks into crawling into the wrong bed or shoved Rapunzel up a tower, never to be heard from again.

Aiden had knocked the camera out of Heather's hands.

Simple as that.

That's what she told herself, anyway. Of course, that ignored the fact that she could have whipped out her gold card to buy poor

Heather another camera. Surely there was some big box store close by that still carried a few digitals.

Amanda rolled her eyes at herself. Why did Heather even need a new camera? Why couldn't she use her phone? Do some artistic editing in Photoshop?

There, Amanda thought with satisfaction. That showed she wasn't a horrible person at all.

Still, Amanda was very aware that her best friend (the poor little waif) had taken hit after hit while she had spent the last decade-plus collecting markers of success. It had all been relatively easy. Almost as easy as it had been when she was a little girl and had racked up achievements playing the old Life board game at sleepovers: a husband and babies, an enviable lifestyle. Being married to Tom, a corporate attorney as well as the majority shareholder in a boat manufacturer and a partner in a growing fitness franchise, meant she had more than a comfortable existence. She had clout. Places to wear gowns at night. Actual ball gowns. To evening galas. Dinner parties and events, so much networking to do. Year after year, she was still sticking blue and pink people pegs in her plastic car-shaped game piece, spinning the multi-colored wheel, working her way around the board.

Amanda had far surpassed Heather in the game of life. When she thought about it, she really did feel a sad mix of regret and guilt about the incident with Aiden and the camera.

And yet, she also felt quite happy.

The happiness was harder to understand. In fact, her happiness kind of stung.

Here's the thing: Nobody ever cheers for a black-hearted villain. Nobody likes villains. Not even the villains themselves. The true quest for a storybook enemy isn't to triumph over good. It's not to conquer and crush the hero. It's to stop being the villain. It's to get on the right side of the story.

And so Amanda sent Tom off with Aiden and the twins for pizza at one of those kids' places with Skee-Ball and Whac-A-Mole. Told him to stay *extra long* because she'd invited Heather over. It wasn't the first time, either—it had, over the years, become something of a habit: inviting her best friend over while the kids were with their grandmother, the husband off fishing with his buddies, like a scene straight out of a 1950s sitcom. Amanda loved the evenings they spent commiserating like teenagers. Only, instead of parents and boys, the troubles were now rent (Heather) and contractors for the additional room (Amanda). By the third glass of wine, there was also Heather's career. Amanda would listen and play with her hair, and when Heather finally wound down, Amanda wrapped her in her mother-in-law's hand-crocheted afghan and let her sleep it off on the Anthropologie velvet-upholstered couch.

Knowing that Heather could not have possibly made her shoot with Liu, Amanda had (without mentioning Liu directly) tonight offered Heather a shoulder to cry on. And an empty house to do it in.

She'd even offered to pick her up. But Heather'd said her car hadn't been quite as doornail-dead as she'd suspected. She'd found a few YouTube videos that helped diagnose and fix her car. Another Band-Aid for another injury, sure to fall off in another thirty miles or so, exposing a still bigger problem underneath.

When the doorbell rang, Amanda expected to find a familiar face wrenched into a giant wad of tears.

Instead, Heather was smiling. And holding up a plate.

"You made brownies?" Amanda asked.

"You love brownies," Heather said with a shrug. "Don't get too excited. They're from the oldies but goodies bin at the grocery store."

Heather had brought treats, even after Amanda's own son had wrecked her camera?

Amanda tried to swallow. It was hard, since she was getting all choked up. She needed a drink.

"I'm so sorry you didn't make it to your shoot," she said after gulping down half a glass of chardonnay.

"Oh, I made it," Heather said, plopping down on the couch.

"You—you did?"

"Sure. Darth Billy came to my rescue."

"Darth Billy? How could he?"

"Hey, don't be so suspicious. Little boys rescue girls all the time. Even mean little evil ones. It happens that way sometimes. Enemies can turn out to be guys waiting for an excuse to quit being jerks. Enemies are guys who play havoc with your life only because they resent not being part of it somehow. Green with envy."

Amanda's smile faded. Was that pointed?

"Yeah, as it turned out, car trouble was catching like the flu. After Ryan filled up, *his* car wouldn't start. Lucky for me, Darth Billy and his mother had been riding bikes near the gas station."

"Were they."

"Yes!" Heather's eyes sparkled.

Amanda recognized this right off. It was a game the two of them had played through the years—trying to one-up each other, story-wise. They'd bragged about make-out sessions under the bleachers and about chance meetings with favorite musicians, and even told a few heartbreakers—about fathers being transferred and having to move, or about being given a semester of detention. It was up to the other to guess which stories were true and which were complete fiction.

"So Billy's mom offered me a bike."

"To go all the way to Goldeneye."

"No! Of course not. To the *bus station*, silly."

"Of course," Amanda said, giggling as she handed Heather the bottle of wine.

"Of course," Heather giggled back.

After pouring herself an extra-large glass, Heather continued, "I had started to pedal away when Darth Billy surprised me by calling out, 'Wait! I'll come with you!'"

"Small wonders."

"*Yes.* And you and I both know that it has been well documented that road trips can work wonders at forging friendships."

"Even when they're on bicycles?"

"*Especially* when they're on bicycles. Darth Billy and I sang in harmony as we pedaled, block after block. 'Pop Goes the Weasel' and a few of Duran Duran's greatest hits."

"Darth Billy knows Duran Duran?"

"Apparently, Darth Billy's mother has a surprising number of '80s bands on vinyl."

"Does she?"

"Yes! At one point, we ended up following a pre-Flag Day parade."

"You don't say!"

"A woman on an Uncle Sam float tossed the two of us red, white, and blue crepe paper streamers. We wound them around our handlebars.

"When the bus station came into view, I hugged my new pal Darth Billy. And I started to say goodbye to one of my fellow crepe paper wavers when I realized she happened to be wearing a name badge declaring she was the high school principal and therefore trustworthy with children. I pointed toward Billy and shouted, 'He lives on Robberson.'"

"What'd the principal do?"

"Promised to make sure he'd get home safely. And return his mom's bike for me."

"As any good principal would," Amanda agreed.

"He called out to me, 'Bye, Heather!' And you know, Darth Billy promised he would never, ever, ever be a jerk supreme again. Not to me, the person who had risen to the top of his buddy list."

"What a tale!" Amanda said through laughter. She loved Heather at that moment. Loved her with all her heart. Heather had told her that preposterous story for the same reason she'd brought sweets: to show her that all was forgiven. Heather bore no grudges.

Yes, Amanda was forgiven. Aiden was forgiven. When her husband returned home, he'd surely ask something like, "What's up, ladies?" She'd sigh and roll her eyes. And before Tom could get the least bit worried about whether his photographer recommendation had put him on some sort of unsteady footing with Liu, his potential future colleague or business favor-doer, Amanda would shake her head, flash a *you should know better* warning frown at him. The same frown she had often flashed at him during his hobnobbery work events. The look that would wordlessly reprimand him before he could blurt something awful, the kind of thing polite society inevitably punished you for saying. The same look that had the weekend before kept him from asking after a business acquaintance's wife. Once said acquaintance had stepped out of earshot, she'd explained, in a whisper, "She ran off with her yoga instructor, remember?" Tom's fingers had searched the thin Georgette of her skirt; finding her hand, he'd squeezed in wordless gratitude.

This would be just like that. Cover Heather's failure, save her feelings. Later on, when they were alone, Amanda would suggest to Tom, "Why don't I go ahead and hire that photographer who worked the Richardsons' daughter's wedding? Pay for a reshoot ourselves? Once it's all over, we could invite the Lius over. Informal barbecue.

And have a good laugh. In the long run, that'll give you more mileage with Liu than a successful shoot with Heather ever could."

He'd agree. And squeeze her hand again. Grateful.

Amanda really did have it all: Heather's forgiveness and her lovely life—the one she adored. The one with the always-filled wineglasses and her children's laughter, the notes of their giggles as easy to memorize as the chorus of a song. Oh, she loved all of it. The loud, boisterous comings and goings of a family she had helped to create. At that moment, it was every bit as delicious as Heather's brownies promised to be. It nourished her.

She was still quite good at the game of life.

"There's only one problem," Amanda said, ready to show Heather that her story was complete and utter fiction, ready for the two of them to fall into hysterics. "Why did you even go to the shoot at all? After that job Aiden did on your camera?"

Heather's face fell. She looked at Amanda in a kind of wounded way, as though reliving the whole scene. Maybe even wondering why Amanda hadn't swooped in to offer her gold-card help.

"The store across the street—you know, with the awning? It was a camera store."

"It was?"

"Yeah, the lady in there gave me a deal I couldn't refuse," Heather joked with a wink.

"So—wait. Are you being serious or not? I mean—is that another story? A made-up one? Like Darth Billy?"

"I really made it to the shoot." Heather shrugged. "Why? Didn't you think I did?"

"No, no, between you and Ryan—you had it covered." Amanda tossed a hand at Heather in an *of course* kind of way.

But on the inside, Amanda's black, festering sore spot began to ache all over again. Her light mood turned instantly dark.

174

She didn't want to feel this way. But she couldn't stop it. She was spiraling downward. She was angry. Furious. She felt like punching drywall.

Why?

Because what she'd wanted to happen hadn't. And that wasn't the ending Amanda was accustomed to.

She was losing Heather. Of course she was. She'd been here before—not with friends as close as she and Heather had always been. But this was how it happened. Success was going to rip Amanda's oldest, best, and perhaps last real friend away.

That's what success did, after all. It sent people into their own private circles. Heather would attend her own galas and hobnobbery work events, and they wouldn't be the same ones Amanda and her husband would attend.

Amanda was about to lose one of the pink pegs in the backseat of her little plastic Life car.

Quite simply, she was terrified.

One of Amanda's three garage doors went up.

"Is that Tom?" Heather asked.

Before Amanda could get her mouth to work, her family was banging back into the house.

"Hey, girls," Tom bellowed.

Amanda's head was spinning. Tom was smiling at her. Tom, the college sweetheart who had started out as her study buddy, the one who still laughed with her, teased her, consulted her, comforted her. She wanted to talk to him like she once had, when it was the two of them out for beers after their Thursday night philosophy class. She wanted to grab him, push him into the dining room and whisper, "You'll never believe what's been going on with me and Heather." She ached to confess her cattiness, tell him all about the business cards and the busted Nikon and Heather making it to the Liu shoot and how horrible it was making her feel. How this was like some twisted breakup in slow motion.

But she couldn't, because more than anything, she didn't want him to know what she'd been up to. She'd be humiliated. And he'd be shocked. He'd think less of her.

Besides, Tom no longer talked to anyone from high school. His friends were all business associates. How could he sympathize?

"Grease fire over at the pizza place," Tom explained. "So we decided to grab us some ribeyes. I grabbed the adults ribeyes, anyway. Got some great squashed-flat patties for the kids. And chocolate chip mint ice cream! Right, guys?"

The kids cheered. Tom opened the back door to the deck. "You're staying, aren't you, Heather? For dinner?"

"Only if you let me take a few family shots," Heather announced. "My camera's out in the car."

"I was hoping you'd say yes," Tom called out to her. "Got you a ribeye too. And it's going to be delicious because *I'm* grilling. Amanda chars meat to smithereens."

"I do not—" Amanda started, but Tom and Heather were laughing. Just beyond the back door, her children were squealing joyfully on the swings. No one could hear her.

It was a little lonely knowing that the two people closest to Amanda never would have guessed that her devious mind was already searching for a new idea. Some way to thwart Heather's momentum.

Neither one of them would have ever thought to look suspiciously at her.

Which meant they did not see both of her hands curled into fists.

From the Studio Walls
Minyard's Photography Interior
1980 - 1989

To a great extent, the studio walls inside Minyard's showcased the photos Sharon had taken across the entirety of Fairyland. People of all ages. Some frames surrounded children at the park—their smiling faces enjoying the rush of a swing swooping high above the tree line, or their tears being wiped from their cheeks as skinned knees were tended to. Other frames held teenagers clustered in rowdy groups outside of Fairyland's movie theater. Or the painted-up, almost clown-like adult faces inside Murio's.

But the section closest to the front counter featured the figures who had once occupied the interior of the shop. Because when Sharon's popularity exploded, interesting subjects started coming to her.

Sure, she continued to venture outside during these busy years, taking photos of Fairyland streets and restaurants and parks,

Fairyland gatherings and celebrations. But some of her very best shots were taken, during this time, without even having to step outside her own door.

And so they were given a special place of honor in Sharon's ever-changing mural.

Some pictures captured full-on crowds. Too many people to count. Hovering near displays, leaning against the glass front counter. Wandering the aisles. Sharon caught individuals with their faces upturned, staring admiringly at *The Art of the Kiss*. She photographed those who showed up for her classes, a brand-new Minyard's-purchased camera in hand. Candid shots of expectant faces racing to see their prints for the first time were easy to come by. Occasionally, the candid studio shots were even used in print ads.

Sharon did not have to ask for permission.

By then, the people of Fairyland were seeking her out. Asking to be included in her studio mural. In the ads for Minyard's. Hoping she would let them borrow, for a slice of time, just a taste of her own fame.

From Sharon's Laptop

She wanted to create a new portrait of the studio. At least, that was the original idea. A portrait, she thought at first, like the studio was a person. She wanted to say something about its chapters. The same way she'd wanted to depict the chapters in the faces of the men in Fairyland's tattoo parlor all those decades ago.

But she quickly realized it was more than that. She wanted to say something about emptiness and time gone by. About her own burst of recognition and subsequent loss of relevance. She wanted to show how, without warning—as quickly as a summer breeze could die—it had suddenly become so easy for anyone to take a snapshot. How the residents of Fairyland had decided they no longer needed her.

She wanted to show, with insight, what that felt like. She wanted to draw viewers into that world, make them feel it too.

But how could she show the passage of time in a single image? With a collage, somehow incorporating all the old images in with the new? Wasn't that too easy? Would a viewer even feel anything staring at a collage?

She wasn't there yet. This image on her screen wasn't right.

Sharon sighed, turning away from her computer and glancing up at her mural of photographs. She'd stopped framing and showcasing her new work right about the time her customers had dried up. Why? Did she think she had less to say? Did the lack of a crowd mean she felt her work wasn't quite worthwhile? Not worth showcasing?

Or was it simply that she was scared? Afraid to show Michael a new photo and see it in his eyes—confirmation that she'd lost something?

That's what happened to old women. Wasn't it? They lost what had once made them special. Sharon rubbed at the inside of her wrist, the spot that held her tattoo.

Who was this villain invading Sharon's mind? The fickle audiences who no longer applauded? Michael?

Or was it herself?

Sharon

Michael was on the radio constantly.

Really—every time I turned it on. The station had started playing reruns of his clips, making sure that everyone in Fairyland heard him.

At the sound of his voice, my jaw would tighten and my frown would deepen, digging all the wrinkles deeper into my skin.

I couldn't escape his words.

Not even when I flicked to a different station. Or turned the radio off completely. Because his words would still be there bouncing through my head. Once those echoes would finally begin to settle down, I'd wind up letting my eyes shoot up toward the ceiling, even as I was trying not to. And I'd see it: *The Art of the Kiss.*

The image I'd taken of us. Our beginning.

The echoes would start in all over again. All those long-winded metaphors—fairy tales and boredom. The station had played the first bit often enough that I nearly had it memorized.

Look, I wasn't mad. Not by then. I was hurt, which is kind of how we feel once anger gives way, isn't it? Almost like we've scorched ourselves on the inside.

(Really, though, while I'm at it, isn't anger little more than a front? A disguise? Isn't it something you can stand behind when you're terrified and need to appear steely and resilient?)

I'd fallen for him *despite* my efforts not to. When falling happened that way, it was overpowering. It engulfed you. And believe me, my love for him may have changed shape—love just *does* as time goes on—but it hadn't left. It beat on, like a second heart.

I still wasn't sure what to do with any of it. Not with what he was saying on the radio. Not with the way I felt. Maybe Michael made sense out of confusion with words, but that wasn't me. I made sense of the world with pictures.

So I'd flip the "Closed" sign to face the street, grab my camera, and head out.

But it wasn't like I could get away from it. Clear my head. Because—this is the truly cruel part—his voice would bleed through open car windows, or waitresses would be listening to him at the diner on the corner, or he'd be playing in the grocery store instead of Muzak.

He was everywhere.

I mean it.

Everywhere.

Even if I managed to find a spot where his actual words weren't filling the air, talk of him was.

"You know, he sounds exactly like my uncle," one of the two women at the convenience store off the square was proclaiming when I stopped in for a cold drink.

"Nah," the other said. "I bet it's my ex. That man fancied himself *quite* the *poet* when we first met. Used to write me these hoity-toity love letters all the time. Would be just like me to cut a man loose right before he came to something."

The two fell into a round of hysterical laughter.

I heard it all in my treks across town: The voice belonged to the high school principal, or the local nightly newscaster. It was somebody's doctor, their preacher, their neighbor. It had become a game, a challenge: *Who is that man hiding behind the curtain of his words?* Like somehow, he'd become the Great and Powerful Oz.

I don't think anybody in Fairyland had ever really listened much to that station. Nobody but me. Now, all this word-of-mouth was drawing them in. Making them think about what he was saying.

He was the literal talk of the town. No wonder the station was replaying his short segments so often.

Michael had moved them. Nearly every single adult in Fairyland. Anybody who had ever been in a boring relationship. He got it. He understood. He was inside their heads, saying all the things they'd never had the guts to say out loud themselves. That was why they seemed so determined to find out who he was.

But I was his target—the one person who was supposed to be moved more than anyone. Wasn't I? Wasn't that the point?

Or was it?

I had no idea how to bring it up in a way that wasn't offensive or accusatory or…

Was he hurt? Was he saying *I'd* hurt him? Was that what he'd been scribbling in his notebooks all this time?

How did it make him feel to finally say it all out loud? Wasn't it embarrassing? Or did it feel, somehow, like a little slice of revenge? Was he really trying to punish me? Not being able to see his face as he read his words meant I had no clue.

I was the visual one. I had to see him to understand him.

Why in the world was he on the radio?

After a while, I'd wander back to the old studio, where our

picture still hung.

The picture no one came by to stare at anymore.

I was glaring at it one afternoon when a knock exploded against the shop entrance.

Mind still spinning, I realized I'd failed to turn the "Open" sign to face the street again. That's why Heather was knocking.

She was back. And jumping up and down in pure excitement as I swung the door open.

Heather

You'll never believe what just happened, Sharon. I was in Charles Liu's office building. And as soon as I walked in, I swear all I could think was, *Oh, my.*

His building—you know, the new one off Commercial Street—it's not a high-rise, exactly. Maybe more like medium-rise. But I'm a ground-floor kind of girl. This place has all kinds of businesses in it—lawyers, architects, even one of those financial adviser places.

Liu's agency was way up on the fifth floor, and it had this giant plaque above the reception desk: *Liu Marketing and Advertising.* Or maybe it was *Liu Marketing Inc.* No. *Liu Strategies...*

I can't even remember now, I'm so flummoxed. Anyway. You get the idea.

Liu's receptionist was busy—flicking her manicured fingers across her phone, moving swiftly from one call straight to another, ignoring me the whole time.

I was getting the feeling that I was the least important person ever to dare to step inside the place. I was also getting the urge to run, to tell you the truth. So I tried to distract myself by staring at the plaque that hung above the receptionist's head. Really memorizing the thing, like I'd once memorized European geography of the Middle Ages in school. There was plenty to go over, let me tell you. The thing had to measure at least three feet long and was made to look like a giant chunk of antique ivory. Then again, maybe it didn't *resemble* at all. Maybe Liu's was the kind of high-end place that could afford ivory signs. It seemed to me that there was some kind of law against importing the stuff, but maybe this chunk had been in the family forever, passed down from one Liu to another.

I started to gnaw my bottom lip as I stared at the pretentious monstrosity. For some reason—probably because I was craving a little slice of comfort—the longer I stared, the more it reminded me of another piece of ivory: a carved piece of scrimshaw I'd inherited when Mom died. A pipe, which I put away in a safe deposit box. I didn't know what else to do with it. Anyway, remembering its history—and the pipe's original owner—seemed to temporarily tamp down my nerves.

My great-grandfather had been the original owner of the pipe. I think he said it was walrus tusk. The bowl had been carved into a pirate head. Where he'd picked it up had been a mystery. He'd used it every day, even after it got old enough to be valuable. He was ancient by the time I'd known him, a squiggle of a man, the same shape as the curl of smoke twirling out the pipe.

The smoke itself smelled kind of pleasant and toasty, but the carved pirate head had scared me, made even my weary, age-weakened great-grandfather seem formidable, tough, intimidating. He'd been a sailor for a time—that was what Mom had always told me. Probably one of those family stories that exaggerated the details of the past, growing like a fish tale with each retelling over the course of three generations. But back then, I'd truly believed that he had been a regular Blackbeard or a Dread Pirate Roberts in his youth, a plunderer who'd sailed the seven seas and even taken a few secret islands for his own.

When he passed away, I didn't imagine him going to heaven. Instead, I pictured him on his boat, white sails drawn tight with a never-ending gust of wind. I saw him drifting off toward one of his stolen islands, a young man again with long black hair and an eye patch and a ruffly poet's shirt, puffing on his scrimshaw pipe all the way.

That probably sounds really strange. But those are the things you think about when you want to run. Your head pings around in all these strange directions. The awful part was, the longer I stood there, the less thinking about that old pipe brought me comfort. Instead, it kind of all got twisted around. Staring at the giant, towering Liu business plaque, I started to feel small. Weak. Conquerable. Like a kid. No—like I was waiting to walk the plank.

I became aware that additional carvings surrounded the name of Liu's business in that showy ivory slab. What was that design?

Sharks! A warning, surely. What did I know of swimming with sharks?

What if these were cruel people—the kind they make movies about? The kind my mother warned me about?

I'd never worked in an office. I'd never filed anything. I'd never worn a power suit. I'd never negotiated.

I was in over my head.

And Sharon, let me tell you, I took a step backward, ready to bolt for the elevator.

But the receptionist started rapping one of her long nails against her desktop in this annoyed way. Apparently, she'd finished answering her calls for the time being, and was ready for me to speak up. Impatience seemed to have found her the moment she'd replaced the receiver.

I fought to remember how to make my mouth work. *It's you guys' fault*, I wanted to say, a phrase I'd heard Darth Billy use on other neighborhood children roughly nineteen billion times. *Come on!* I could have added. *Ivory towers, swimming with sharks? These are not exactly subtle hints.*

I sighed, shrugging helplessly at the receptionist. After I finally squeaked out Charles's name and something about my one o'clock appointment, the receptionist motioned with one of her long nails for me to follow.

But my fears didn't cool off now that we were wading deeper into the massive office suite. If anything, they were worse. I felt like I really had jumped straight into dangerous, choppy waters, filled with hungry sharks and nasty pirates looking to take photographers hostage.

I muttered, "Quit it" at myself. But not as quietly as I'd wanted to. The receptionist tossed a rather haughty look over her right shoulder.

The office assistants and fellow advertising gurus (I was at a total loss regarding their official titles) were all dressed to the absolute nines. Even the women in what appeared to be the art department wore five-inch heels. They'd had their hair professionally styled. Everybody smelled of perfume. Real perfume, not that Eau de Watery Stuff I'd received a time or two for Christmas.

It occurred to me that any person who worked in Liu's suite would be used to perfection: three-hundred-dollar jeans and makeup counters and fancy cars. They did not have to put up with cold fingers in the winter or washing machines with semi-busted agitators. They'd never pinched their cheeks instead of buying blush or spit on a mascara wand to make it last longer or fought with a heater named The Creature who made it a habit to cough soot all over their T-shirts when they tried to relight the pilot. They had never taken the city bus because they did not know what it was like to turn an ignition key and have their car shrug in return.

A person in my position puts up with just about everything. I'm used to self-manicures and purses with Super Glued handles. My venetian blinds are repaired with mailing tape, and my twin bed-spread has unicorns on it because it was on sale (discounted to nearly free) at Walmart, and if my flip-flops last more than a week, I'm impressed.

I figured these people had never had to say, after trying some cheap solution, "That works," or "That's good enough." Maybe, as a result, little imperfections stuck out to them.

And maybe—no, more like probably—that was all Charles Liu would see in my work. The flaws.

I tugged nervously at the lapel of the boyfriend jacket I'd dis-covered at—yes, where else—Goodwill, and hugged my framed pho-to a little closer to my chest.

I was regretting showing up at all, at that point. Charles Liu was going to laugh at me. If I was lucky, he would laugh. Most likely, he would become enraged and kick me out.

When his own assistant—yet another woman in a tailored suit that cost the same amount I'd spent on last month's rent—reached for his door, I imagined Charles sitting in a large leather chair, overstuffed with wings, that smelled like thousand-dollar bills. I was already betting he had taxidermied heads—not of animals, but of conquered business adversaries—on the wall above him.

The door finally opened all the way. Charles Liu was not, in fact, sitting at a giant carved Presidential English oak Oval Office-style monstrosity. And there were no heads mounted on his walls. Instead, he had a very basic metal workspace for a desk, with clean beige walls and no drawers or cabinets anywhere. Obviously, he ran a paperless work environment.

He did have a small indoor fountain in the corner. The sounds of water trickling over a stack of marble stones instantly allowed me to relax. A little, anyway.

(It also kind of made me want to pee. Then again, that was surely my nerves too.)

"Heather," he bellowed, greeting me warmly. Had he always been warm? Had I been too worried about myself to notice it at the park?

Or was he being nice in front of his assistant? Acting like he was Mr. Jolly Good Guy, and then, when she was gone and he finally got a chance to see what I'd brought him—what he'd paid me for—his eyes would turn red and fangs would grow out of his mouth, and I'd wind up being his first official taxidermied head?

"Have a seat," he invited. "How are you?"

But I didn't want to chitchat—I wanted to get this thing over with.

I handed him my photo. And I took a breath. The last clean breath I'd take before his anger began to incinerate the walls, filling the atmosphere with smoke.

Charles accepted the frame. His face first looked slightly surprised, then confused, then amused.

Here we go, I thought. *Here we go, here we go…*

"Look, if it's not what you had in mind," I began, "we can certainly schedule a more traditional reshoot. For no extra charge, of course. I didn't mention it at the park, but I had…" I paused to lean on one leg and chuckle a bit. "You know, it's kind of a funny story. You won't believe it. I had a real snafu with my camera. To give you the full picture of how it all happened, I should really start by telling you about this kid I call Darth Billy…"

Charles held up his hand.

I widened my lips with a grimace, exposing my clenched teeth. If I could have clenched my ears, I would have. I was ready for the shout. Humiliation. Two security guards. A citizen's arrest. Couldn't a girl be arrested for inciting one man's outrage?

I took a step backward, toward his door.

"I'd never reshoot this. This—it's amazing," Charles announced, his voice mirroring the happy surprise on his face.

My head turned a somersault. Actually, my head was doing an Olympic tumbling routine. "It—is?"

"I don't know how you did this. I was told you were talented, but this is astounding. What you captured. It's—it's *us*."

Sharon

"Can you believe it?" Heather screeched.

"Told you he'd like it," I said. I was trying to smile. But in reality, her words made me feel like she'd torn all ten of my fingernails in the quick.

Because I was remembering that old professor of mine. That first photography class, and being told that I had something. His words had made me feel like I had some sort of power. Enough to make something really wonderful happen for myself.

It was all so far away. The scene was, anyway. What did that say about the power?

"Mr. Liu told me to bring him more of my stuff. Said that if it was what he was looking for, he'd send some work my way. He does marketing and ad campaigns. Social media stuff. I guess that was obvious from the name of his business, wasn't it? Which I mostly got wrong, I think, but still." She shrugged, flustered and thrilled to the point of seeming kid-like.

She sighed with happiness, tilting her head back. The photo

caught her attention again—the one of me and Michael. Her face turned serious as she admitted, "The funniest thing happened." But it was like she was talking to the photo, not to me. "I got this urge to celebrate. And to tell Ryan, you know, how important that ride turned out to be, because things feel like they might finally be starting to take off. And he..." Her voice trailed.

"He what?" I pressed.

"He kissed me. And I—wished I had a picture of it. Like that one up there."

"That good, huh?"

Heather shook her head. "That confusing. I wish I could have seen it, to understand it better."

I barked out this weird laugh. I couldn't help myself.

"It is kind of silly, isn't it?" Heather asked with a blush.

When I didn't respond, she shrugged, asked, "Is it okay for me to come back? To develop the extra pictures I take for Liu? I want to put together a whole new portfolio."

"Develop? So you're going to use the old Nikon, then?"

"Of course. You said it yourself. It's..."

"...magic," I finished quietly.

On Air

Prince Charming.

I worry about that guy.

Sure, it appears he's got nearly everything a man could ask for. He's handsome—and usually rich—powerful. He's got some sort of status. So much in his life is settled. The one thing missing is love.

Or so we're told.

What else do we really know about him? I mean Prince Charming as a person. Does he like music? Does he prefer ketchup on his eggs? Does he get teary-eyed at sentimental coffee commercials during the holidays? Does he follow football?

I think he is, arguably, the worst character in all the fairy tales. The least interesting. Because he's the flattest. He's Mr. Perfection. He can do no wrong.

Only, that can't be right. No one can literally do no wrong.

Seems to me, poor Snow White should have been far more interested in one of the dwarfs. All seven had such strong personali-

194

ties, they were stamped right into their names: Sleepy, Dopey, Sneezy. You remember.

Prince Charming never even has his own name. It's a generic *Prince Charming* in one fairy tale after another. Not Prince Harold or Prince Arthur.

Prince Charming, the lot of them sharing the same overly sweet-sounding moniker.

Prince Charming is the grand fantasy, you say. When he frees the damsel from a spell—and he's always freeing some poor damsel— why, that's a metaphor for the awakening of a heart. He's a symbol for what it's like to fall in love.

Could be. It's nice to think that way. I'm a big fan of metaphors, after all.

But I can't get past how painfully *dull* the guy is.

The girls in fairy tales, all of them, have far more to recommend them. We see their kindness, their hope for a better life, their perseverance in times of trouble—and their beauty. Lots and lots of beauty.

Excerpt from
The Fairyland Times
Entertainment Section
May 7, 2018

Local rock band The Tommies brought their talents to the stage of Murio's last Saturday, and judging by the audience's enthusiastic reception, it won't be their last appearance. The Tommies, founded by childhood friends Ryan Withersby and Fayth Johnson, are a somewhat eclectic foursome. Still, the band manages to successfully blend strong pop-rock melodies with infectious hip-hop beats. Withersby and Johnson write all the band's original material, as they have since The Tommies (a shortened version of their original name, Tomfoolery) were formed by the two in high school.

"We've seen a few drummers and bassists come and go over the years," Johnson admitted. "But this time around, I think it's safe to say we've finally got the perfect lineup."

Asked if she or Withersby could have foreseen it taking twenty years to assemble the kind of lineup that could garner three encores, as the band did last weekend, Johnson replied, "Sure, it took a little longer to get there than we planned. But Ryan and I have been dreaming about creating a whole lifetime of music together ever since we were kids. It's the dream that you never let go of that tastes the sweetest when it finally comes true."

Michael

Explaining life's mysteries in fairy tale terms had begun to infiltrate the entire town. My words acted like germs, infecting and swirling through everyone's heads.

Fayth Johnson listened to my latest radio spot as she biked to band practice. "Prince Charming," she grumbled. "You gotta be kidding."

Maybe it was a little old-fashioned to listen to the radio, but Fayth preferred it. There was something about bumping into the just-right song at the just-right moment that felt like fate. Like you'd run headlong into someone you were about to fall in love with.

Deciding she'd heard enough, she fumbled with the dial, attempting to search for a new station. She didn't hit the frequency dial, though. She accidentally hit the volume. My words pounded through her earbuds at about the same level as a hundred jackhammers. She flinched, swerved without meaning to. Her front tire whacked the curb, and the bike wobbled ferociously.

She recovered quickly. It's what Fayth did. She recovered quickly. She'd always lived up to her name.

198

She steered toward the ugly shed behind the gas station—space the band had been renting for months. She locked her bike to a nearby lamppost, wondering—like everyone else in Fairyland was at that point—who the guy spouting all the fairy tale stuff could possibly be.

Somehow, bumping into my words already felt like fate, every bit as much as finding the just-right song at the just-right time. Like something she was supposed to hear.

She tugged out her earbuds. A frown etched itself into her face as she tried to figure out how she could have found so much truth in the words.

Had she, for the vast majority of her life, been personally acquainted with a real-life Prince Charming?

Fayth let out a short *get real* guffaw.

Preposterous. And yet…

Ryan had exploded into her mind as soon as she'd heard me mention Prince Charming. Ryan, her best buddy for more than two decades. They'd gravitated toward each other time and again. Comforting each other, crying on the other's shoulders, hanging out in-between loves.

But then again, that's what friends did.

That did not mean she had been thinking of him in any kind of romantic way. Ever. Prince Charming. Come on.

Ryan's car pulled into the gas station. He waved at her through his rolled-down window. Fayth waved back limply to the one person in the world with whom she had shared everything: her childhood and her trials and her hopes. She and Ryan knew each other's favorite desserts and had written songs for each other and slept in the band's van all curled up in each other's arms.

Did friends really do that? Had something else actually been going on all along? Had another feeling been growing inside Fayth?

199

The kind of feeling that had been forced to live in the shadows beneath their friendship?

Fayth frowned, a new question hitting her with the force of a Midwest windstorm: *What have we been doing all this time?*

A good hour and a half later—long after the other two members of the band had shown up, plugged their instruments into amps, and kicked the practice session into gear—Prince Charming struck another sour chord.

He growled, throwing his arm out wildly, accidentally scattering emptied soda cans and takeout containers from the top of a Marshall amp. The band had all chipped in to purchase the amp together, with the idea that someday, it'd be perched on a stage in front of a sprawling crowd, the size of which would merit using a whole wall of giant, powerful amplifiers.

Had Ryan been an actual rock star (at the height of the era of much-adored yet pampered and indulgent rock stars), his actions might have been seen as cool—or, at the very least, tolerable. He could have immediately struck a pose while whipping his long hair behind his shoulders and twirling a silk patterned scarf, perfect for the cover of *Rolling Stone*.

"Poor tortured guy," his fans would have said. "Oh, well, bet it'll lead to a really good album."

As it was, in a cramped, dark, cheap, and often somewhat smelly space behind the mid-town gas station, it seemed pathetic.

And annoying. Really annoying.

Matt raised his sticks and thumped out the "bah-dum-pah" drumroll usually reserved for punctuating the end of a joke.

Ryan growled in frustration. He felt like a joke. An even bigger joke than their crummy practice space.

Fayth read his mind, recognized his mood. She'd seen it before. After all, they'd been friends and confidants since the days of kickball and lunch boxes.

But is that all? The question kept swirling through Fayth's mind, growing louder and more insistent with each appearance.

She clenched her jaw, resenting me at that moment—even though she didn't so much as know my name. Why'd I have to hijack one of the few radio stations in Fairyland? Start in with all that fairy tale nonsense? Get everyone talking? Make her switch over from the stations she usually listened to, the Top 40 stations, the hip-hop stations, the rock stations that never would have put these thoughts in her head? Why'd I have to make her question everything that existed between her and her closest friend?

Especially since everything, before she'd started overthinking it, had seemed perfectly fine. Comfortable. Solid.

"Take ten," she sighed. Not only to give Ryan a little breathing room. She needed a break too. His incessant mistakes, leading to constant do-overs, were killing her voice.

"You don't get it together soon, poor Fayth's going to start growing polyps the size of cannonballs," Matt grumbled.

Ryan grunted as he propped his guitar into the instrument stand.

"You want some tea, Fayth?" Matt asked.

"Oh, come on. I didn't *injure* her," Ryan argued. "She doesn't need to be babied."

"Hey," Matt barked. "I gotta have Fayth." On cue, Drew plunked on his bass and began to sing the chorus of the old George Michael song. Matt's joke had truth to it. The entire band was protective of its lead singer, whom they'd collectively referred to as "their girl." She was the band (as Matt frequently liked to remind them all). Fayth and Ryan had grown up together, but she had come up listening to mostly hip-hop and R&B, and her rhythm and phrasings were different from the rock and pop sensibilities of Ryan and his music store co-workers. She gave the band a different sound. Without Fayth, The Tommies would be a different band completely—one of those dime-a-dozen old-school garage bands.

At least, that's what Matt said. More than once. More than often.

Like Fayth would have ever left Ryan for another group.

Now, she wondered if that was because of her devotion to music...or to him.

Ryan walked outside and slumped down on the back step. He leaned back on his elbows, trying to relax.

Fayth grabbed a beer from their small cooler and followed, plopping down on the step beside him.

The summer evening draped itself like a cool bed sheet across the back of her neck. In the distance, a familiar song poured from a car radio in the gas station parking lot. One from their high school days. The Goo Goo Dolls. Ryan still loved old pop songs—three-minute bursts of pure emotion. He'd made sure Fayth loved them too.

But the song wasn't nearly as forceful as the echo of my words, still ringing in Fayth's head. *That guy doesn't know what he's talking about,* she told herself. Some crazy old guy who doesn't think Prince Charmings are ever interesting. Why, Ryan was talented and kind. Didn't you have to be exactly that in order to be "charming"? And his music—that showed personality, didn't it? Maybe that guy on the radio wasn't looking hard enough. Maybe he'd been distracted by bibbidi-bobbidi-boos and glittery wands.

That had to be it.

So why was she still feeling so defensive? Why was she thinking of him as a Prince Charming at all? And if she wasn't a princess,

202

then who was she to Ryan? What role did she play?

How about Tinker Bell? The bright spot in Peter Pan's life. Not one of Grimms' characters, but a fairy who fixed things. And one, it seemed, she had been somewhat fond of as a kid.

Fayth cringed against the idea. Wasn't Tinker Bell really no more than a Peter Pan groupie?

She raised a perfectly sculpted black eyebrow at Ryan. The kind of eyebrow raise that she'd often used to call him on his b.s. This time, the raise told him she knew all those excuses he'd tried to give for his poor playing for the past hour and a half were lies: everything from having a headache to struggling with a hangnail to worrying about rent. They both knew what was really going on. His head wasn't in it today. Because of his breakup with Heather.

Fayth felt no reservation about calling him on it. In the going-on thirty years they'd known each other, she'd never missed an opportunity to call him on his b.s.

Yeah. Most definitely not a groupie.

He sighed. "I know. Sorry."

She leaned back on her hands, knees jutting up into the sky. She'd worn her shortest cutoffs to rehearsal, along with a floppy striped shirt hanging off one shoulder, vintage *Flashdance* style. Not that she truly expected Ryan to notice.

Did she want him to notice?

Why was she thinking about this?

Now that she didn't have to stand in front of her first-grade classroom, she'd dyed her teeny weeny Afro purple. It'd be black again come fall, but this was when Fayth felt the prettiest. When she was herself, short shorts, purple hair, and all.

At that moment, she figured any other red-blooded guy—especially one recently single—would have looked at her with his own sense of *what if* floating in the back of his head. Another guy would have leaned closer to her, whispered something slightly indelicate, even borderline risqué. Tried to get a laugh or at least a smile. Wormed his way closer to something physical.

Ryan grunted and looked away.

Why would she have suspected there'd be even the slice of a chance he'd respond differently? With all that history between them? Their friendship had started before their ages had turned double-digits, when Fayth had attacked a playground bully who was teasing him—for what, who could remember anymore? Poor bully had underestimated her. But then again, how could he have known she was already working on her green belt in taekwondo?

And besides, there was a chance that Prince Charmings did not like the fact that they'd been rescued themselves. Maybe that one act of childhood kindness at the start of it all had forever erased the possibility of there ever being something more between him and Fayth.

That couldn't be right.

Could it?

Itching to find out for sure, she dipped her toe in the water by joking, "So Prince Charming got a chance to rescue the girl and it's messed with his head."

"What's that supposed to mean?"

"Last weekend—Heather. You rescued her."

"I told you, I gave her a ride. That's all. She called. She needed help. She didn't have anyone else. So I helped."

"Huh-uh. Rescue. In your head, it was a rescue. Wasn't it?"

Ryan rolled his eyes.

Fayth nudged him, encouraging him to take the beer bottle from her hand. She liked the dark stuff—the porters and stouts. He still hated the taste of any kind of alcohol, but if he didn't at least take a swig, he knew she'd probably use it as an opportunity to tease him about being a softy.

He took a sip, surely grateful it wasn't the Four Roses whiskey Fayth was also fond of.

"I'm telling you, that girl doesn't want to be rescued," she warned. "Maybe she and I aren't exactly besties, but she's been around enough for me to figure her out. She's doing it all on her own. She could have done a hundred different things. Gotten married. Gotten a real nine-to-five. Anything. But she's in that crummy apartment by herself, working her tail off. Seems to me, the last thing she wants is somebody to rescue her."

"I didn't think I was."

"You have a thing for it. Saving damsels in distress." *Is that part of the reason why you've never seen me in that way? I'm too headstrong. Too independent. Is that it?*

"I do not have a thing for…It was just a ride. Besides, she came back to see me yesterday."

Fayth's stomach bottomed out. "She did?"

Ryan nodded. "Yeah—to thank me for taking her out there to her shoot. And to tell me that it could open up to a better job for her."

"And?"

"She kissed me. Or I kissed her. I think I started it. But she kissed me back. I mean, not like a *kiss* kiss. Kind of a peck, but…"

"*And?*"

He shrugged, running his fingers through his hair.

"You're so pathetic," she grumbled. "Seriously."

Why did it pinch to hear that Heather had kissed him?

"It's barely been any time at all since we split. I'm supposed to be completely over it, with somebody new?"

"I've seen you do it before."

"I'm older now."

"And oh-so-much wiser, eh?"

He shrugged again. His eyes grew distant as he relived the kiss. Fayth could read his mind.

"This breakup hit you hard. Heather got to you." Fayth wasn't trying to convince him of Heather's worthiness. And she wasn't trying to put the two of them on an even plane—two girls who would never need saving. She was trying to shake some sense into him at that point. And—okay, so she was also trying to find out what he really felt. She needed to know how serious he was about Heather. She needed to know if he'd ever once thought of her the way she was beginning to think of him now.

Knowing what was in Ryan's heart could help her make sense of her own feelings.

She squirmed uncomfortably on the step.

"She did not get to me."

"Bull." She could hardly breathe. She found herself wishing he would fight her on it. Prove he didn't care. Not about Heather.

It was such a strange feeling. Especially after all these years.

"She chooses her photography over me. Every single time. I'd had enough."

"You're such a hypocrite!" Fayth blurted. She couldn't help herself. It was so stupidly sexist. "How many times have you been over here practicing—or at a gig on a weekend—instead of fawning all over her? And that's okay. You assume it'll be okay. But when the tables are turned, and she's the one chasing after her dream, it's not."

"Not true," Ryan argued, but he had that look on his face like he was going to be sick.

"I think that sometimes, we see what we expect. Not necessarily what's actually there," she said. But how was he interpreting her words? Now her stomach was absolutely churning.

"You should embroider that on a pillow."

She shoved his leg, making his knees clang together.

"Don't get defensive and dismiss what I said. I've seen you with plenty of girls before, and you've never moped about a breakup like this. It's like you're still hanging on to it for some reason. You need to decide. Let her go or ask her to take you back. Just get off the fence." She stood, brushed off the seat of her cutoffs. "Either way, be sure to leave Prince Charming at home from now on. Heather's not the kind of girl to go for that crap. Very few of us are."

Nobody with half a brain is. You like Heather—and she's sweet, but she's got her own toughness. Don't you see that? You like tough. I'm tough.

"You coming in?" She held the door for him, but he shook his head.

Inside, Fayth lunged to a spot where she could still see him through the small window.

What was he going to do?

He pulled out his phone. Fayth held her breath, hoping that she had pushed him enough to decide, right there, that his instincts to call it off had been right. Hoping that he would erase Heather's number. Go about unfriending her on all his social media accounts.

Instead, she listened as he began to leave a voicemail. "Hey, Heather. Uh, it's me. Ryan. I was talking to the band, and we—the band, I mean—we all agree that we need a photographer. Someone to take some live performance shots. At one of our next gigs. Something other than those crummy posed shots. We, uh, we need them for the website. And online stuff. Help advertise our gigs. So. Let me know. Okay?"

Fayth pulled her face away from the window. What had she done?

Sent her maybe-Prince Charming back into the arms of another woman. A woman he was obviously really attracted to.

Of course, she tried to assure herself, there was still a chance Heather wouldn't accept Ryan's offer.

Then again, what princess had ever turned down her chance to show up at Prince Charming's ball?

If only Fayth had a Tinker Bell she could count on. Someone who'd sprinkle a little fairy dust and make everything better again.

But no—it was all on Fayth's shoulders. She would forever be her own rescuer. Her own Tinker Bell. Fayth, the now-black belt in taekwondo, would tackle emergencies herself.

Did that radio guy know anything about heroines like that?

Sharon

"A shoot!" Heather announced as we descended back down to the studio basement. "Over at Murio's."

"Murio's?" It was starting to get a little uncomfortable, frankly, the way Heather was moving in on my territory. Only, it wasn't really territory, exactly, was it? An old camera I didn't use anymore, a bar I'd stopped visiting.

I'd made a decision long ago to stop traveling the same ground, stop following my own footprints. Why did it hurt so much to find Heather standing in them?

"…Ryan's band plays there. Needs some shots…" Heather babbled. "My best friend, Amanda, she's the one who got me interested in taking pictures. You know I took her senior photo? Preserved for all time in the annals of high school. But she was always into artistic stuff. Music…"

Amanda. The name had filled the darkroom frequently as Heather and I developed her rolls of film. Shot after shot—images she had once intended to take back to Liu. Now, she was acting like these were all practice shots. Like she was training, getting ready for this night with her ex. Hoping to use images from Murio's as the entirety of her portfolio.

I had my own Murio's portfolio. One that Heather had never seen. I'd never shown her. Why wasn't I now?

Heather kept on chatting and chatting about her oldest friend, this Amanda person. Maybe, at first, it was only to erase the silence in the darkroom. Maybe it was a way to seem friendly and not like an imposition as she brought me yet another roll, developed for free.

There were times, when Heather spoke of their friendship, that I was carried backward—not necessarily to the faces of my own old friends, but to my feelings about them.

"We used to call each other," Heather confessed. "Me and Amanda. After we should have been asleep. On these really basic early cell phones. The two of us with our comforters over our heads, whispering into these flip phones both our parents had bought us."

What did they talk about? I wanted to know. Oh, the same old stuff. Boys. And teachers. Their parents. Hopes and fears and music and the world. The kind of things that seem like kid stuff later on, but are the whole world when you're whispering through the night. They talked the way we all dream of being able to talk to someone as adults, but so rarely do.

Her story brought back the way I'd once sneaked downstairs while Dad was asleep to make calls to my own teenage best friend. Kathleen, that was her name. Kathleen, who had a line in her room and a fancy phone that could light up instead of ring with the flip of a switch. I could call her and her parents were none the wiser. Two girls talking and giggling and pledging secrecy through the night.

"Sometimes, things seem different now," Heather admitted. "A little distant, kind of." She twisted her face, showing the explanation for it was something she couldn't quite put her finger on.

They were older. In different places in their lives. It's easier when you have the same teachers and go to the same school and are the same age and going through all the same milestones—dating and learning to drive and figuring out college. When the struggles are the same, the triumphs are more easily celebrated together.

I couldn't remember the sad slow loss of a close childhood friend. It didn't even seem like I'd gone through this—no post-college time of friends drifting off in their separate directions.

It had happened, though. It had to have. The same girls who had once had extra toothbrushes in Dad's bathroom. Who had helped with chocolate chip pancakes after sleepovers. Who had spent hour after hour on the phone. They were gone from my address book.

Why hadn't I noticed?

I frowned, reaching for my tongs. Before I could pull Heather's latest image from the fixer, the answer came to me, giving me a shiver: *Because I had Michael.*

He'd come into my life fairly soon after college, when I was so absorbed with my business, with making my own way. I was just so busy. Before I had a chance to so much as take a deep breath and wonder where everyone had gone, he was already there. Filling all the spaces my close girlfriends had once occupied.

Underneath every single one of the titles he'd worn in relation to me—boyfriend, fiancé, husband—he'd also been my friend.

At that moment, with Heather's ramblings in my ear and Michael's face at the front of my thoughts, I found myself aching for another long, winding, aimless conversation—the kind you can only have with a best friend. The kind that went nowhere and to all the exact-right places at the same time.

From the Studio Walls
Bottom Step
2

The bottom of the stairs to the basement—the same step where Sharon's father had once sat at night to listen to the fights and talk to his daughter—was empty.

Well. Empty except for the one last can of Pabst, anyway. A wordless toast to the man who had told Sharon she *could*. Whatever "could" amounted to at any given moment. Photograph the world, go into business, be married, not be married.

He'd drummed it into her head. She *could*.

One brief look at Sharon's picture and you'd know the entire basement was empty. You'd swear it echoed with loss.

And you'd be right.

Not because the basement's darkroom was gone—and had been for some time. Because *he* was gone. The man who had acted as her bodyguard while simultaneously making sure she had her own pair of boxing gloves, one that would protect her knuckles from every blow he wanted her to give the world.

Sharon had inherited her father's estate. It was hers to break apart, folding some things into her life with Michael and selling or giving away the rest.

His house was the biggest part of everything he'd left behind. And yet, she was selling it. Letting someone else take up where he had left off.

Was that always true? Were the biggest parts of us the things that had to be let go of in the end? Even our hopes? Our fears? Who we'd really been? Did we let that go with the last beat of the heart?

She wasn't sure, but avoided developing the roll that contained the shot as long as she could. Six months. Until the "Sold" sign appeared in what had once been her front lawn.

She'd hung the picture in her studio as a tribute.

And then she'd tucked away her 1967 Nikon F. Not just back into its case. She'd put it in the farthest reaches of the studio shelves, behind the rest of her portrait equipment.

Over the next few years, the camera would eventually drift out of the studio, into the junk closet upstairs. But that was the day she officially retired it, the camera that had started everything.

It was time. Her father was gone. Sharon's beginning was over. Besides, she'd thought, maybe the ache of missing him would be a little less if she used a different camera. One that had not been purchased with her father's money. One that had never had his fingerprints on it.

A foolish idea, born in grief.

"Buck up," she could still hear him chanting. "Can't quit now, just because I'm not around." And she'd chuckled a bit, turning from the old camera case for what she thought was the last time. It was the one thing that would make him proud. Keep going, keep pushing, keep adapting, keep moving ahead, his tenacious little fighter Sharon.

Excerpt from

The Fairyland Times

About Town

March 7, 2001

The best young talent in Fairyland performed on the Central High School auditorium stage last night to a standing-room-only crowd.

Performers from all three Fairyland high schools battled for several titles: Best Singer, Best Band, Best Dancer, Best Comedy Skit. The Central High band Tomfoolery took the trophy for Best Overall Act.

Fayth Johnson, Tomfoolery vocalist, and lead guitar player Ryan Withersby accepted the award to a round of cheering and deafening applause—so loud, in fact, their thank-you speech went largely unheard.

Audience members Heather Scott and Amanda Pierce, both juniors at Fairyland South, left humming "Worlds Apart," an original song written by Tomfoolery members. "We've never heard that band before," Pierce said, "probably because we all go to different schools. But they were so good. And so different. I wish they had an album out. If they did, I'd play it until my next-door neighbors knew all the lyrics. *Definitely* deserved to win."

Sharon

Listen, I know Michael's all about slow burn and getting to know the characters and using a bunch of literary acrobatics. Me? I like the *now we're getting to the really good stuff.*

And trust me, nothing makes a story juicier faster than a villain getting more villainy. Like Amanda was doing.

Yeah, I used the word: villain. You already know where I stand on Michael's fairy tale stuff. But I can agree with Michael on this much: Amanda was getting to be quite the bad guy.

Besides, I know these people. I get Heather. And Amanda's family had been the snoots of Fairyland for generations. The sort whose overt displays of wealth never did seem to quite match up with their résumés.

Which sounds a little judgmental. But I'm just trying to say I'd photographed them all. Which means I had to really *look* at them. Every one of those Pierces.

216

So you can trust me on this part. Every single word…

Amanda's gated community had a pool, which should have been a perfectly fine place to take Heather for the afternoon. The two could have stretched out on neighboring beach towels while the kids played, and Amanda could have bled Heather for information on what, exactly, was going on with Liu. The adjacent game room and bar, the pricey tropical plants in the landscaping surrounding the kidney-shaped pool would have done quite the job of reminding Heather how far down she still remained on the social scale.

And yet, Amanda decided instead to drag her—and all three of her kids—to the pool at the country club.

It had to be the most devilish thing Amanda's rebellious little heart could think of.

Oh, sure, Amanda could reason her way through this decision too. Paint it in a way that made her look helpful. Why, she was inviting Heather to the club for her own good. Preparing Heather for the realities of the big-time world she was about to enter. The world of the Lius and corporate jobs and advertising was no place for wide-eyed girls who wore lipstick from the Dollar Tree and talked about promising their dying mothers to lead with kindness. The world didn't respond to little darlings. It responded, quite frankly, to straight-up intimidation.

And money. It always responded to money.

Amanda would be doing Heather a favor by toughening her up. She needed to help the girl grow a few calluses. Enlightenment—she could provide the exact dose Heather needed.

It was bound to be an uncomfortable enlightenment. And a big part of Amanda found that absolutely delicious.

Her twins bolted ahead of the group. Heather carried Aiden. Amanda, in sync with their current atmosphere, carried a crocheted beach tote from Nordstrom. And a few brightly colored Lilly Pulitzer beach towels, draped over one arm. (Nice. Tasteful. Designer. But nothing too ostentatious or over the top.)

The girls were so anxious to get inside that they sprinted through the wrought iron gate the moment Amanda used the coded keypad to swing it open. They cannonballed into the cool water before Amanda, Heather, and Aiden even stepped onto the stone patio.

Amanda paused to breathe in the smells of broad-spectrum, oil-free sunscreens and lightly tinted lip balm. And smiled—only a little, nothing that might give her away. Things were about to get interesting. After all, country club members abided by an unwritten code of conduct. Rules of behavior. An intricate hierarchy. A meaning existed behind everything—choice of drink, choice of bathing suit, where you sat…Amanda could have written her own book explaining the etiquette of a country club pool.

The rules applied, even here, in a town considered on the small side in the middle of Missouri. Or was that *especially* here? After all, if a woman couldn't make it at Southern Hills Golf & Country Club, what were her other options? Fairyland wasn't exactly brimming with country clubs. Just one.

Rules were important. And the beautiful part was that Heather knew none of them.

In the first place, single women of Heather's age were generally in a somewhat precarious position at the Southern Hills pool. Should they appear lacking the proper degree of ladylike decorum, they were promptly punished with the ever-feared cold shoulder. A woman Heather's age did not wear a string bikini. She was not to pretend to be seventeen. She wore a structured bathing suit. She usually had a ring on her finger. And if she didn't, she made it quite clear (through her choice of modest attire and by sitting near other women) that she was not out to snag a few good times with anyone's husband.

A woman Heather's age did not drink too many fruity drinks with umbrellas. She did not douse herself in oil and sunbathe, putting her toned body on display. Single women of her age did not play in the pool, either, splashing and squealing and drawing undue attention. Nor did they attempt to align themselves with one of the grand dames who generally sat in the shade beneath large straw hats and designer sunglasses and shapeless sundresses, not to mention gold earrings and necklaces, never once sliding out of their closed-toe sandals.

The grand dames ran the show. If they shunned you, good luck ever being able to strike up a conversation with anybody at the pool for the rest of the summer—maybe even two summers. They reigned supreme in their own supercilious closed community of sorts, right there under the eaves of the pool house, complete with an invisible (but very real) gate. Having arrived without the proper credentials, Heather would only be allowed to admire them from afar.

She was bound to screw up. How else could it go with a girl like her, who had no knowledge of the rules of proper behavior?

Heather put Aiden down, giving everyone at the pool a full view of her first faux pas: her outfit. She was wearing cutoffs. Daisy Dukes. The kind she'd made herself, with scissors, and washed a few times, so that white strings dangled and danced down her toned thighs. And an ancient T-shirt commemorating some summer music festival she and Amanda had attended together a lifetime ago. Amanda chuckled softly as Heather quickly tugged it off, exposing a bikini top, the kind that tied on around her back and neck and had no support whatsoever.

Amanda expected Heather to jump into the pool with the rest of the kids—to play with the girls, who had learned to swim last spring. Instead, she followed Amanda to the wading pool.

"Can't leave my boy, now can I?" she asked Aiden.

The other women sitting poolside to watch their own toddlers smiled at Heather—there she was, using *Amanda's* son to show herself to be uninterested in any of the husbands, and like a real sweetheart to boot, the kind of woman who never ran out of patience with the most trying little kids—even, dare Amanda think it, the *brats.*

In fact, as the women smiled and nodded and waved, it was instantly clear that Heather's bond with Aiden was endearing enough to make the women completely forget the swimsuit faux pas in a matter of seconds.

What *was* it with Heather lately?

Amanda tried to turn her face into a blank page as she and Heather sat side-by-side at the wading pool. Aiden wore floaties on his arms and filled a cup with pool water, emptying it again and again, over and over. The other women drifted back into their conversations, none of them giving Heather a single narrowed side-eyed glance.

Heather was getting along at the Southern Hills pool perfectly fine. The only judgment she seemed to be receiving was coming from Amanda. And that in itself was really starting to tick Amanda off.

It was also, quite frankly, making her crave a tequila sunrise.

But it would be wrong to jerk the kids away from their games. And besides, it would also look bad, especially here, at the wading pool of all places, where the women all appeared to relish time with their babies. Fighting the urge to scream, Amanda graciously allowed Heather to play with Aiden until she knew, from the look on his face, that he was hungry. A pouty, grumpy kind of hungry. And then with a smile and a chipper clap of her hands, she led everyone to the clubhouse.

220

Her kids ordered hamburgers, as did Heather, while Amanda stuck to her single piece of skinless, grilled lean chicken and quinoa.

She couldn't believe it. Heather was wearing a bikini and eating kid food. Here, in the ornate members' dining room.

Yet again, nobody seemed to care.

Heather had also ordered one of Amanda's tequila sunrises. Just one wasn't going to hurt anybody. Or so she'd said.

"Hey," Heather barked, pointing skyward. "It's that guy."

"What guy?" Amanda grumbled. Heather was getting awfully giggly. Suddenly, *everything* was funny. Even the tablecloth.

"The guy—you know," Heather persisted. "On the radio? The one everyone's been talking about? The fairy tale guy? They're tuned in to that station. Here. At the club. You know which guy I'm talking about? Sure, you do."

"What's with you?" Amanda hissed.

Heather blushed. "Haven't had anything to eat yet today. Plus, being out in the sun—I guess it's hitting me kind of hard."

"Since there's no question I have to be the one to drive home, finish mine," Amanda muttered, sliding her glass toward her. "I'll drink water."

She might as well. What would it matter if she didn't get to enjoy her favorite cocktail? Nothing about this day was turning out to be very enjoyable. Yet again, Heather was escaping being taught the rougher truths of the world. She was living in her usual sickeningly sweet little bubble, the same bubble where she got to cry on Amanda's shoulder, complain in confidence, then snag really fantastic jobs using Amanda's own husband's contacts, skipping through life, tra-la-la.

Never-ending youth. That was what Heather had. More than anything, that was what irked Amanda. Come to think of it, maybe it had been annoying her for eons. Maybe that was why she'd chosen

"Sweet Child o' Mine" as Heather's ringtone. How was it that everybody on the planet grew up at some point, with the glaring exception of one person? And why did the one lucky person have to be her own best friend? Most of all, why would Heather's youth not stop pounding Amanda with the force of a tornado?

Pushing her emptied cocktail glass aside and picking up Amanda's, Heather asked the twins, "Ish your mom gonna to let you girls spend your whole shummer here at the pool? It's 'a only place on *earth* I'd wanna be, if I were your age." She said it too loudly. And her words were running into each other, like the colors in one of those watercolor portraits the girls had brought Amanda home from school the year before.

Heather wasn't tipsy anymore. Heather was flat-out drunk.

"Whersh my fork?" Heather asked, giggling as she picked up Aiden's plate and looked underneath it.

Amanda glanced across the room. One of the grand dames from the pool was staring at them.

Amanda prepped her face in order to share a look with her. One of those *Can you believe this silly woman?* kind of expressions.

But the grand dame, Amanda realized with horror, was glaring at *her*. Not Heather. She was angry at Amanda for bringing this ridiculous girl into the club and upsetting the upscale, sophisticated atmosphere.

It was Amanda's fault. Yet again.

Women all across the room took turns scowling at her. Younger women. Shaking their heads. Making disapproving *tsk-tsk* sounds as they lovingly patted their children's backs.

Amanda had allowed alcohol—and a drunk woman—around her own children. Amanda was being a Bad Mother. Shame on her.

She felt like standing up, slamming her hands on her hips, and shouting at the world, "Hey! What gives?" Lately, every single time she tried to take a spin at the game of life, Amanda felt like she only wound up landing on some awful square that declared she had encountered a new setback or a thwarted plan.

She glared at Heather. She wanted to flick her little plastic game piece off the board.

"Shhhh," Heather said, putting a finger to her lips.

Where did that come from? Why was she trying to quiet Amanda? Could she hear her thoughts?

"I have a secret," Heather whispered.

A secret. Right.

"You don't believe me," Heather said.

"Sure, I do," Amanda said. "I have a secret too. I don't know what I'm going to do with you. You're kind of a cheap drunk."

"A really *good* secret," Heather insisted, swaying in her chair.

"Fine. I'll bite. What is it?"

"It's about the *camera*."

"I know Liu liked your picture," Amanda said with a toss of her hand, no longer in the mood to drill her for details. "Tom told me about it. How he offered you a chance at a job."

"Noooooo!" Heather leaned forward and shook her finger at Amanda. She smelled coconuty. It was an obnoxious smell, actually. Strong. Cloyingly floral. Cheap.

"The camera—that film thing I've been using? It's a Nikon F. Mostly. It's mostly a Nikon F." She giggled. "It's got these replacement parts from a long time ago. And it's also *magic*."

Amanda rolled her eyes. "Come on—I've got to get you home."

"No, no, no. I mean it. It's why she gave it to me. It was magical for her."

"For who?"

"Sharon. Minyard. The one who owns that photography studio. I told you about her. I think I did, anyway. She *gave* me this camera. The film one. It was magical for her, and it's going to be magical for me. It *is* magic. It's really magic. It's why I took the picture Liu liked. And he's going to hire me. I know he will. Because see, the thing is, I'm taking him a portfolio."

"Uh-huh." Amanda grumbled. "I think we covered that already."

Heather leaned back slightly. "Guess *what*? I even know what he wants."

"Who?"

"Liu."

"How do you know that?"

"I emailed Tom." She grinned.

"My husband? You emailed my husband?" A fire was bursting and billowing inside her.

"Yep. I'm *net*working. I asked him what Liu is working on. *He* said he wants to get into entertainment, not boring toothpaste and stuff." Heather tapped the side of her head. "Smart of me, huh?"

"I don't see what that—"

"It's perrrrrfect! Ryan called. And I'm going to take pictures of his band—at Murio's! A live gig! And it's going to show Liu I can work in entertainment. See? My whoooole portfolio's going to be this gig. That I'm going to shoot with my magical camera. And everything will be so perfect. I'll live happily ever after." Heather grinned again.

"Okay, okay, Annie Leibovitz," Amanda grumbled. She was seething. But she had to do something with Heather. "Right now, I've got to get you home."

"It's a rotten apartment."

"Not your home. Mine. Where I can watch you."

"Good idea. I think. I think it's a good idea."

Amanda helped Heather into the front passenger seat and

buckled Aiden in while the twins climbed into their boosters. She drove to her house feeling defeated and lonely. Because she *was* alone. There. She said it, finally. When had it happened, exactly? When had her life gotten all carved up, little slices of it divvied between so many people—her husband or other country club wives? So much of Tom's working life was outside of her purview, and with the other wives, she always had to censor herself. There was no longer anyone in her life who really shared all of it, even the ugly parts, the way she and Heather once had. Back when they were kids and they'd whispered through the nights to each other on their flip phones. Back when boys were mysteries to fantasize about, when the future was a glorious anything they could imagine, when they both believed they'd conquer the world, arms linked and walking in time with each other. And in the meantime, before all that conquering could be done, they'd commiserate together about having to abide by the same set of unfair rules.

Now there were four other people in her car, and Amanda was the only sober adult having to abide by a set of strict, unchanging, unbending rules. It made her feel like a chaperone. And she hated it.

In the garage, she draped Heather's arm around her neck and led her inside. She tugged a sheet out of the laundry basket in the living room and covered the couch before dumping Heather on top.

"You guys go get out of those wet suits," she told the girls.

Aiden stood next to the couch, tugging on Heather's hand. "Okay?" he kept asking.

But Heather was asleep. And snoring.

Aiden giggled. And put his fingers across her mouth.

Amanda changed him in the living room, tossed his suit along with the girls' in the wash.

While Aiden drove his cars across the carpet, Amanda opened her MacBook. She Googled "Sharon Minyard."

She was greeted by a seemingly unending stream of results. A Wikipedia page. A listing on several photography sites.

Magic? Could it be? Was it possible?

Please. Why would she even consider Heather's drunken ramblings?

Only, this other woman—this Sharon—had certainly hit it big. At least for a while. Gone surprisingly far. Especially for someone with an old photography store in Fairyland.

Heather certainly believed it, all that magic stuff. Maybe that was all that mattered.

Maybe, Amanda's little black heart mused, *this day isn't turning out to be such a failure after all. Maybe it's just what I needed.*

As Heather snored from the couch, Amanda clicked over to eBay. And began to search the listings for a vintage Nikon F.

This Story

This is the story of a man. And a woman.

And it's about a young girl, this Heather, who blustered into their lives.

You know all that. You were promised as much right at the beginning.

But it's also about Fayth. Hasn't Michael already gotten into her head, told you a story about her and Ryan? About their decades-long friendship? How Fayth is beginning to suspect she feels something more?

And didn't Sharon just get inside Amanda's head, tell you about her fears, her resentments, her attempts (however misguided) to hang on to the best friend she will probably ever have in her life?

It's true. When someone comes bursting into your world, they never come alone. They wind up bringing the entirety of their own lives with them. Every last person in it.

Heather certainly did. All those dreams. All the longing and the hopes. So many hearts aiming in so many directions, you almost need a chart for it all.

A whole constantly-moving crowd.

Michael's words, broadcast regularly on the radio, were stirring all of them up into a bigger frenzy. Heather might have still been in the dark about Amanda becoming her nemesis, but Michael's words had certainly pushed Fayth to view Heather as a villain. To see her as the one directing Ryan's attention away from her, the same way Cinderella's stepsisters strove to take the prince for themselves.

In Michael's world, Heather was stealing Sharon's attention. He saw Heather as a villain too.

But isn't that the way it always goes? Aren't we all, at this very moment, participating in not just one fairy tale but five, ten tales at once? Aren't we the princess of our own fairy tale and the arch-enemy of another's? Wasn't Heather the princess of her own story at the same time she was acting as the wicked barrier between Fayth's and Michael's goals? Wasn't Fayth a Tinker Bell, a supporting character, but also a star? Michael feared Sharon viewed him as her foe, but weren't his listeners viewing him as a Prince Charming?

It does explain how Heather could have been a force strong enough to lift Sharon and Michael from their rut. She wasn't doing it by herself. She'd brought a whole crew with her. An entourage, each member with their own baggage, their own ongoing stories.

With a crowd, momentum becomes unstoppable.

Michael and Sharon were swept up in winds far beyond their control.

The same way the people of Fairyland were getting swept up in Michael's words.

Once a crowd is involved, there's simply no escaping.

Such is the insidious power of a crowd.

Sharon's Favorite Photo Album

*I*t was initially Dad's scrapbook. The one he wanted me to fill with all my successes. But the first image was Michael, anyway. The headshot I took for his column. And for some reason, the next picture I slipped in turned out to be the one I took of Michael and Dad together on the front porch, two cans of Pabst between them, obviously engaged in some sort of spirited discussion.

Dad liked him from the start.

No. He loved him. Maybe even before I did.

After that, I just kept filling it with pictures of Michael.

In most of them, he's writing.

He ages, of course, as the album progresses.

When I fell for Michael, it wasn't about attraction and gooey eyes and a handsome face. Please. I fell for his view of the world. It wasn't unlike my dad's, really. They both shared the idea that all things are possible. While Dad championed hard work, Michael tended to think success hinged on innate talent. But both believed, above all else, that dreams came true.

It was almost childlike. Not naïve. But I rarely saw that kind of pureness of vision in an adult. Usually being knocked around by the world meant you no longer viewed dreams as things that were destined to be realized.

Still. According to Dad and Michael, dreams came true. Period. They did, if you were talented enough and worked hard enough. Nothing—no detour or tragedy, no disappointment or frustration—could ever darken or dampen their belief.

I don't think Michael's faith in dreams becoming reality is clearer than in those pictures I took of him holding a pen. They've always looked to me like he was revising. Scratching out all the "no"s the world liked to dole out and replacing them with "yes"es and "of course"s and "just watch us"es.

He scratched out all the old rules, too, those loaded with "can't" and "don't" and "not good enough." Because Michael wasn't so much a traditionalist, I learned over the years. That wasn't why he loved his hometown and the Fourth of July bashes and the three-legged races, every year, right on cue.

It was because he loved people as he found them. Old, frumpy, silly, grumpy. He took people as they came. He accepted them without reservation. And he celebrated the seasons, the markers of the time he'd spent with the same faces.

He took me as I came. Me and my dream. And my plant-killing ways.

All of me. Back then, I was sure of it.

And in return? I learned not to judge a man by his stuffy dress shirts. I accepted his notebooks piled to the ceiling and the way he invited any fellow Fairyland resident who promised a juicy story to join us at our table in our favorite diner. I accepted the fact that there was no Christmas lightning ceremony or Easter egg hunt or Veteran's Day parade that we wouldn't be a part of. I accepted that Bingo on Tuesday was a must-do, because Michael promised the guys at the Eagles Lodge we'd be there. I accepted that when Michael told Gladys Miller that we would be by the junior high to see her grandson's picture in the seventh-grade art exhibit, we were *going* to that exhibit. And then we'd find Gladys on opening night and make it a point to tell her grandson what we liked the most about his drawing.

I photographed it. He wrote it. We exchanged our pieces. We smiled. Or we debated. We challenged each other. "That's simplistic," we'd say of each other's work. Or "That's not it." Sometimes, "That's perfect." In the midst of it all, our edges got a little less defined. Parts of ourselves ran into each other. Our colors started to mix.

You can see that in the pictures I took of him. You can see, as the years progress, that he is anything but flat. Anything but simple. He is both solid and reliable and somehow also ever-changing. Able to absorb pieces of me and remain himself.

After a while, because of Michael, I grew to love all the everyday, recurring parts of living in Fairyland. I became a part of the town in a way I had never been before. I saw it differently. Appreciation. That's a good word. And maybe that changed the way people saw me in return. I, too, was absorbing other pieces while remaining myself. Because after a while, I'd started to believe it right along with him. Dreams came true. Even dreams of love.

I got all that from some annoying Clark-Kent-minus-the-superpowers character who wouldn't stop bugging me in a record store.

Imagine that.

Excerpt from
The Fairyland Times
September 25, 1989

Winners of the Missouri Associated Press Excellence in Newswriting Awards were announced last Thursday in Kansas City. *The Fairyland Times*'s own "Observations from the Tower" columnist, Michael Minyard, took top spots in the categories of Opinion Writing and Public Interest. It is the fourth year Minyard's award-winning column has been recognized.

"I don't make my column special," Minyard said in his acceptance speech. "The people of Fairyland do. My neighbors and fellow townspeople have been graciously allowing me to document their comings and goings for decades. I have traveled with them through their trials and triumphs. Seen their vacation slides while we shared pie and coffee. Attended funerals, and sat with them on porches or in backyards long after the reception was over, listening to them tell me about their loved one. I have sat on the town square and listened to soldiers and mothers, the young and heartbroken, the gray-head-

232

ed and lonely. People who had lost loves or money or work. People at a crossroads. People who still didn't know how their own stories might end. I've also been delighted by the voices who called my name on the street, the people who raced to my side, breathless, anxious to tell me about a happy new turn. I have listened as night began to encroach or rain began to fall on myself and the storyteller, neither one of us daring to move. Not while there was still more to say.

"I can't remember the last time I've gone out to clear the snow from my front walk or pick up the dry cleaning or even just collect my mail without being met by a Fairyland resident with a story to tell. The people of Fairyland have trusted me with their most private possession: their stories. They've acknowledged me as a safe place. They opened up. Let loose with feelings and insights.

"Fairyland is a medium-sized town not unlike every town throughout our state. The people of Fairyland are just like your own neighbors. Your own families. You see yourself in my column because the people of Fairyland have been honest with me. Without them, there would be no column.

"I believe...no, not just believe. I *have* become a better writer as the years have gone on. No doubt about it. But not because of practice or experience. The people of Fairyland made me a better writer. They taught me to listen. And by listening, I found out what makes a good story. A powerful story. The people of Fairyland gave that to me. And they did it all by simply letting me into their lives."

Sharon

My phone pinged, signaling another incoming message.

The ping sort of echoed gloomily throughout the store.

The thing was, with Heather around, I decided it was time to get serious about ordering film. It didn't make sense that I'd let my stock get down so low, anyway. Why'd I keep the developing solutions but not the film? Where had my head gone?

At any rate, I told myself I was going to have to do plenty of scrounging around for suppliers.

Or so I'd initially thought. Turned out, *scrounging* wasn't the right word at all. My online searches taught me there were still plenty of old-school die-harders out there.

It was a funny thing to discover. Just when I'd settled deep into the assumption that the world had moved on completely, I was having to face—with each new ping—that maybe the truth was that I hadn't been looking in the right places. Too much staring at my own empty aisles and not enough reaching out. All this time, my own life, the one I thought had wrapped up, was still going on? For other

234

people? Without me?

I frowned at my phone and the texts I was receiving from film aficionados. All with their own recommendations. A few suppliers even reached out directly.

Odd how the digital age worked. Send out a feeler and suddenly, you were bombarded with answers. Almost like getting back some weird chain letter.

It should have comforted me, I guess, all the pinging signaling new incoming messages. Suggestions. Somehow, it made the old shop feel emptier than it ever had before.

I stared at the radio propped on the counter.

Should I or shouldn't I?

I twisted the power switch, finding Michael in mid-sentence:

"...ever notice the age of fairy tale stars? The Snow Whites and the Cinderellas and the Rapunzels?

"They're always young."

I crossed my arms over my chest—protectively, really. As Michael rattled on, I slowly made my way across the studio, pausing to look up at our portrait. *The Art of the Kiss.*

A bunch of echoes bounced against the walls. And not from my phone, either. Echoes of the past, of former customers' voices: "Do you sell prints of that one?" If I'd been asked once, I'd been asked upwards of ten thousand times. And now, staring up at our portrait, I could hear them all—young and old, male, female...Their familiar request like the chorus of a song sung in a round.

I'd refused. Sell my love story? It was one thing to put it on display. But put a price tag on it?

"Nah, you should be displaying your own pictures," I'd reply, hoping each time that it came across as friendly and kind. Hoping it didn't sound more like a *not in this lifetime* or *you gotta be kidding.* I couldn't stomach the idea of that photo hanging up in everybody's living rooms, surrounded by hotel prints and piles of dirty laundry.

Michael would grin every single time they asked, a geyser of satisfaction bursting from him with each request. There'd never been any denying he'd played a big part in *The Kiss*'s success. After all, without his handiwork, without him resurrecting the camera from the dead, there'd have never been a photo.

A similar satisfaction—or maybe it was sheer pride—oozed from me each time someone realized Michael was none other than the writer behind their favorite *Fairyland Times* column. Why wouldn't it? As much as he helped in the shop, I helped with that column, listening to his ideas, asking questions, helping him refine his topics. Giving him ideas he ran with from time to time.

We were together in it all. What a high it was for both of us to be in a shop that buzzed with admiring voices, all that attention. A couple of small-time celebs. Every once in a while, we'd glance across the shop, catch each other's eye, share this knowing look.

And still, people came. Still, people asked for a print. *The Art of the Kiss*.

In the evenings, though, a new feeling would find me. By this point, Michael and I were several years into our life together. The newspaper article about our traffic jam had yellowed a bit around the edges. In the quiet, I'd flip the evening's "Closed" sign and grab a hammer. Nail between my lips, I'd scan the walls, searching for a different spot to hang *The Art of the Kiss*. A better spot. Must have been a thousand better spots during those hectic years—spots, I told Michael, that wouldn't block seasonal displays or the checkout counter.

"I know they come to see our picture, but we've got to keep the customers moving in here," I'd say, trying to sound convincing.

Eventually, I settled on a place so high up, the top of the frame brushed the edge of the ceiling. It would still grab everyone's attention. But it'd bug people to keep their heads tilted back too long.

236

That would finally, finally, *finally* ensure the clustering was limited to the briefest of moments.

That was what I told Michael, anyway.

In reality, clogged aisles had little if anything to do with my decision to hang that picture as high as possible. I'd hung it there so people would have to look at the rest of my work and, by so doing, finally see me. All of me, not just my love story. My whole life, not a single moment of it.

I loved the attention *The Art of the Kiss* brought. I appreciated it. I recognized the power it wielded. Everything it did for me.

And yet, at times, so much of me still felt ignored.

"…What do old people do in fairy tales?" Michael was saying now, his voice pouring through my radio. "Old folks are never given a Prince Charming role. They're around for no other reason than to put roadblocks in the main characters' way—to throw them in towers, turn them into toads, or feed them poison apples. That, or they become helpmates. They're fairy godmothers. They don't have a story of their own. They're around to help somebody else—the struggling star of the current tale—find their way.

"Think about that. Old characters don't have a story of their own anymore. They're not cast in the starring role. Ever."

I flinched, flicked the radio back off. He was still talking about me.

That time, I was sure of it.

Worse yet, it was like he was in my head. Didn't I think something very much like that, when I was on my laptop trying to work on a portrait of the store, one that showed the passage of time? Hadn't I thought about how long it had been since I'd shown Michael one of my pieces? Hadn't I wondered if I was afraid of having lost my special something, the talent that defined me?

I'd become a secondary character. A fairy godmother helping

Heather on her way. An old woman who had supposedly gotten her happily ever after.

My own story was finished. Wrapped. *The end.*

That's what us old women are supposed to be, isn't it? Over. Through. Used up. Michael was right; that's what stories have taught us.

But what were the words that had roared through my mind when Michael brought the Nikon downstairs?

This camera's not done yet. Neither am I.

I glanced down at the inside of my wrist, at my faded tattoo.

When had I started to let the outside world dictate to me who I was? Now that I'd gotten a few decades under my belt, was I simply going to let the world tell me I was unimportant, unseeable? Or that my only role was helpmate? Observer?

My phone pinged again. I flinched. I didn't want to think about film and the old ways.

Time for a fresh start, Sharon. Time to shake the place up.

Which meant I didn't even want one of my digital cameras. Not the ones I'd used before. I chose a new camera from my display of professional-grade options—and started charging it. New life, new camera.

Time to become the main character in my own story again.

PHOTOGRAPHY FACT

Sharon Minyard's
Intro to Photography Class
1984

Aperture. Shutter speed. F-stop. Sounds fancy. Technical.

I've worked in this medium so long, I don't think of these terms as technical at all. I think of them as emotional terms, like *love* and *want* and *desire*. It's a language that lets you talk to your camera. Tell your camera how to create a fixed image of what's in your heart.

Did you come to this class believing that photography was about objectivity? Documenting the world in front of you in a factual way?

There is no knob that lets you view the world in precise terms.

Lenses aren't perfect—they contain some degree of distortion. Recognizing this, you'll wind up picking settings that capture subjects in the way you're interpreting them at that moment in time. You can't remove yourself from any scene. What looks like truth to you can be a skewed presentation according to the person standing next to you.

Photography is about the subject, but it's also about the photographer—how we personally see the world. How we want others to see our world. That much is inescapable. You might not even realize it at the time you take a specific photo. But you will. Later on, with distance, you'll look at a photo, even if it's of an inanimate object. A street. A building. And you'll know instantly where you were at the time. You'll remember what you were going through. You'll see it imprinted in your image. You'll see your own thoughts and hopes exposed for the world to see.

Photography is not merely an objective documentation. It's not simply preservation of a moment.

Every image is, unavoidably, a mix of facts, lies, and dreams. It's a conversation between the photographer and the camera and the viewer.

But even in the best of conversations, someone can always misinterpret. Mishear. Get the wrong message.

Don't start with vague images that are open to misinterpretation. You shouldn't rely, either, on pretty accidents. Taking hundreds upon hundreds of shots and just hoping something interesting shows up in the darkroom.

Have a message. And be as clear as possible in your message. Make sure your viewer will understand what you're trying to say.

Make them feel what you want them to. Love or revulsion or shock or peace.

In this class, I'll show you how to use all those technical tools.

And then it's up to you to make sure your story is heard.

Michael

Emails were no longer arriving in a slow, steady stream, forwarded occasionally by the radio station. They were coming by the truckload.

I'd push my glasses up my nose and squint at my computer screen, determined not to miss a word. Reading them, I could hear their voices—high-pitched, gravelly, whispers, shouts. Like they were all standing in the room speaking to me.

So *many* of them. I began to doubt I'd be able to keep up with them all.

Ever notice how sometimes, something can be gone long enough that it doesn't occur to you to miss it? Years ago, people had come to me. To tell me stories they hoped would inspire a new column. To invite me to their special events. Sharon and I attended high school band concerts. We tasted every single pie entry at the fair. We shivered along with the rest of the town as the Christmas lights went live on the square.

The stories dried up with my retirement. But the times changed too. The sense of community disappeared. The people of

Fairyland stopped picnicking together. Stopped celebrating together.

Suddenly, though, they were back. Reaching out to me.

And I realized, with the arrival of each new email, how much I'd craved it. Their words echoed through empty spaces I hadn't even known were there.

They wrote for as many reasons as there were messages. Some debated my choice of words. Some flat-up disagreed. Others asked questions. Some of the messages were marriage proposals. Can you believe that? Ancient me.

My favorites, of course, shared their personal tales. They told me about their spouses—good and bad. They related snippets of fairy tales gone awry. They told me about their own plans and daydreams.

I heard love. Or, at the very least, the hope for love. In each letter.

As I read, I could also hear Sharon's and Heather's engaged, excited voices floating up from downstairs. Their conversations weren't only about photography. I could just barely make out fragments of personal anecdotes. Their lives. Heather's boyfriend, her best friend. Story after story.

I'd listen for a while, but it was hard to keep at it when I only caught bits and pieces. Tired of trying to fill in the blanks, I'd go back to reading my emails.

It seemed so strange. Once, Sharon's *Art of the Kiss* had made everyone in Fairyland really feel our love. Now, my fairy tale talk (which was a thinly-veiled attempt to talk about my life with Sharon) was kind of waking the town of Fairyland up.

My words were making everyone think. Or feel. Or relive. Almost the same way that Sharon's picture had once invaded the hearts of everyone in town.

Looking at Sharon's picture, Fairyland had believed in the magic of love.

Listening to my words, they were coming back to that old belief. Dusting it off. Finding it as sturdy as ever.

Happy endings seemed possible to them all once more. That much was evident in their messages. Even after failures and disappointments. It was the thread that connected every single one of their notes.

Their words were brave and admirably honest. Listeners confided in me because they trusted me again. They trusted me with their stories. They did not know who I was, and yet, because I'd laid bare my own feelings, they felt an affection for me.

In an unexpected way, I'd gotten what I wanted. Part of it, anyway: I'd been hungry for love. Isn't that what had sent me to the radio station in the first place?

And now, my inbox had an actual heartbeat.

If I could have written them all back without exposing my true identity, I'd have told them the same thing. The answer to every one of their questions: that I'd never been a magical person, no real-life sorcerer—not until Sharon came into my life. Magic had happened to us. Not me. It never would have happened to me alone.

In the evenings, Sharon and I would chat superficially about what was on TV and whether the windows were collecting too much moisture.

We didn't talk about Heather. Or my emails. Or the radio station.

The people of Fairyland might have opened up to me, but Sharon hadn't.

I was afraid to find out what she thought of my on-air readings. Isn't it strange? The one thing I'd wanted to talk about more than anything, and suddenly, I was afraid. That's what time does. It lets fear saturate everything. Fear can talk you out of anything.

Even love.

Which meant that every night, the person in my bed felt a little farther away than she ever had before.

I'd become the most adored man in Fairyland.

And I was the loneliest man in Fairyland.

Sharon

The more I thought about it, the more Heather's idea appealed to me. Taking pictures of kisses. She'd mentioned it in the most offhanded way. But a single photo of a kiss had changed the course of my young life. And now, I was beginning to wonder what a photo of a kiss might do for me a second time around. The idea began to burn increasingly hotter in my mind.

Would anyone ever let me, though? Take pictures of such private moments? Real kisses? Impromptu—not posed.

Seemed like the ultimate invasion.

I trekked around the edges of the Fairyland square, camera in hand. Knowing this idea would most likely become a dead-end exercise.

And still not being able to get it out of my head.

I raised the new camera to my face, hoping the viewfinder would help me.

Help me? Really. Seemed I'd been listening too intently to Heather.

"You a spy?"

I jumped at the voice. Instead of lowering my camera, I swiveled to face the direction the voice had come from.

An older man with white hair—or what was left of his white hair, anyway—appeared on the opposite side of the viewfinder. Sitting on a bench outside of an old secondhand bookstore. Frowning at me.

I shrugged. "A photographer."

"*Clearly*, you're a *photographer*," the man sighed. "Are you a spy too?"

"Pretty bad spy if I'm taking pictures out here in the open like this, aren't I? I mean, being a spy requires a girl to be a little more covert." I edged closer.

"Didn't ask if you were a good one."

I chuckled as I finally lowered my camera—only a little, to chin-height. "What would make you think I was a spy?" Frankly, it was the most interesting thing anyone had accused me of being in years. Now that the camera was no longer obscuring a large chunk of my vision, I could see that he wasn't alone.

He elbowed the woman beside him. Her own white head of hair and the easiness between them had me guessing she was his wife. "Told you she was a spy," he told her. "They always deny it."

Turning back toward me, he asked, "What is this, *corporate* espionage? You going to open a bar across the way from Murio's? Trying to get a handle on the competition's secrets first?"

"No—affection espionage," I dared to say.

"Come again?"

"I'm attempting to uncover Cupid's secrets."

The man propped his elbows on the back of the bench. His frown evaporated, and he appeared in the mood to play a bit. Actually, truth be told, even the frown had probably been more of a tease. He stretched his feet out in front of him, as if readying

246

himself to tell a good long story. "You want to know something about real affection."

"Yes."

He glanced over at his wife, who smiled back at him.

"Not passion?" he pressed.

"Passion's another subject entirely."

The couple let out a burst of laughter. "Yes," the man eventually agreed, staring into his wife's eyes. "I suppose that'd be right."

The couple was no longer merely looking at each other. They were reliving the decades they'd spent together. There it was, all that time, reflected like moonlight in their faces. I wanted to ask them how it had all started. I wanted their story. I wanted to know where they'd been before they were each other.

But then again, if I really was going into the business of affection espionage, I couldn't exactly come right out and ask, could I? Wasn't it going to require me to be a bit sneakier? Silently probe into secret moments like this one? Edge stealthily closer to it?

Emotions and memories whipped through the air. I wanted to capture it, take this very moment with me. Like it was a map, a way back to Michael. When their lips touched, I was quick to snap their photo.

"Oh!" his wife exclaimed, surprised. She touched the fringes of her windblown hair. Then tossed a hand at me in a way that said she was only putting up a halfhearted fight at best. She didn't really mind being photographed. Not if she was the subject of my great investigation. Not if she was someone a photographer might want to preserve, highlight, shine her flash on.

I thanked the pair and turned to go, but stopped to offer, "If you don't mind sharing your address, I'd be happy to send you a print."

I almost expected them to laugh again. A print. How old-fashioned could it get?

But instead of laughter, a dig ensued, all three of us diving into purses and pockets. I was the first to unearth a pen and an old receipt. A flurry of thank-yous fluttered into the air before I walked away, leaving the pair smiling, holding hands—deeper in private conversation than before.

Excitement burned inside me, giving me strength. Where could I find other couples willing to be photographed? No dead ends today.

I smiled and took a shortcut to the Fairyland bus station.

Excerpt from
The Fairyland Times
About Town

September 3, 1974

Local photographer Sharon Minyard said of her upcoming show, "It might sound odd, at first, the idea of holding a photography exhibit at a bar. But I've spent the past few years documenting the nightlife at Murio's. My pictures have changed over time, of course. My own life changed enormously as I was taking them. I got married, got my career off the ground, opened my studio. I see my own story here in my pictures of Murio's after-dark scene, even though I'm not in a single one of the shots. I've spent so many nights here, I really can't imagine hosting the show in another location. I can't think of a better backdrop for my photos than the actual walls of the building where the images were taken."

Murio Vargas, owner of the namesake bar along the southeast corner of the Fairyland town square, added, "Reinvention's what it's all about. Isn't it?" He pointed out the wooden platforms along the sides of the establishment, areas where he claimed the original business, a mortuary, drained body fluids from the deceased. "Kind of a frightening sight, if you think about it. Now," he was quick to point out, "folks dance on them most nights."

Vargas welcomed the idea of hosting an exhibition of Minyard's work, stating, "The thing about a town is that it's not just one person who writes its story. We all do. Heck, this bar could be a book by itself. Sad chapters, dark chapters, gruesome chapters, triumphant chapters. A story's not much of a story without all of that. The people of Fairyland have been helping to write the story of this bar for years. Sharon's show adds another new chapter—a happy one."

Sharon

Ryan would be the first to tell you that sometimes, a song showed up fully formed. It bumped and crowded you, demanded you pay attention. A new song could fill up the space in your brain until it felt like you were stuck on an elevator with a stranger. At a certain point, there was no ignoring it. You might as well extend your hand and introduce yourself.

Other times...

This particular song—the one he and Fayth had been struggling with for the past two hours—had turned into pure, undeniable torture. Every time he managed to get closer to capturing it, it wound up shooting in another direction.

Much like Heather.

He kept replaying the scene in his mind—her showing up to Slade Music, knocking on his lesson room door before his first student arrived. Thanking him for driving her to the Liu shoot. How he had kissed her. Without thinking. And she had...

Nothing. She had done nothing. Said nothing.

Just sent a business-sounding text confirming she'd be at their gig at Murio's. To photograph the band.

Why hadn't she even mentioned the kiss? Why didn't she call him to talk? Say, "About the other day, at Slade…" The possibilities tortured him.

His idea had been to write a song saying how he felt about her. In his head, he had planned that it would be a momentous thing. A soaring, beautiful love song. He would play it during the same gig at Murio's Heather had agreed to photograph. After the first chorus, she would realize that the song was about her. She would lower her camera. Stop snapping pics. The rest of the world would melt away. It would be the two of them, Ryan and Heather, sharing the spotlight. Their hearts would beat in time, to the same rhythm as his song.

And he would know. She would know. *Meant to be.*

It was outlandish and laughable—Ryan knew that. But it was the story he told himself, the beautiful, happy ending he held to.

Every single time he strummed a chord, he could already feel that spotlight. He could feel Heather standing in front of him. Listening. Because he'd attached so much importance to the writing of this song, nothing felt good enough. It all sounded mediocre. Ordinary. Slipshod.

Fayth tapped a pen against her notebook. As a first-grade teacher, Fayth was well-versed in all things sparkly and organizational in nature. Her whole apartment was cataloged, coordinated, and systematically arranged, down to the last paper clip. The cans in her kitchen cabinet were perfectly aligned, the eyeshadows on her bathroom counter were artistically assorted (greens on one side, purples on the other), and even the to-be-read books on her coffee table were stacked alphabetically by author.

At least somebody's life is in perfect order, Ryan caught himself thinking sourly.

"Want me to get my rhyming dictionary?"

Ryan grimaced. "God, no."

"Might give us some direction. If you grab a word you like the sound of…"

"No, no, no," Ryan grumbled. "I hate writing songs that way."

"What way?"

"A contrived way. Cut and pasted. I want it to sound like I had something I had to get off my chest, something I had to say or I'd burst. I don't want it to be a bunch of refrigerator poetry, and I don't want a bunch of blue and moon and cutesy stuff."

"I kind of figured, from the sound of your call, that you did already have an idea for this masterpiece. I figured it was about Heather."

Ryan slumped, scowling. Why had everything gotten so complicated lately? He'd kissed Heather, and he could not stop asking himself why Heather hadn't been moved by the kiss. Had she considered it kind of perfunctory? Nothing more than a congratulations?

He'd kissed her, and now, he felt rejected. He didn't even have the right to feel rejected. He'd broken up with her, after all.

Like he'd broken up with all the others.

Ryan had never been dumped. Not once.

Which meant he'd never been rejected before.

Poor Ryan's thoughts turned into whirlpool, circling around the same questions: *Was I afraid of her not wanting me? Was that why I really broke things off? Reject before being rejected?*

A surge of feelings bubbled inside of him, threatening to burst. He needed to release the pressure.

Mostly, right then, he needed Fayth to stop staring at him.

"I think I'm tapped," Ryan finally said. Not that he meant it, really. He just hoped it might snag him a little sympathy. "Three-chord pop songs have to be written by seventeen-year-olds. I don't think I can do this anymore."

He shot her a pitiful hangdog expression, expecting one of her b.s.-calling eyebrow raises any second.

"Good grief." Fayth uncrossed her long legs, capped her pen, and shoved her feet into a pair of sneakers.

"You're not giving up, are you?" Ryan challenged.

"You want me to sit here while you pout?"

"Yes! I do!" he announced, realizing it was exactly what he wanted. "I'm heartbroken and I can't write a single decent song. The best pop songs—rock songs—country songs are all about heartache. It's the number one source of inspiration for musicians. And I can't write one single decent verse? Can't come up with one measly hook? That's a sign. It's a sign that something is seriously wrong."

She glared at him from beneath her purple hair. She turned toward the kitchen, filling a cooler with ice and Cokes and grabbing a couple of insulated drink containers. Still the picture of preparedness.

"Keys. Come. With me. Now," she ordered.

He could have argued. But there was rarely any arguing with Fayth. And besides, Ryan was anxious to get away from it all—away from the song he couldn't write and the questions about Heather that remained mostly unanswered. Ryan grabbed her keys from her coffee table and tossed them at her.

Fayth wasn't one for long drives, but she steered her Toyota with the enormous bike rack toward the city limits, zipping past the "Leaving Fairyland" sign. She slipped onto the highway, the late afternoon slowly fading away. The car purred beneath her, seeming to be grateful for a chance to make an out-of-town getaway. The evening air was delicious pouring through the open windows. Ryan hummed—still working on that awful song about Heather.

Fayth clenched her jaw and turned on the radio, successfully redirecting his thoughts.

Until she cut the engine.

Ryan's eyes were still closed.

"We didn't come out here so you could daydream about Princess Flashbulb," Fayth snapped, whacking the side of his arm. "Out," she barked, and popped her own door.

Ryan finally cracked an eye, finding that Fayth had driven them both to a cemetery. An ancient and familiar one at that—little more than a cluster of headstones beside a dirt road. The remnants of a family burial ground on farmland that had once belonged to Ryan's great-grandmother.

Ryan chuckled. He knew exactly why they'd come.

He headed straight for the hollow base of an old oak tree.

"It's still here." He reached into the trunk, pulling out a bag of small gardening tools.

"Of course it is," Fayth said softly.

They found a spot inside the rusty old barbed wire fence that surrounded three crumbling headstones, and they dug a shallow hole.

They buried what they'd always buried at this spot, starting way back when they were kids: all their bad feelings.

A childish thing, perhaps. "A bunch of tomfoolery," that was how his great-grandmother had put it.

Ryan buried his doubt. He buried the overly critical voice that was keeping him from writing a decent song.

What did Fayth decide to put away? The unexpected feelings that had surfaced? Her hope that friendship would give way to love? Could you ever dislodge those feelings once they'd taken root?

They didn't tell each other exactly what they buried, but then again, they never had. Not even when they were kids and had come up with the idea.

Fayth tagged Ryan in a *You're it!* kind of way, and took off running.

A mile away, they were still walking along a stretch of old

railroad tracks, like they had when they were twelve. Pretending the tracks were a bridge, and the first one to stumble would actually fall to their death.

Ryan laughed. He laughed in a way he hadn't in ages. That free way children have, when they laugh with their whole bodies. And when they looked at each other, they both acknowledged, silently, that burying bad feelings had cleared the air.

Fayth still wasn't sure she wanted her feelings to stay buried. She wasn't even sure they were bad. Unrealized hopes weren't necessarily things you needed to get rid of.

Often, they were something that needed pursuing.

Had she rescued herself yet? Sure didn't feel like it.

They both wanted to keep walking. Keep the game going. Oh, it was so much fun to play-pretend like this. To make things up. To live in a world of complete fantasy.

Take my hand and make-believe. Ryan was chanting it, like a chorus.

Fayth joined in, harmonizing, their voices a perfect fit.

They started playing with lyrics. Even songwriting stopped being a torture and started being a game as they sang and danced along the railroad tracks.

I'll be the king and you'll be the queen. Take my hand and make-believe with me.

They were together, and it was easy. So easy.

They were still singing when Ryan forgot to pay close attention to where he planted his feet. He slipped on the track.

Fayth scrambled to catch him or at least brace his fall. Instead, they both went tumbling, a regular Jack and Jill, falling into the wildflowers beside the silver tracks gleaming in the orange-red hues of sunset.

"Owoh—" Ryan yelped, lifting his fingers out of some purple

blooms. "Those stupid flowers stung me," he moaned.

Fayth took his hand in her own. A giant bumblebee squirmed, still attached to his palm. Her hand was warm as she brushed the bee away and gently removed the stinger. He stared into her dark eyes.

"Who would've known flowers could be so dangerous?" he croaked.

Fayth quickly opened the insulated cup she'd brought from home and poured ice into the palm of his hand to kill the pain. Just like that. So, so easy.

"What are these things, anyway?" Ryan asked, nodding once at the blooms.

Fayth raised her dark eyes again to meet his own. "Cupid's darts."

Excerpt from
The Fairyland Times
Michael Minyard's
"Observations from the Tower" Column

March 12, 2012

For more than five decades, Murio's has been open for business on our Fairyland square. A bar, some might call it when looking at the building from afar or passing by on the sidewalk.

But to designate Murio's as nothing more than a bar is to oversimplify.

Murio's is a gathering place, a lingering melody. It is a keeper of stories told and retold again, a site for first dates and ten-year anniversaries. Through the decades, the ever-changing fads—polyester collars and sideburns, parachute pants, torn jeans—one thing has stayed the same: Murio's has thrived.

To have ever been young in Fairyland is to have known Murio's.

Murio Vargas, longtime owner of the establishment, has announced he will retire at the end of this month. No need for sad goodbyes. Murio's Bar and Grill will simply sing another chorus under the leadership of Murio's son, Sebastian.

The baton will be passed without missing a beat.

And so we bid Murio a happy retirement. Sad to see the end of his era, glad to have shared so many years with him.

It is similarly with a sad heart—but also a glad one—that I announce my own retirement. I have loved listening to and delving into the stories of Fairyland. It has been my honor and privilege to translate your stories into print. As you know, this column has never been the place for breaking news. No car crashes or political scandals, no indictments or exonerations.

In this column, I was proud to celebrate Fairyland. But I am now laying down my baton. The column will print its last story next week. *The Fairyland Times*, like so many papers, is cutting back, shrinking. My column will end.

If this column ever moved you, entertained you, made you smile, honor it by gathering at Murio's, just as you always have. Let Sebastian pour you a drink, and share with each other all the stories that you once told me. Should you see me on the street, the old story man who used to accompany you through your first cup of coffee each morning, say hello. Tell me a tale or two worthy of retelling.

It is my hope that the wonderful stories of our Fairyland will live on.

As stories always should.

PHOTOGRAPHY FACT

Sharon Minyard's
Black and White Photography Class
1998

So much of photography these days is sheer trickery. Mostly because it's getting easier and easier for anyone to manipulate their captured images. All it takes is a computer program. A few clicks of the mouse.

That's what has me so excited, to a great extent, about this class. As a photographer, you should explore every single tool available to you. But here, we're getting back to basics. Black and white film.

I'll admit, black and white felt like my element from the very start. Some people work in watercolor, some prefer clay. For me, it was black and white film. Yes, the kind you develop in a darkroom.

You'll find your own perfect medium. Maybe in this very class.

Maybe black and white will fit you like it fit me. Maybe not—maybe you'll still wind up gravitating toward a bit of the new digital trickery. That doesn't mean you won't take some of the more traditional methods you'll learn here and apply them to your own work.

Promise me this: you won't allow trickery to define who you are as a photographer.

Images can get less and less clear the more you try to play with them. And by less clear, I don't mean they lose their visual sharpness. I'm not saying, for example, that the objects in your pictures can get blurry when you try to enlarge them. I mean they lose their emotional punch. They no longer have the same impact. Because by that point, they've lost their original context.

For me, it's why so much photographic trickery falls flat. It may be kind of fun to look at for a few seconds—for instance, at the stormy sky that doesn't match the sunny day below. The kite flying when the tree below isn't rustling in the wind. The gurgling water fountain in the desert. But what is the real context? What is the story?

What will those images say about us—or to us—tomorrow?

Think about it.

Sharon

My kiss pictures grabbed me. Redirected me. Refused to let go.

I was no longer just waiting for Michael to be at the radio station. I was leaving at all times of the day, offering no explanation other than the "Closed" sign turned toward the street. I was inspired. I was chasing that inspiration.

And I was determined. Michael's words, his bit about old women being nothing more than fairy godmothers, had smacked me right in my face. Stared me down the same way those men had back in the tattoo parlor in what seemed like a lifetime ago.

I couldn't stand to be "sweethearted" back then, and I wasn't going to be "old ladied" now.

I wasn't done yet.

I could still do this.

Just watch me.

But how did the whole thing really start to take off? With the couple on the square?

Or had it been the Fairyland bus station?

When I got to the bus station, it didn't feel like anything was taking off. I just kind of paced around aimlessly, not sure where to stand or even what I wanted to do. And probably looking plenty suspicious to the guard.

That is, until I heard the final call for Bus #82—Fairyland to Chicago, leaving in two minutes. I zoned in on my subjects quickly: a young man and woman, facing each other and holding hands, heads turned mostly downward, struggling through a reluctant goodbye. A college couple? Seemed the spring semester should have ended about a month ago, but then again, maybe they'd been trying to hold on a little longer, relish a few stolen summer weeks together.

It was impossible to know the true details of their story, but from where I stood, I could feel the sadness pulsing between the two. The obvious uncertainty—perhaps they would never be together again—combined with a wish to pause time, or to roll it back. As they stared at each other, I raised my camera. I watched through the viewfinder as they drew still closer, his hand touching her cheek, her hand finding his waist…

And then—a kiss.

I pressed the shutter button.

They pulled away from each other as the flash exploded, both of them turning to glare at me. I made the same offer I'd extended to the older couple, to send a print. But only one, to one address. Which meant that if the picture was to be shared, there would have to be another meeting.

My offer softened the air around them. Desperation wasn't as black and suffocating as it had been a moment before.

With the girl's name and address in my purse, I thought again about the contacts I'd made with others who still loved using actual film. Two people this young should have hated the idea of snail mail. Of a print. But somehow, judging by the looks on their faces, it appeared my offer seemed special. Maybe, to them, I was even saying their moment was special, or their story was. Maybe that was what they heard.

Maybe, like film, prints weren't completely dead, either. Maybe a physical object not attached to a screen was special.

I waited another twenty minutes for an incoming bus. A soldier in fatigues stepped into the depot, his arms outstretched to catch the woman racing toward him. *Welcome back, welcome back.* Their kiss was filled with hunger and warmth and joy.

They laughed as they gave me their address. "Can't wait to see it," the man said, wrapping his arm around his wife's shoulder.

Ever notice how sometimes, when you squat down in a patch of clover, you don't find one four-leaf lucky sign, you find a whole cluster?

That's exactly what happened. Suddenly, after that visit to the bus station, there were dozens of pictures begging to be taken, kisses popping up like clover all over town. A teenage girl and a boy in swimsuits, their fingers clutching the chain-link fence that circled the public pool, shy and smiling their way through an awkward first-ever kiss. Two boys at a car outside the high school, where throngs of summer school students raced out of the building's exits, unabashedly kissing hello.

A couple on church steps—white dress, black tux—lips pressed together and hands locked as if in a sign of victory.

A woman at a playground kissing her toddler on the cheek.

A Schnauzer in a dog park kissing the tip of his owner's nose.

The winner of a 5K run kissing the side of his trophy.

Kisses were everywhere for my taking. Sweet or passionate or triumphant.

A mother leaving her nervous child at daycare. A man leaning over a woman on a hospital stretcher—moments before she was wheeled into surgery. I was getting increasingly brazen by then. Telling the couple they'd have something to share when it was all over. Their moment of uncertainty conquered.

Still, more: A kiss behind a shared book on an afternoon riverbank. A kiss beneath an evening's streetlight. Two men, two women, children, friends, kisses on cheeks, kisses on foreheads. All of them meaning something different. Passion. Adoration. Unconditional. Uncertain. First. Last. So many stories, so many emotions, all expressed the same way.

With kisses.

Back in the studio, I edited the photos on my computer. The results surprised me. Everything surprised me, as I adjusted color temperatures and contrast, as I experimented with layers and effects.

I could say different things now, couldn't I? Different things than I had all those years ago?

It stopped feeling like trickery.

What did that mean about the first camera? How could it have also worked so well for Heather? What about that story she'd told me about the park? The camera showing her the way? Had that camera done something to me? Taught me something in those early years? How?

Why was I even entertaining these thoughts?

I flicked on my small transistor radio, searching for Michael's voice, wanting to hear what he would say next. Grimacing a bit when I found the station playing yet another rerun.

I'd been hoping for something I hadn't heard before.

I leaned on the counter top, the coolness of the glass seeping into my forearms. But his words were seeping into me, too, as they always had. Even if I occasionally bristled, they still eventually found their way under my skin.

Wasn't that how it had been at the very beginning? Wasn't that what his words had done to me out there during the Fourth of July picnic, or during our first dance down in Dad's basement?

My mind flipped about wildly as Michael insisted, yet again, "...can't get passed how painfully *dull* the guy is..."

Think, Sharon, I scolded myself as Michael's thoughts about Prince Charming filled the shop. *What did he really tell you in Dad's basement? On that July day when he returned your camera?*

"The girls in fairy tales, all of them, have far more to recommend them," Michael insisted on the radio.

And suddenly, I knew. Like I maybe always should have known.

Back in Dad's basement, he'd said we'd be good together, of course, but looking back on it, through the lens of time and distance, with Michael's metaphors dancing through my head, it suddenly felt like he'd been asking *me* to see *him* as every bit as capable as I was. That he could rise to the occasion of being with me.

And not the future me, either. The twenty-three-year-old me, that me in the basement, with nothing yet to show for my efforts. He didn't see me as a woman who hadn't arrived yet. He saw me. He was asking me to see him too.

I turned to my computer screen, flipping through my kiss images. He'd hurt my feelings going to the radio station. He'd made me angry. But he'd gotten in my head. He'd made me think. In a way I never would have if he'd just come to me. Because we weren't face-to-face, my defenses weren't up. Not all the time, at least. Which meant I heard him. Over and over. The words had a chance to permeate. Soak beneath the surface. Once they were there, deep inside, they vibrated. They resonated.

He wasn't flat or dull at all, not like the Prince Charming he described. As always, I found him to be the most intelligent, interesting, most thought-provoking, often funniest, most infuriating man

266

in all of Fairyland.

And I knew, from past experience, that he was the best stupid kisser too.

His words had pushed me out the door, back into the world, back into my work. Yes, I'd retreated. I hadn't even realized how far. And he had pushed, with no warning, before I'd had a chance to get myself ready. Sometimes, though, a push is exactly what you need.

With his voice in my ears and the memories as clear as the images on my screen, Michael came roaring back through me. In the most surprising way. There'd always been love. But this felt different. It reverberated inside of me like a just-struck gong, rather than a gong that had been clanged long ago, growing less and less audible as time passed.

What was I supposed to do about it? Me, the one who had given away the object that had preserved the moment the two of us fell? The object that Michael was convinced held the magic of our love? That was it, wasn't it? The magic of our love. Not my success.

That was why he'd felt it was so special.

And there was no way to Photoshop that scene into something else. I'd done it. I'd given our magic away.

Guilt burned inside me, right beside that tender sense of a new kind of reawakened love.

Michael

I saw her. Sharon.

There she was, on the north side of the square, stopping traffic with her camera.

A smile broke across my face as I hugged my notebook to my chest. I felt it all over again, just like I had that first day on the square. The lunch hour I'd watched from afar as she set up her equipment for the perfect shot.

She intrigued me no less. I wanted to get closer.

Especially now. Didn't she seem energized? Focused in a way I hadn't seen in so long? What was she working on?

But there was so much distance between us. Sure, it was a measly twenty feet or so, but it was also decades. Day after day piling higher and higher, and it was filled with dandruff and socks with holes and ant traps in the kitchen and garbage bags and oil changes every three thousand miles.

It sounds absurd. If I were watching this on the big screen, I'd be shouting into the movie theater, "How hard could it be to just *talk* to someone?"

But it is. It is so hard. When you are that tangled up in a person, it is like having to confront yourself. You are staring into someone else's eyes and seeing yourself at the same time. Your own history and your own tomorrow morning. And the horrible part is, that reflection also has a life of its own, and might just want to walk away entirely, taking the parts of your reflection that you like the most.

Sometimes, the stack of calendars takes you someplace you never anticipated you'd be. Instead of a groom, you're an old man with a heart that feels a little like a ghost town. Uninhabited. Desolate.

I wanted to approach her, but was shackled by everything I had on the line. It had been easier when we were strangers meeting for the first time at Bleeker's Record Store.

I daydreamed about her framing these new pieces, hanging them on the studio walls.

Like old times.

Maybe Sleeping Beauties didn't wake up all at once, but in stages. Maybe the first stage was about Sharon waking up to her work. She hadn't yet reached the stage of waking up to me. To us. To the idea that I was her partner, not her bad guy.

I squeezed my notebook tighter. And felt the weight of everything unsaid inside my own throat.

As I watched Sharon disappear around the corner, I was more anxious than ever to get to that radio station's microphone.

This Story

This is the story of a man. And a woman.

In the midst of a dust storm.

Everything has been disturbed. Nothing is clear.

Perhaps you feel they have lost their senses of humor at this point. Perhaps this man and this woman seem more serious now than they did at their *once upon a time*. Fear isn't funny. Dust storms aren't funny. Danger can't be laughed at until triumph is won.

Perhaps they also seem more concerned with themselves than with each other. But when a storm hits, you forget that anyone else is around. You only know that your own life is being disrupted. The only reaching out you can do is for something sturdy to grab onto. All you can think about is hanging on for dear life, in the worst of the winds.

But haven't Michael and Sharon found something? For Michael, isn't it his radio spot? For Sharon, isn't it her kiss project?

With something to anchor them, hasn't the time come for squinting into the chaos? For calling out to each other?

What would it take to finally clear the air?

Michael

Stories teach us there is love and there is hate, and they are on two separate ends of the spectrum.

The hardest thing I've ever had to learn is how wrong that is. Emotions are never absolute—never simply white or black, either-or, no shades of gray, no shadows in the middle. It's not like you either love somebody or dislike them with no in-between. You can adore someone at the exact same time you find yourself absolutely resenting them.

That's life.

To some extent, that's marriage. It's sharing yourself with someone and still feeling like you don't completely know them. It's loving them and watching them act in ways you don't quite understand. It's wanting them to know you and not wanting them to see the less than perfect sides of you.

Ah, but friendship is tricky, too, isn't it? At least, it was for Amanda. Her heart was being pulled in competing directions as she stared at the doorbell hovering right in front of her, wondering what the brown gunk was in its center. This was Heather's apartment, after all. That gunk could be anything.

She began searching her purse for a Kleenex or one of her daughters' cloth headbands—something to provide a barrier between her fingers and the gunk.

"Hey!"

Amanda swiveled, but the parking lot was empty.

"Up here!"

She tilted her head back, gazing up toward a second story balcony. As she squinted into the sun, she grumbled under her breath about the stupid layout of the place. Heather's apartment had a kind of castle-meets-storage-unit feel, with sorta-turrets and square chunky sections of apartments. Almost like Aiden had built it with his blocks, and every once in a while, he'd come along to pile on some new addition. It sat on the fine line between avant-garde and down-and-out. Typical Heather.

But no—the voice wasn't coming from the second story after all. It had come instead from a wide branch on a nearby oak tree. Darth Billy lay stretched out, his feet dangling down. "Sometimes, she doesn't hear the bell. She's in the *zone*," Billy told her.

Sometimes, she doesn't hear the bell because it hasn't been rung, Amanda thought as she gave a half-hearted wave to acknowledge his presence. She took a deep breath and knocked. When Heather didn't answer, she texted her.

The door flew open.

"Amanda!" Heather exclaimed, brushing strands of hair away from her flushed cheeks. "You never come here."

Amanda held up an armload of clothing.

"What's that for?" Heather asked.

"Suits."

"For?" she repeated.

Amanda sighed, her shoulders slumping. "The big shoot at Murio's. Of Ryan's band."

272

"Are you serious?" Heather backed up, letting her inside.

"Of course. What were you thinking of wearing, jeans?" Amanda chuckled at her own sarcasm. When she saw the embarrassed expression on Heather's face, she groaned, "Don't tell me—you weren't."

"I mean, I'll be working. And it's a bar. Right? Why would I need to dress up?"

"Ugh. You cannot wear jeans. You cannot wear secondhand clothes. You're a professional woman. It's a good thing I came. The shoot's tomorrow night. And you..." Amanda's words trailed off. She pointed through an open doorway. "You turned your bathroom into—what? A gallery?"

"Yeah," Heather laughed. "I guess I did. Ran out of wall space. I've been trying to develop a critical eye. That's what Sharon's after me to do, anyway. I fix my makeup in the kitchen now. That's why I stuck a mirror to the fridge door."

Amanda craned her neck. Sure enough, there it was. Between the blender and the toaster, a plate had been filled with mascara and eyeshadow palettes and blush brushes. It reminded her a little of their college dorm.

"You can go in the bathroom if you want," Heather offered. "Check out what I've been working on lately."

Amanda took a cautious step inside.

Heather lunged in too, hoisting the venetian blind covering the tiny window behind the toilet. Natural light seeped in, illuminating an entire clothesline of images strung all the way around the room.

Amanda's scalp tightened up as she eyed her photos. Heather had been taking action-based shots. Student athletes jumped toward basketball hoops. Women jogged down runners' paths. Metal shopping carts careened through a grocery store parking lot. Stuffing

273

exploded through the air at a Build-A-Bear. Dogs twisted through canine obstacle courses.

"I wanted to practice," Heather admitted. "I figured what I'm really going to do for Ryan is take pictures of movement, you know? They'll be performing. I want to make it feel like their performance leaps right out of the pictures."

Amanda nodded.

"Sharon—the one who's been helping me develop the film—she says I've got good timing."

Amanda nodded again. She didn't really know about all that. But she did know that the images were astonishing. Even better than she'd assumed Heather was taking.

The longer Amanda stared, the more that infected black sore inside her began to throb and pulse.

She marveled at the photos. And she hated them. She wanted one of her own. And she wanted to throw them all away.

Her heart swelled with pride at knowing Heather, this woman with such talent. This woman who had stuck out pursuing her dream, learning and growing through the hard parts. What had she learned to do this well? Amanda the music freak had never even learned to play the piano. Never strummed a guitar on her own. Because it took too much effort? Or because she'd followed everyone else's rules, convinced it would help her win the game of life?

"So you're still using that old camera?" Amanda managed to croak.

"Yeah—there's something about it. If my timing's better with it, clearly that's the kind of camera I want to use. It responds so differently, you know?"

"And?"

Heather smiled. "And it kind of feels like my good luck charm. It's silly, I guess. But I believe in it. It's gotten me this far. Right?"

She gave Amanda a look that said she was waiting for her to tease her.

Amanda questioned, in that moment, if Heather had honestly believed that old camera was magic. Had the tequila at her country club acted like truth serum? Or had the tequila instead helped her make up another wild tale, not unlike the story she'd told of Darth Billy and the pre-Flag Day parade?

Amanda couldn't quite tell for sure. So she let her eyes bounce through the collection of images. Slowly, she made her way into the living room, where the walls were completely papered in black and white photos.

Until she found it. A picture that made her stop breathing for a moment.

"Oh, that thing," Heather grumbled, seeing where Amanda's eyes were pointed. "I didn't even mean to take it. I hit the shutter button accidentally."

Amanda's internal temperature gauge shot upward. Anger found her. Pure, flame-throwing rage. And utter abhorrence. For the same person she also loved.

In the photo, Heather was walking down the street, her hair flying behind her. Taking enormous strides, holding her camera chest-height with both hands. Her reflection in a business's plate-glass front window was somehow both clear and full of purpose but also slightly blurry around the edges with motion. Heather looked like a woman with direction and a plan, a woman with a dream she was about to pluck right out of the air, make her own.

Tug down from heaven, like little Aiden.

The longer Amanda stared at it, the more it also began to sink in that Heather was walking away in the picture. Amanda'd been fearing it was happening. But in that image, she had visual proof. She didn't just suspect anymore. She could see it with her own eyes.

It was such a beautiful picture. Startlingly beautiful. Surprisingly beautiful.

And Heather had taken it accidentally. The fact that she could take a photo so powerful without even trying proved Heather was truly mastering her craft.

As Amanda stared, terror splashed like acid on her black internal wound. Heather, little Heather, in her rattrap apartment, with all her inane complaining, was about to conquer the world.

"'Manda?"

Amanda jumped. "Sorry," she said, trying to avoid her friend's eyes.

"The suits?" Heather asked.

"Right."

Blinking away tears, Amanda examined the living room, with its ratty brown plaid couch and its stained pink side chair. She cleared her throat. "Is your—camera—in here?"

"Sure."

"Show it to me. I know you had it back at the house—the night Tom showed up with the ribeyes—but I didn't get to see it up close. I'd love to see how it works." Her voice broke on the last word. She faked a cough to make it seem like she had something in the back of her throat.

Heather picked her camera up off the small end table where she'd once told Amanda she ate her meals while watching TV. Back then, Amanda had rolled her eyes. At their age, it almost seemed animalistic.

Now, though, it seemed right. This was where Heather was supposed to be. Where Amanda wanted her to be.

As right as it was, it also hurt.

Amanda leaned over the couch and gently placed her armload of clothing down on the roughed-up cushion.

The jackets and slacks didn't lay flat. They couldn't. Not with the case underneath.

One that Amanda didn't want Heather to see.

"You wind the film like this," Heather started, showing Amanda the various buttons and knobs.

Amanda had never seen Heather exhibit such passion. She'd enjoyed her photography, but since she'd met Sharon, something had changed. Photography wasn't just an interest. It drove her.

The sore inside of Amanda started to ooze and pulse, ripping far deeper and wider than ever before.

Finally, as Heather rattled on, Amanda could diagnose it. She knew what that black hole was.

It was jealousy. As simple and obvious as that.

Where had it started?

When she and Tom had taken Heather and Ryan out to eat? It would make sense. Didn't Ryan being a musician hurt because his abilities stole the thunder from the one stupid thing she'd had on Heather? The thing she'd known more about? Amanda'd been the one whose teenage years had revolved around the radio and discovering new independent acts online and obsessing over her collection of vinyl. She was the one who'd known all the lyrics. And the dances. Suddenly, at dinner, hadn't it felt as though Heather was stealing that too? Taking up with a musician boyfriend when Amanda had given up her vinyl and the concerts, cut that part of her life free?

But it was more than that. Staring at the accidental self-portrait, Amanda knew her jealousy had been with her longer than any few weeks or months.

It had been with her for years. Decades.

It had been in Heather's pretty blond hair. And the fact that everybody liked the way she put together her secondhand clothes, complimenting her in high school more often than they'd complimented Amanda's designer jeans. It had been in the easy way she'd gotten through Algebra II and how people giggled at the funny, wild stories she told, and called her the sweetest girl in the entire school.

It had always been there. Jealousy. Ever since the very beginning of their friendship.

But isn't that what all villains really felt, deep down? Wasn't that awful queen jealous of Snow White? Didn't the stepsisters envy Cinderella's natural beauty? Isn't that why they felt the need to push her down, make sure Prince Charming never saw her?

Wasn't jealousy really at the core of so many vicious plans?

Now that Amanda recognized it for what it was, did that change anything? Was Amanda going to finish the job she'd come to do? Or would she see it as a bad idea, a mistake she didn't have to make?

"Going to do any more practicing tonight?" she asked, pointing at the sea of pictures.

Heather shook her head, replacing her camera on the end table. "Nope. I figured it was best to take it easy. Rest up for tomorrow night."

Amanda nodded. Swallowed hard. The black wound inside of her hurt worse than it ever had before. "Guess you're almost all set."

"Almost?" Heather got a funny twisted look on her face.

"I really have to remind you? You don't have the outfit picked out yet. Come on, come on, this is the fun part."

Heather brightened a bit.

"How about we start with the Calvin Klein?" Amanda offered a light gray seersucker to Heather.

"Where'd you get all these, anyway?" Heather asked.

"I bought them, of course. I still know your size. Since you're the same size you were in college." She grimaced, acted like she was suppressing a gag.

"All of them?" Heather asked, looking horrified.

"It's easy enough to take back the ones you don't want. The best way to see them is in your own setting, not in some stuffy department store," she lied. "Go on, go on. Try that one on."

Heather scurried out of the living room.

The question pounded Amanda again: Was she or wasn't she?

She folded the remaining suits back, exposing the camera case she'd brought.

She felt dizzy. She put her hand to her sweaty forehead.

It was hard to breathe.

She didn't have much time. Slowly—so as not to make any clicking noises—she flicked the latches open and removed the vintage Nikon she'd purchased on eBay and had delivered express. She tiptoed across the carpet, to the end table. She repeated the same action with the latches. And she exchanged the cameras, putting her own eBay purchase in Heather's case, then carrying Heather's magical camera to the case she'd brought from home.

She quickly covered all of Heather's magic with the rest of the suits.

"How's it going in there?" Amanda asked.

"Fantastic!" Heather shouted.

"Same here," Amanda murmured, before she could stop herself.

Excerpt from
The Fairyland Times
About Town
June 27, 2018

Murio's Bar and Grill on the downtown Fairyland square will be hosting a public birthday party for Murio Vargas, the establishment's original owner, this Saturday, June 30. As part of Vargas's eightieth birthday celebration, Murio himself will be in the bar all night to mix his signature drinks and reminisce with all his old regulars.

"We're really doing it up," said Sebastian Vargas, Murio's son and the current owner. "We're pulling out all the stops. And by 'we,' I really mean 'my dad.' I tried to tell Pop to relax and enjoy the night as our Guest of Honor, but he'd have none of it. He'll be behind the bar, and he's insisted on being in charge of decorations. Hauling out the old disco ball. Hanging a bunch of old photos taken years ago, when the bar—and Pop—were young."

The Tommies, a local Fairyland band, will play a wide selection of both their own original songs and dance hits from the past few decades—including a few of Murio's own personally requested favorites.

Cocktails will be buy one, get one half off all night.

"It's going to be quite the shindig," Sebastian Vargas said. "A regular Fairyland ball."

PHOTOGRAPHY FACT

Sharon and Heather's Basement Chat

2018

There's a kind of conversation that goes on between you and your camera, Heather. You already know that. You're feeling it more and more as time goes on, but...

Listen, the thing is, you have to acquire a ton of faith to be a photographer. Faith in your ability. Faith in yourself to try new methods of setup or lighting or even something as simple as a change of subject matter. I know at the beginning, you think you'll always be experimenting. But once you master a few techniques, it's easy to succumb to doing the same thing over and over again. It worked once. So why would you ever deviate, right? Why would you go through that awful period of floundering and failing and trying to master something else?

282

You can't just spin your wheels. You have to grow. To do that, you have to believe you'll eventually master a new technique you initially saw as something of a long shot.

You have to have enough faith to keep moving out of your comfort zone.

You also have to have faith that your camera will do its job. You have one shot at it, to get the image right. Having faith in your camera means you can think less about the mechanics and more about the emotion of the moment. You can explore, even in that split-second of time you have to take the picture. You can search for the artistry. You can truly find your own way behind the lens. A way unlike anyone else's.

If you know that the tightrope beneath you will never snap, you can suddenly take faster, bigger steps. The kind of steps you might not have believed possible.

And yeah—that's pretty magical, isn't it?

On Air

Ah, the moment of truth.

That's what we live for, isn't it?

Those times, in our favorite stories, when our hero loses everything.

The worst happens.

The dark night arrives.

And our hero seems doomed.

We love that. Not because we want our hero to suffer. But because that means we can now feel the moment of resurrection and redemption is on its way.

Once he has lost, our hero can triumph.

Yes, that's what we live for.

We live for the scenes in which love wins...

Let's Go

Invitations arrive from professional printers, sometimes in linen envelopes. If we're lucky, they arrive with handwritten messages across the bottom. Lovingly addressed to us. The more elaborate, we assume, the better. The more exciting the event will surely be.

Someone has thought about us. Someone wants us to be with them at some life-changing ceremony.

Often, the most important invitations we receive don't even really sound, at first, like personal invitations to special events at all. It's a phone call from Ryan offering Heather a job photographing the band. A notice in the newspaper of a birthday party for Murio. It's a casual text from Liu to Tom asking him to meet him for drinks at Murio's—"and be sure to bring your lovely wife."

It's a note left on a kitchen table from Sharon to Michael: "Heading out to Murio's. Won't be gone long."

It's warm weather on a pitch-perfect lovely Saturday night.

A night with bright stars and a glowing neon sign.

It's a tug in your belly—maybe even out of nowhere—that says you need to head out.

And so you do.

Michael

Murio's—and its pulsing silvery blue neon sign—shone that night like a castle on the edge of the Fairyland square. A solitary wolf in a white shirt and black jeans paced back and forth in front of the entrance, making sure the night's clientele were of proper age—no potential troublemakers allowed.

This wolf's name, if I'd heard him right, was Cody. He had a long nose and small, dark, deeply set eyes. There was something slightly threatening in the way he held himself, pitched slightly forward rather than leaning back against the bricks, snarl on his face, a lock of black hair across his forehead. His muscles bulged as if any minute—at the right provocation or for the right prey—he could pounce. Like the many wolves who had come before him throughout the decades, it was clear, simply by looking at him, that he had spent quite a few nights devouring Red Riding Hoods only to spit them out again come morning.

I slowed on the sidewalk as I got closer to the entrance. Cody was engaged in a long, rehearsed recitation of the history of Murio's building as he checked IDs and took cover charges. "Used to be a..."

He snapped his thick fingers a few times, searching for the word. "A mortuary! That's it. When you go in there, look at those wooden platforms along the walls. It's where they used to lay the bodies—you know, to *drain them*."

The girls' eyes widened as Cody piled adjectives onto his already rather gory tale.

I did my best not to laugh. Same old wild story. After all this time, it hadn't changed. Here he was, repeating it just as I imagined he'd learned it from the last wolf, the one who had handed this job over to him. Repeating it like a fairy tale. A warning, just as Red Riding Hood's original tale offered warnings to children about talking to strangers. In Cody's tale, of course, the dangers were inside, and Cody was himself the grand rescuer. If Cody was at all the drinking kind, the details would be greatly exaggerated after a beer (or four).

As he moved slightly closer to one of the girls, I got a funny feeling suddenly, as if the past had folded back around to tuck itself into a corner of the present.

It was all still here. The wolf at the door. The old story, the gruesome details.

But another question immediately begged to be asked: *What else still remains?*

It came back to me, the nights I'd been here with Sharon. The two of us on that very sidewalk exchanging knowing smiles as we waited for the current wolf to finish telling the story to the current group of young girls so we could hand over our own cover charge.

I remembered stepping inside and ordering a drink, watching her work. And God, how I loved watching her work. Taking her nightlife photos. A project that had begun before we'd met and continued on strongly for a while, somehow fizzling out without announcement or any kind of big triumphant fairy tale turning point.

Standing there on the sidewalk, enveloped by a strange mix

of history and facts and memories and old times and new times that did not look really so much different, I felt myself spiraling through one emotion after another, each one increasingly deeper than the last.

Finally, at the end of it, the feeling at the root of it all lay exposed. Underneath the aching quiet and the agonizing small talk, beneath the feelings of being ignored or left out, beneath the sadness of having seen my own youth cool and fade like a sunset, beneath the hurt of watching her give our magic away—there it was: I missed Sharon.

Simple as that. I missed her. And I missed who we'd been to each other.

I stumbled a little closer to the door, pausing long enough to glance over my shoulder, toward the radio station where I had recorded a piece earlier that day, to be played during Murio's birthday party.

Tony wasn't on air at this time of day. Another DJ was currently seated at the microphone.

"No way he won't play it. Not if it's yours," Tony'd tried to assure me.

I'd hoped that was true. But this DJ certainly didn't have to. All it had been was a request. A suggestion. A Post-it note on a desk, easily ignored.

Even after all the messages, the emails, the calls to the station, I half-expected interest in my tales to dry up at any moment, leave as quickly as it had arrived. I'd seen it happen.

I tried to shake it off. It was Murio's birthday, after all. It was a night for celebrations. I'd come to wish him well.

I didn't just come for Murio. The words popped into my head, and I slipped my hand into my pocket, where I found the note Sharon had left on the kitchen table.

Was she already here? I'd taken a shortcut. Had I gotten there first? Where was she? Already inside?

Cody the Wolf was getting really worked up. Boasting, "… and remember, if you have any problems in there, you come find me." He offered this crop of vulnerable Riding Hoods an almost vulgar, toothy grin.

I waited in line for a chatting twosome to slip their IDs back into their purses and make their way inside the bar. Mostly, tonight's girls came in clumps. Except for one, who appeared to be on her own. She leaned down to gather something at her feet.

A camera box. A familiar one at that.

There she was. Heather. With bulky bags of camera gear over both shoulders. She almost looked like an unsure new parent, carrying too many just-in-case bags. But in that split second, seeing her move through the entrance, I was hit with a wave of anger. I wanted to make her vanish with the twirl of a magic wand, the innocent-looking villain who had dragged Sharon father away from me than she'd ever been before.

Once Heather disappeared inside, Cody nodded at me. No need for an ID, not with my shock of white hair and six million or so wrinkles.

I stepped inside to find the bar completely packed. So many people—all ages, all sizes—and interwoven so tightly, like threads making up a piece of cloth.

Where had Heather gone? I didn't want to lose her.

I pushed my glasses up my nose and wormed my way through the crowd. Was I a mere spectator at this ball?

I didn't want to be.

No—I wasn't going to be. Once, I'd been a Prince Charming. On a quest for the perfect girl. Making sure that I charmed her enough to ride into the sunset.

Once, I'd gone after what I wanted.

I was going to do it again.

I was going to get that camera back.

Which was to say, I was going to prove I'd never been Sharon's villain. I was going to do the honorable thing.

I was out to get magic back.

The same magic Sharon and I had created together.

Sharon

In fifty years with Michael, I'd never left a note for him, not like the one I'd placed on the kitchen table before stepping out to Murio's birthday.

Ever since I'd seen the notice of the celebration in the paper, I hadn't been able to get it out of my mind.

I wasn't telling Michael I needed to be on my own. I'd left him that note hoping he would follow.

Which was a little strange. I wanted Michael to follow me. To join me. When we already lived together.

I just didn't want the two of us to keep looking at each other in the same way. We needed a different backdrop.

At the bar, I handed over my cover charge, the old faded-to-blue ink in my tattoo visible in the glow from the nearby streetlight.

I paused to glance around the square, hoping to see him.

And tried not to hang on to disappointment when I didn't. Plenty of night left, I had to assure myself.

Oh, but the worries stopped pummeling me in the moment I stepped inside. Because it was like stepping into my old skin, especially as I removed the lens cap. The walls had aged, but the atmosphere hadn't changed. Different faces, an entirely new crop of them, were still painted up as brightly as they'd been decades ago. The same familiar dreams made the air feel muggy and dense with hope.

What did they see in me? A woman in a bar by herself.

Ah, but I was old this time. No old woman is up to no good. No old woman is bad. Old women are done. They have had their happy ending.

I was simply here to revisit mine. A reunion with my past.

That's what they thought, anyway.

In part, they were right. My beginning really was there. It danced and pulsed around me. Back then, my life had seemed like little more than a prologue. I'd tapped my fingernails impatiently, anxious for the rest of my story—the real meat of it—to get going. Not enough time had elapsed yet for drama to kick in. Or so I'd thought. But that was so wrong. Beginnings are loaded with uncertainty. What's more dramatic than uncertainty?

Murio's bubbled with firsts: first dates, first time being introduced to a friend of a friend. First time in a long time seeing Murio. First time seeing what Murio's son had done with the place. First time to be back inside the old bar in ages.

I understood firsts differently from this spot, a good distance from any first of my own. I wanted to capture it all. I snapped. And snapped.

I told myself I wouldn't be distracted. Not by the heat in the room. Not by voices and shouts and bumps.

I wasn't done yet.

But my early determination splintered when I found myself distracted by a familiar face.

Mostly familiar, anyway.

I lowered my camera and headed back toward the bar.

"Should I have brought another permission form?" I shouted at Murio, now as white-headed and wrinkled as I was.

He rolled his eyes. "Get real, kid. Don't get schmaltzy on me. Get out there and do what you do best."

Smiling, I pushed myself away, like a swimmer pushing herself from the side of the pool, ready for another lap. I raised my camera, letting the crowd draw me from one direction to the next.

Until I saw them, through my viewfinder. My pictures. My night shots. They were back.

Oh, sure, the article about Murio's party had said something about old pictures. But I certainly didn't suspect they'd be mine.

Every single wall was filled with the photographs that had been displayed during my exhibit years ago. Copies I'd given to Murio as a thank you. He'd framed them, hung them again.

I stood on my toes, looking over the crowd.

Back at the bar, Murio shrugged, held his hands out to the side, then waved me on in a *go on, get going* kind of gesture.

He'd remembered.

It did something to me. Just being remembered. *Do what you do best.* It shook and strengthened me all at the same time.

But saying that sounds flimsy. That's not enough. How can I describe it? To be remembered, you had to have really been seen in the first place. Someone had to take the time to develop your image in the darkroom of their own mind. They had to think enough to frame you, preserve you.

I didn't think I had been. Suddenly, I was surrounded by proof I'd gotten that all wrong.

I didn't want to shake off the surprise. I wanted to let tears prickle in my eyes. I wanted the lump in my throat. I wanted to be rattled.

Staggering forward I few steps, I found it. Near the stage,

there it was, my favorite nightlife image: the woman dancing alone, out in the middle of the floor.

It was so good to see her again. The woman still daring the world to come at her with their suspicions and their prejudices, their rules and their standards.

At that moment, while I was buzzing with the past and staring at my work and realizing I wasn't quite as forgotten as I'd thought, it happened. Like something out of one of Michael's storybooks. A woman walked up to my picture and made the exact same pose. Stuck her face up, her leg out, and hiked her long, gauzy skirt slightly, imitating the pose.

Was she teasing? Tipsy? Playing some sort of game?

The shape of her upturned face, the smirk...I took her picture immediately. Then lowered my camera to ask, "That's you, isn't it?" as I pointed at the fifty-year-old black and white photo.

She let go of her skirt, covering a leg dotted with a few unmistakable markers of time. The veins, the sun-thickened skin.

We exchanged names for the second time in half a century. We shook hands. I gathered her address, in exchange for a print.

"I remember that night," she agreed. "I'd come to visit my sister here in Fairyland. What else could I do? My life felt like it was falling apart. I was on a losing streak. And then, out of nowhere, the man who said I wasn't enough changed his mind. Came after me. Followed me straight to this place. Murio's. That night, for the first time in my life, I said, 'Too late. You're not enough for *me*.'"

"He was there?" I asked, my head swimming. Why hadn't I asked about her story all those years ago?

She nodded, her eyes growing hazy beneath her thick white bangs. And she told me about the long upswing that followed the night I'd taken her picture. My chest warmed as she shared the details of her story.

When she was gone, all I could think was that I'd done her a disservice with that picture. I'd zoomed in too close. If I'd pulled back, I could have told the story of the crowd's reaction. Surely, the onlookers would have revealed shock, pity, admiration.

And I could have captured him, too, there in the throngs. The man she had was standing up to. *Just watch me. I'll show you.*

By shooting the bigger picture, I wouldn't have diminished the woman's importance. Just the opposite. Including other faces would have said more about her.

If I were to take the same picture again, it'd be different.

What else would I take differently? My thoughts zipped through those years of photos, all those nighttime images.

Until I came back to Michael. He'd been there, too, while I was doing my own dancing, of sorts. He'd been beside me through all those years when I had the spotlight on my face.

He'd seen me. The way the woman in the center of the dance floor wanted to be seen.

But that wasn't all. It wasn't simply that he'd let me dance. He hadn't watched from the fringes of a crowd. He'd been part of it. All of it. From the very beginning. We'd been dancing together in Dad's basement, the night I took *The Art of the Kiss*.

If I hadn't had what it took, *The Art of the Kiss* would have never had a follow-up. No exhibits, no editorial work. The shop would have closed shortly after opening.

I'd followed my own dream. *And* we'd been in it together. At the same time. It had been there all along, but I was finally seeing it. The big picture.

I needed to tell him.

Where was he?

I turned, bumping into another familiar face.

Heather. Here to take her shots of her ex-boyfriend's band.

I'd seen my camera in her hands before, but this was different. Here, in Murio's, surrounded by the photos the Nikon and I had taken together. Here, engulfed by everything the Nikon and I had shared with Michael: passion and purpose and a partnership and a best friend and a wealth of genuine affection.

It was a hard sight to see, that camera in Heather's hands. Almost as hard as looking at an old love—one you never quite got over—in the arms of another.

JULY 5, 1969

Michael's uncle had spent his working years as a watch repairman in a tiny hole-in-the-wall shop, the kind of little bitty place that was once all a man needed to keep his family in new shoes and living beneath a roof that didn't leak.

He had shown his curious nephew the ins and outs of his craft—the delicate little structures, the tiny gears and moving pieces. "Like miniature hearts," his uncle had whispered. *A timekeeper*, that was what Michael's own mother had called him. Michael grew up believing his uncle to be a wizard of sorts—a man who created and kept control of the time.

Uncle Vincent, father of three girls, seemed to enjoy Michael's company. He'd helped Vincent with the watch repair starting when he was still small enough to fit on his lap. It was easy for him, what with his little fingers. And his abundance of patience, which was unusual for a child.

But why wouldn't Michael be patient? He and his uncle were keeping time. Without them, horrible things could happen. Why, Saturday, the most deliciously lazy of all the week's days, might disappear forever.

He learned to love all things intricate. By the time he was ten, he was taking apart anything with screws: the toaster, a radio, a vacuum, the lawn mower motor.

So it wasn't unusual that after the Fourth of July fiasco, he had gathered the pieces of Sharon's camera, bid her and her father good-bye a good three hours before the start of the fireworks, and taken a city bus to the edge of the Graysons' neighborhood, where he could pick up his Pontiac then head straight to the offices of *The Fairy-land Times*. The paper had a room in the basement full of not-completely-busted typewriters and rotary phones and, yes, cameras. The Graveyard, everyone on staff called it. Only, the castoffs weren't completely dead. Some pieces were still in decent condition. Kept around *in case*. Everyone knew replacement pieces could help you out in a jam—say, if a reporter happened to find himself wedged between a rapidly approaching deadline and a suddenly malfunctioning typewriter return bar.

Michael had begun work early in the evening, stopping only to curl up on The Graveyard's couch with the broken springs somewhere around one in the morning. A vicious crick in his neck had roused him less than two hours later. He'd splashed water on his face, his beard like a Brillo pad beneath his fingers, and dashed off his latest column, about the pre-fireworks Independence Day picnic, only to return immediately to his most important task at hand.

At a quarter after six in the morning, he flinched against the door flying open at the top of the stairs.

"Minyard, what in the Sam Hill are you doing down here?" thundered Reed, his editor.

"Already turned my story in, boss," Michael said, still sifting through the boxes.

"You'd better. News doesn't stop for a holiday."

And still, he clomped closer.

But Michael was lost in his work. In the salvage and restoration of Sharon's Nikon. He had disassembled another camera just to see how it all went together, laying the pieces out across an old desktop strategically, so that he could keep track of the order in which he'd removed the parts. It was different from working on watches, but also not so different. Tiny little pieces, screws.

Even with Michael's experience, though, it should not have been easy. It should have frustrated him. Doubt should have crept into the process. He should have, at some point, shaken his head at himself, wondered out loud, "How could I have ever thought I'd fix this?"

And yet, he didn't.

He'd launched into the task with hope and joy and excitement in his heart. Those feelings had never lessened. Now that he was fully enmeshed, he had started to feel it all absolutely clicking. Sliding into place. Somehow he could dig through a box of parts for the next needed piece, and it would come to him, like his fingertips were magnets.

He would not quite be able to explain it when his editor got close enough to demand some sort of answer.

All he knew was that he felt certain this was it. A fixed camera was his way to show Sharon how much he cared, even though they barely knew each other. Sharon had made it clear, more than once, that she wasn't interested. He knew he was riding a fine line, at this point, between being a man with a crush and man Sharon suspected of hiding in the bushes watching through her bedroom window while she phoned the Fairyland sheriff. Without the camera, any remaining time with Sharon could disappear.

That, he knew, would be far worse than the disappearance of Saturdays.

300

Reed reached the desk Michael had commandeered, slamming his hands down on the top. His tie was loosened, his sleeves rolled up. But Michael had long assumed he actually dressed that way each morning, sliding the Windsor knot only part of the way up and never once making use of cufflinks.

"Minyard," Reed barked. "Didn't you hear me? I said what in the Sam Hill are you doing?"

He had often used the same tone on Michael at a quarter to five, when he broke out his bottom-drawer bottle of scotch. "You stay away from the skirts," Reed would warn, dragging his feet about going home to wife number three. Michael would accept the bottle Reed offered, take a sip, and he would nod. *Yes*, he would agree, *a bachelor's life forever. That'll be me.*

But he didn't feel that way anymore—if he ever really had to begin with. He needed to ready his face. He needed it to show Reed how different this woman was. Sharon was a single moment in time, the kind that could drift up to you and waft away before you really had a chance to even recognize it. And if he didn't do this one thing to show her everything he felt for her, everything he'd been daydreaming about, she really would slip right on by. She'd forever be this wonderful thing that had almost happened to him.

He couldn't let that be the story. He had to pause this moment just long enough for her to see him. To stop dismissing him.

This was it. His one shot. It had to be done.

Michael raised his head, meeting Reed's eyes. Slowly, Reed's frown smoothed out beneath his head of wiry gray hair. "Shoulda known it was about some woman," he grumbled.

He turned to go.

He was wrong, of course. It wasn't about some woman. It was about *the* woman. If he'd ever met Sharon, he'd have understood.

But Michael didn't have time to argue. He rubbed his scratchy eyes and returned to his work. To sliding pieces into place, one after another. Pieces that should have fought him every step of the way.

He began to hum softly. Sharon would see the magic he had worked on her camera. And she would know that together, they could be every bit as magical.

His fingers worked nimbly as he filled the gadget with all of his dreams.

Michael

I got bumped, my beer sloshing over the top of my glass.

"Sorry. Sorry." Apologies bubbled all around me. A group of three had arrived and were balancing their own beers as they searched for a table. Or a decent place to stand. Two men, one woman. The men had a business relationship. The formality of it was a dead give-away: the slacks, the straight backs, the polite discussions, the way they held each other's eyes. Sometimes, eye contact becomes like a handshake—firm and unwavering, a testament to a person's intentions. Each of the men refused to be the first to glance away.

The woman who accompanied them seemed on a different sort of mission—mostly, to dissolve. Shoulders curled forward, head down toward her chest, auburn hair like a curtain.

Heather recognized her. "Amanda," she called. Poor girl must've said it eight, nine times before the woman finally looked her way.

Amanda. A name that had floated up from the basement,

through the floor grates in the apartment.

Up until that moment, I'd been focused on Heather, on that camera in her hand. But as she hugged her old friend, I realized every last character in our intertwining story had all arrived in the same place, at the same time: Heather, Amanda, Ryan, his band members. Introductions and hellos meant that I also knew Amanda had come with her husband and Charles Liu, the same Liu whose shoot had sent Heather to our door.

But I was after the camera. The magic. Sharon's dream. Me. I was good at fixing things. I'd fixed them before. Inexplicably. Sometimes, when you want something enough, you will the universe to bend just enough so that this one little measly miraculous thing can happen to you.

Yes, that was the way it had felt back then.

The universe had bent enough to let me put together all the little delicate pieces of Sharon's camera. And now, the universe was going to bend enough for me to put all the delicate pieces of us back together again too.

The universe couldn't let magic drift away that easily.

I kept my eyes on the girls, trying to take it all in. Trying to listen for clues. Some way to edge myself in, get my hands on that camera. I wasn't sure what I had in mind yet. I was just waiting for some opportunity to open up.

It felt like I was crouched on the starting line, listening for the sound of the starting pistol. And still the girls rattled on about clothes. "Thanks so much for the suit," Heather said into Amanda's ear. "You were so right."

Ryan called out to get Heather's attention. Heather smiled, juggling her gear enough to be able to wave back while Fayth watched from the stage, frozen in place, hands on her hips.

"Gotta go," Heather told Amanda. "Hey, maybe I can get

Ryan to play that old song from high school. The one at the talent show. You remember, the one you liked so much? Think they still know it?"

Amanda offered a limp attempt at a smile before Heather turned to bump her way through the crowd, banging the camera case along the way. I could almost feel a new bruise form on my body every single time she clunked the case against a table.

Heather caught Sebastian's attention quickly. He leaned forward, seeming to drink in Heather's attributes. She stood out, of course—for the same reason I'd once stood out in Bleeker's all those years ago, a man in a tie on a Saturday. Yes, there she was, dressed in a linen suit that had to be growing hotter by the millisecond. She slipped her arms out of the jacket and handed it to Sebastian for storage behind the bar, leaving herself in a sleeveless white blouse.

Ryan began to gain speed, trying to catch up to her, his face registering anger. There was no need for Sebastian to look her over quite so hungrily, he was surely thinking. She wasn't exactly fruit that needed to be inspected for flaws.

I laughed softly, edging my own way through the crowd. Two princes, ready to do battle to win the fair maiden's heart.

Heather did look prettier than I'd ever seen her. But it couldn't have just been about new pants and a blouse. Was it because she'd freed herself from Ryan? Moved on? It happened that way with women sometimes. Breakups didn't necessarily send them crying over cocktails. Often, after a bit of introspection, they bloomed.

Fairy tales never say that. But the prettiest women are the ones who stand on their own feet, have their own lives. That's the true beauty—not the rosebud lips and long wavy hair.

Regardless, Ryan would never accept that Heather had gotten prettier in the days without him. What man would? It would have to mean that he wasn't a Prince Charming at all, but a frog.

Ah, but Sebastian wasn't the only one in Murio's who'd noticed her. A man about Heather's age pointed at an empty stool next to his own.

Another wolf. Vicious, dangerous, salivating. Holding his arm out in a chivalrous manner.

Don't fall for it, Ryan seemed to silently cry out as he collided with the edge of a small table. He glanced about as if realizing wolves were all over the place, inside the bar and guarding the door. Smacking their lips—on the prowl.

Heather shook her head, waving the wolf off. No need for Ryan's intervention; no rescue junk for that one.

Heather passed some of her gear over to Sebastian for safe-keeping behind the bar too. She maintained a firm grip on the camera case.

I slipped between the bodies, coming closer to them both. Close enough to hear Heather telling Ryan, "You know, I was poking around online, and I saw this thing about another bar—a couple states over, but anyway, the place does open mic nights that give bands a shot at a record deal."

Prince Charming's eyes widened and his head jutted back. He looked startled, as if he'd been stretched out on one of those legendary mortuary platforms—like her words had completely and totally drained him. I could read it all in his face: Did Heather think he was struggling? Failing? Unhappy? Wished he was someplace else? A place with more fans? Didn't she know what she said was coming across as downright cruel? Unthinking?

"What's that mean?" he asked. But she didn't seem to hear him.

"I'm paying my bills," he shouted at her over the din, "and I'm surrounded by music. Even my day job involves music. And I'm playing at night. We've got a couple of videos up on YouTube. They don't have millions of views. I have to pay attention to what I spend. But so what? Isn't that actually living the dream? To make a living doing what you love? What's success, anyway? Does it have to be worldwide fame? Do you have to have millions in the bank? Is there just one definition?"

"But if you're not constantly pushing for more," Heather argued, "doesn't it get boring? Shouldn't there always be a new challenge, a new rung to climb onto? Otherwise…" Her voice trailed before she could finish.

What's the point? Those words dangled in the air, unsaid.

Funny, the power unsaid words wield.

"I'm not as good as you? I'm somehow not living up to your standards?" he asked. "What, you got a little slice of success, and now, I need to catch up? Is that it?"

It was Heather's turn to jut her head backward in shock.

"I mean, you were always into my stuff. It didn't matter to you back when I first heard you singing my song in your car whether or not I was signed to some big-time label. Right?"

"Why wouldn't I—and you—want to strive for more? Why would either of us stop? Isn't that why I'm here?"

"You're here," Ryan said, "because I wanted to see you."

"But not because I can do the job better than anyone else?" Heather asked.

Ryan frowned.

"Don't you believe?" she asked.

"In what?"

"In me. In—more."

"In more," Ryan repeated. "There we go again."

Their words began to swivel, like the dots of light coming from the disco ball. Two different viewpoints, each of them swirling and swirling and chasing one another, never stopping to rest on the same point.

Fayth appeared with the rest of The Tommies in tow, ending what had become a somewhat prickly conversation. She carried a tray of shot glasses with one hand, shoulder-height.

"Sorry," Fayth said. "Didn't mean to intrude. Just thought I'd start a new pre-gig tradition." She pointed to one of the glasses, telling Heather, "Got you one too."

"What is it?" Heather asked. She peered into the brown liquid as the drummer and the bass player reached for their own shots.

"What is it?" Fayth repeated, in a tone that insisted it should have been obvious. "A shot of good luck!" And she winked. "A toast!"

"To good luck!" Matt bellowed, holding up his sticks triumphantly.

"To good luck," Ryan echoed, grimacing a bit as he raised his own glass.

The band—and Heather—all clinked their glasses together at the same time, but Heather seemed less than enthusiastic.

Ryan handed his empty shot glass back to Fayth, a look flashing across his face that said it had finally begun to occur to him what—or who—might actually be the true symbol of his own good luck.

~From Michael's Notebook~
2018

Dear Sharon,

Here's the truth, which I have been too afraid to say. Not because it's bad, not because it would inflict some sort of damage. Because it is the bareness of everything. It is the vulnerable, the exposed. And that's terrifying. But here goes, finally:

You are, without question, the most exciting—and the most aggravating—woman I have ever met. There is a world inside you. A whole world. With landscapes and rooms and hidden corners. I think I knew, when I first saw you on the street, taking your photos, that I could spend decades trying to see it all.

I still think so. I think that much is left to explore.

You took a hit when people stopped coming by the shop.

Of course you did. How could it have happened any other way? You don't go from causing traffic jams to being ignored and not have that hurt.

But don't you see we're one and the same? I invited people, Shar. In my last column. "Come find me," I told them. "Tell me your stories."

They never did.

I retired. The world promptly disappeared.

I know how it feels.

There's a loss. Part of you is dead. And nobody even seems to have cared enough to mourn. Nobody but you.

Still. You withdrew inside yourself, putting out a very obvious "No Visitors" sign. The message blared like neon.

If they didn't want you, why, you didn't want them back.

It's understandable. Nobody gets that quite like I do.

But I live in that outside world too.

Do I wish we were back there, in those early years? Yes. I wish it because we were closer then. Why wouldn't I want to get back to that?

I never thought you had to have that camera, Shar. Not the one I fixed. You used the camera —it didn't use you. But the fact is, I *was* there. That was me helping out at the shop. And more. That was me dragging you out to all the boring Fairyland events. The bowling tournaments. The parades. The picnics. I was the one who made you see it all in a certain way, changed your mind—made it fun. And didn't it have an impact on the kinds of pictures you took?

My abilities and yours, all tangled. I said that to you at the very beginning. What you accomplished wasn't because of me. But I was there. I was part of it. My hand was in it.

I never stopped wanting to be part of it, all of it. All of you.

I wasn't trying to put the blame for where we wound up on you. Not when I was on the radio. But I was desperate. We don't be-have the same way when we're desperate as we do when we're calm.

310

We overshoot. We broadcast instead of whisper. I just wanted to reach out to you.

Look at me here, an old man talking to his wife in a notebook.

You don't even read my notebooks. Not anymore. You used to sometimes, remember? I'd leave them lying around for you to find. Or you'd listen, head on my chest, while I read pieces to you out loud.

They were love letters. Did you know that? All of them. Even when they weren't about you. They were still because of you. Because you were the thing that electrified me. Not so much my inspiration as the person I wanted to impress more than any other.

You don't read my notebooks, and I don't look at your pictures.

We've been living side-by-side, really. Almost like neighbors in the same house, reaching out only for polite chain-link fence talk.

How can that be? We rode into this sunset together, remember?

I never imagined I'd get so much attention being on the radio. People were listening. You know what that's like when people pay attention.

It takes over. Lights a fire.

But so does silence. The silence between us, anyway.

For my part, my dear Sharon, I'm so sorry.

All I wanted was to get closer to you. To impress you. See the "No Visitors" sign come down, be let back in.

The world inside you is an amazing place. Every time I get a glimpse of it, I can't catch my breath.

I'd give anything to get back there now.

It is, in fact, the only place I never truly wanted to leave.

Sharon

"Everyone is here tonight," Heather shouted in my ear.

Her smile trembled.

She said something else to me, but it was hard to hear over the band. The same band that she was so excited to have been hired to photograph.

So why wasn't she?

Heather rubbed her forehead. "I think that shot Fayth gave me did something to me. I need some water."

She tried to motion for Sebastian's attention. But he was wrapped into some wild conversation with his dad and a group of other former regulars.

And that band—they were so loud, their amps buzzed with feedback. Playing something about make-believe.

Heather gave up on Sebastian and turned her big worried eyes back at me. "My maybe-boss even showed up. Mr. Liu."

I nodded.

"I *really* need this to go well," Heather groaned.

I clenched my jaw. She had my camera. My entire past right there in her hand. What else did she need?

On the other side of the room, Fayth's voice wobbled. She backed away from the mic. She shook her head.

The band faltered, falling out of time. The song clunked to a stop.

Fayth climbed down from the stage, the crowd parting as she raced toward the entrance. Toward Cody, the protective wolf who surely wasn't going to be able to make things right. Not for her.

But she was Fayth, after all. She would make things right for herself. It was what she'd always done. Right then, it meant refusing to be in the room while Ryan sang to another woman using the song she'd written with him. Refusing to participate as he offered someone else his heart.

"Sorry, guys," Ryan said into Fayth's mic. "We've got some technical problems. Back in ten." He slipped his head back out of his guitar strap and hurried off the stage, following Fayth's footsteps.

"Fayth!" he shouted as he raced to catch up.

Now, I will assure you, this scene was entirely real. I know it doesn't seem like it. It seems like one of those rom-com scenes we've all watched play out a thousand times. The *When Harry Met Sally* running down the street, racing to catch up to the one person in the world you suddenly just *had* to declare your undying love to.

Sometimes, though, don't we mimic our favorite scenes? Don't we fall in line with the way our favorite stories tell us to behave?

I think we do. I think Michael definitely gets that part right.

But listen, the bar itself? Murio's. That was real. Fayth and Ryan weaving through the crowd, struggling to get outside. Yes. Real.

This next part? It's primarily blanks that have been filled in. Oh, sure, Heather'd told me all about Fayth and Ryan being long-time friends. If I felt the need to verify it, I could have. Their friendship could even be found in archives of the paper, in all those stories about The Tommies through the years. But how they all really felt? Well, okay, that's me telling you how I'd react if I were in their places. I know what it's like. I've been there before. I've loved. I've also seen the most important person start to slip away.

Just not with the same speed as Fayth racing for the exit.

"Fayth!" Ryan shouted again, calling for his best friend. His co-writer. His lead singer. The voice that had been in his head every single day. It had always been so easy to be around her. Maybe too easy. The kind of easy that you can take for granted.

Fayth had dreamed all his dreams. Stayed beside him in his jerk moods. Taken him out to bury his bad feelings. Goofy as that was, it had also been wonderful.

Ryan's face displayed a whole album worth of soaring senti-mental ballads, love songs. He wore the kind of desperate expression that begged her to stop, to listen.

This wasn't about the hurtful thing Heather had said. Or be-ing on the rebound. It wasn't even about realizing, finally, that he and Heather really had fallen for two different reasons. It wasn't about needing to cover up the burned spot Heather'd made on his heart with someone else. Anyone else.

It was about Fayth.

The moment had smacked him upside the head, hard enough to finally wake up.

My feet were moving, and I was weaving, scooting, rushing, my eyes on Ryan. I'd been hunting down kisses long enough to know one was coming. The tension between these two was as electric as the seconds before a summer storm.

I slipped outside as Ryan grabbed hold of Fayth's arms. There it was. Recognition of what they had. Knowing where they could go together. The understanding, finally, that an all-consuming love had

314

long been boiling over and spewing between them. "My God. Fayth. It's been you. All along, hasn't it?" he said. "How could I have been so stupid? It's always been you and me."

I raised my camera.

Emotions pulsed through the air, changing the color of the space around them. Rolling heat rippled, warming the atmosphere.

They wrapped their arms around each other.

I waited for the acknowledgment, the concession, the agreement, the *I love you*.

Fayth's eyes grew wet. She slipped her arms around Ryan's waist. He lowered his face.

It happened.

The kiss.

I snapped, flash flying out into the world, feeling a familiar rush of emotion. That from-the-gut feeling that assured me the picture I'd snapped had not just been good, but important. How could it not be? That was a first kiss decades in the making.

The rush turned into a cold splash of remorse as I turned back toward Murio's and saw Heather's face in the window.

JULY 4, 1970

Sharon waited all day. All eight agonizing hours of red, white, and blue. Of the humid summer Missouri heat. Of picnic blankets. Of mosquitoes and heavy potato salad and lemonade that didn't seem to soothe the dryness at the back of her throat.

She waited.

She waited through the hot dog dinner; the same hot dog dinner she'd been enjoying for years, but suddenly tasted like slop, each bite growing in the most unappetizing manner the longer she chewed. She waited through yet another slew of stories her dad told Michael about growing up Sharon style. She maneuvered through the crowd, but every last nerve in her body had frazzled, and she was having trouble focusing on a subject for new pictures.

She waited as the sky turned ever…slowly…oranger…and finally, finally started to darken.

Her father squeezed her shoulder as he hoisted himself off their picnic blanket.

Now that twilight had arrived, slinking across the park like a cat, it seemed the rest of Fairyland was waiting anxiously. Readying themselves to enjoy the spectacle in the sky. Just a few more minutes.

But Sharon's own agonizing wait was over.

She reached for her camera case and removed the small felt box. Suddenly, she didn't have just one heart but thousands of little tiny ones, each of them pumping and thundering away.

Her mouth felt drier than it had ever had—including her first and last attempt at running the city's half marathon. Glancing down at her tattoo, still visible in the last dregs of hazy evening light, she urged herself to buck up and get on with it.

"Michael," she started, but he had angled himself away from her and seemed intent on digging into the pocket on his slacks.

"Michael," she repeated. He still wasn't paying attention.

"*Michael.*" She nudged him repeatedly, until he finally turned to face her.

"I—well—" She cracked open a box, exposing the man's ring. Her father's wedding band, which he hadn't worn for decades. The same band he'd given to her with a teary-eyed smile when she'd admitted out loud how she felt about Michael—and what she wanted. The same simple gold band that she'd taken to a jeweler, requesting the inclusion of three new small diamonds.

"Why are you pounding at me, woman?" he teased. But when he finally saw the ring box, a frown dug deep into his face.

"This last year," she started. But as usual, she fought for the right words. She'd rehearsed this, but now, all of it felt hollow.

It had been a fresh, lovely flower of a year. The two of them out enjoying the best of Fairyland. Her work beginning to draw attention. Michael becoming a recognizable reporter. A year of interwoven fingers and the feel of him beside her on park benches and movie theaters. The sound of his familiar voice on the phone. Slowly, her fragile uncertainties had grown sturdy beneath her.

If she'd felt it, surely Michael had too.

She pushed the ring closer to him, avoiding words. Wanting the ring to say everything she couldn't. Didn't it already?

"Are you proposing?" he asked, just loud enough to make a few nearby heads turn their way.

"I—"

"No," he said, scrunching his face and pushing the ring box away.

"What do you mean, 'no'?" Sharon challenged, fighting the hot surge blasting across her cheeks.

"I mean no."

"Really!" Sharon shouted. From the corner of her eye, she could see her father's large frame swiveling toward them.

"That's the stupidest thing you've ever said," Sharon announced. Now she didn't have to search for words at all. Her anger was finding them for her.

"Stupid? Why? Because I turned you down—"

"Stupid because you know how this is between us. You know."

"And how is it?" Michael asked, stretching his legs out in front of him and leaning back on his hands.

"Is that a smirk?"

"A smirk?"

"On your face."

"Must just be I'm squinting into the sunset. You were saying?"

"I was saying you're being an idiot. All the time I've known you, I never thought you were an idiot. Annoying at first, maybe. But never an idiot."

"And yet?"

"And yet, here you are, refusing to acknowledge what we have. Sure, you and I are a strange couple at first glance. We look like opposites. Only, we're not, are we? We're both a couple of outspoken,

318

opinionated—whatevers. You no more than me. And don't ask me why, but you can bounce your column ideas off me and I can show you my work and we don't give each other nice, fluffy answers. No 'Gee, that's swell's. We tell each other what we really think. And it never hurts. Because we know it's not said to be mean. It's honest. It's said with respect. And we want each other to be great. Because we're in this mess—"

"Mess?"

"Thing. Whatever it is. Together. You and me. We fell for each other. I mean *really* each other. You don't care that I can't cook pot roast or keep a plant longer than half an hour, and I don't care about your stuffy button-down shirts."

"Well, you mostly don't care about my shirts. I'm pretty sure you'd have me in longer hair, maybe with a tattoo of my own—"

"Shut up! Really! Are you even listening? Haven't you been paying attention? Don't you know that I like it? I want to go to Macy's and buy stuffy button-down shirts. I want to show you my pictures and know that you'll tell me they're great or they stink or they're not quite there. I want to hear what you're working on. I want to know that you trust me for solid input. Like I trust you. None of this is the way it usually is. I mean, usually, somebody in a relationship has the upper hand, right? Somebody has a more impressive job, or makes more money or something. One's the more admirable one. But for some reason, here we are, and we look up to each other. It's like some weird perspective trick that shouldn't be real but is. Like some Escher drawing of staircases that all go in circles, and all look to be on the same floor, no step any higher than any other."

When he didn't respond, she shrugged, hoping that her analogy wasn't too over the top. In a calmer voice, she added, "Of course, we both know I'm the one who's probably going to make gobs more money." Mostly, she said it to fill the air. Make him laugh. Get a reaction. Why was he just staring at her?

Finally, Michael's grin began to widen, but only a little.

"That—right there—that was a smirk."

Michael shrugged.

The night grew still darker. The Fairyland Orchestra made a bunch of dissonant noises as they tuned up for the "1812 Overture." Fireworks would start soon.

"So?" she pressed.

"So what?"

"What do you think—about any of it? Come on. Look at us. It fits. All of it. Think of where we'd be in fifty years. I bet we wouldn't even have to speak at all. We'd be able to just read each other's thoughts. How could this possibly go wrong?"

"I think it already has. I think you're screwing everything up."

"Me? How am I screwing it up?"

"Because." Michael leaned to the side, reached into his pocket, and finally pulled out a felt box of his own.

They laughed hard enough to make a few more nearby heads turn away from the wide black star-studded heavens to stare at them. And they exchanged rings underneath a sky that had only just started to explode in color and fire and splendor.

Michael

Heather stumbled across the floor of Murio's looking utterly shattered.

I might have called out to her. But how could she have heard me over the radio Murio had turned on in an effort to fill the air now that the band had scattered? Two of The Tommies were onstage tinkering with equipment, the other two still outside.

Next to a far wall, Mr. Liu continued to chat with Amanda and her husband.

Or should I say the two men were involved in the conversation, taking turns shouting into each other's ears.

Amanda's eyes—and her full attention—were on Heather.

Beneath the swirling disco ball lights, the room moved in slow motion.

Heather seemed completely disoriented. Her chest heaved as she fought for breath. She looked confused. Hurt. Ryan had kissed Fayth. Sharon had preserved it in a photo. Even I had seen all that through the front window, same as Heather. Had Heather loved Ryan? Was her heart broken?

Or was she embarrassed? Ambushed? Did she feel like a fool?

She hadn't called him back after the kiss at Slade Music. Why? Because she didn't know what to say, or because she'd already accepted it was over?

If she had, why was she upset? Because Ryan had chosen someone quickly? Because he'd chosen Fayth? It was hard to find out someone you'd spent so much time with had decided you were nothing more than a mistake they needed to make, to learn from, so they could finally recognize the face of their true happiness.

It was pretty clear Heather was trying not to notice Sharon, who had stepped back inside the bar. She didn't want to talk about what Sharon had just photographed.

But I was still convinced she would talk to me. If I could just get close enough for her to hear me. She would listen. I didn't have many powers, but I had that. I could make people think. My time on the radio had convinced me. I'd make her realize how unfair and unjust it was for her to have that camera. It had fallen into the wrong hands. She'd see this was my quest. She would realize the right thing to do would be to return my magic.

She could stop being my villain. She could lead with kindness.

Yes, I would wield my words like a gleaming knight's sword, and she would understand—and comply.

Before I could reach her, Heather took a deep breath and did her best to collect herself. She started to bring the viewfinder toward her eye, but stopped suddenly, a look of utter horror spreading across her face.

"Oh, no," she murmured, turning the old camera over in her hands. She sneaked the briefest of glances at Liu, then turned back toward the Nikon. "Oh, no, oh, no..."

Sharon

Heather thrust the camera at me.

"Look," she insisted.

"What happened?" I asked. "This isn't mine." It couldn't have been. The dents and scratches were gone.

Anger broke like sweat across my skin.

"I don't know," Heather kept saying over and over, her words gaining speed. "I know I took the camera out of the case when I first walked in, but I didn't look at it too closely. I mean, why would I think the camera was different? It's an old Nikon. But it's not yours. How could that happen?"

She rubbed her forehead, looking sick.

"When did you have it last?" I asked.

"Yesterday. In my apartment, when..." Her voice trailed.

"When what?" I pressed.

"Amanda," she blubbered, gesturing toward her friend. "She came over last night. She had some—she—she—"

"She *what*?" The room was swirling, past and present colliding. I felt like I was still in the park. On that first Independence Day with Michael. Like something that had been broken then was being broken all over again.

Only this time, it was maybe shattered forever.

"She brought me these clothes," Heather was saying, pointing at her blouse and pants.

Laughter bubbled up around me. And cheerful voices. The sounds of a birthday party. I wondered how anyone could feel like celebrating. Didn't they know how wrong everything was right then?

"Can't be," Heather muttered. "Amanda—she's my best friend. Since we were kids."

Meanwhile, Amanda was looking everywhere but our way.

"What do I do? I mean, I can't bow out. Not in front of Liu. But what else is there? How will I ever get it to work? This isn't your camera. Yours was special. It knew how to help me. I need it."

How could you? I wanted to yell. *You were careless. Where is it? Don't you understand what I created with it? My career. My life. My whole life.*

But did I really want to yell it at Heather?

Or me?

She blubbered some apology, some plea for advice.

My eyes bounced over Heather's shoulder. I couldn't stand to look at her.

Looking at the walls on the other side of the bar didn't help, either. Because the confusion—the swirling lights and the constant-ly moving crowd—was creating a mirage. Making my old images appear to have come to life. Michael was stepping out of one of the pictures and heading straight toward me.

Only—no. It wasn't some mirage. It wasn't some fifty-year-old picture. It was really Michael. He'd followed me. My heart lurched. He hadn't simply seen my note and shrugged, turning back to scrib-ble in one of his eighty million notebooks. He'd come for me.

324

Michael grew increasingly closer, heading my way.

I took a step away from Heather, feeling for a second like I was falling into a black hole.

Did it even matter that Michael had arrived? Was it too late? All time had done was steal from me. *Everything* had vanished. My youth. Dad. The baby I didn't even know I had. Admiration. The easy ways Michael and I had enjoyed. All those things I had come to count on, including my own abilities. Any talent I might have called my own. The camera. It was gone now too.

Which meant that magic was gone. Even in Michael's silly fairy tales, that never happened. Plans were thwarted. Evil came roaring onto the scene. But the heroes never lost their own magic.

I had. I'd let it go, let it out of my sight.

What would I do without it?

And still, Michael grew closer.

All I knew right then was that I didn't want to keep being reflected in Heather's story. I didn't want to meet the same bad ending she had just met with Ryan.

Impossible! I tried to tell myself. But then again, how could Michael and I have even gotten to this place? When we had been so perfect, so much the same? When we had fallen for the same reasons, the right reasons. Fallen for who we really were, not pretty portraits with our flaws airbrushed out.

"It's gone," I moaned. And in those two simple words, I let it all pour out: missing him and the kiss pictures and everything I wanted to get back and everything I feared—more at that moment than ever before—might have already vanished for good.

"What's gone?" Michael blurted. "What are you talking about?"

"The camera. *Our* camera. I don't know where it is."

Michael

As her words hit the air, utter joy broke through me.

It didn't matter that the camera was missing. Not anymore. It wouldn't have mattered if I never saw it again.

Because Sharon kept blubbering, "I want it back. I want that camera. It's *ours*. How could I have let it get away in the first place?"

It was all I needed. What I'd truly wanted all along. Sharon recognizing how special that old gizmo actually was. That it didn't deserve being shunted to the junk closet, along with a bunch of old everyday items.

I was no longer looking at her face. I was looking at fifty years. Triumphs and heartaches and surviving. I was looking at her heart and mine. I was looking at this woman who had never needed me, who would have been fine without me. This woman who had chosen me anyway. Who chose me still.

I was looking, in short, at a beginning.

Our beginning.

The second one.

As I stared at her, I saw her face shift—like she was reading me, somehow.

"It's been gone for a long time, though, hasn't it?" she asked.

I shook my head, knowing exactly what she meant.

"We let it get away," she went on. "Didn't we? We got lazy. We put it away, like some sort of heirloom. And then we let it out of its safe place. And now, what are we going to do? It's *gone*."

"Asleep," I tried to correct.

"Dead," Sharon cried out. "Or—dried up." Like somehow, she'd killed it right along with the houseplants.

I laughed as I reached for her. "No. We didn't let it get away. Love hasn't dried up. It's *asleep*. Which means it can be awakened. Like Sleeping Beauty. Don't you feel it?"

"Do I—" Sharon's voice trailed. "I don't feel anything most times but what's missing. How could that be? We didn't start like them." She nodded once toward Heather and once toward Ryan, still with Fayth just outside the bar. "We can't end up like them. Can we?"

"Look how we started. With a camera that should have been broken forever. Look where we are. At some creepy old mortuary. Things around us keep rising from the dead, Shar. You want to know what magic is? What it *really* is? Two people coming together. That's it. When that happens, even the impossible is possible."

At that moment, the song playing on the radio stopped.

But not because the radio had been turned off, not because the two Tommies onstage were about to start playing some instrumental piece.

Because—it surely sounds like I'm making it up—the song on the radio had simply faded to its final chord. And its notes had given way to my voice. To my recording. Here it was. The latest of my fairy tale pieces. The one I'd put together in honor of Murio's party.

"What's a good fairy tale without a ball?" I asked as the entire room grew quiet around us. "Oh, it's the climactic moment of any tale. Where hope is at its zenith. You go—whether you're Prince Charming or Cinderella—because you believe that something you need to change *will* change. Your life will greet you at the door. Your dreams will be yours for the taking."

Those were my words—I'd crafted and spoken them—but I was hearing them for the first time. Seeing their impact on Sharon, watching them dance across her face.

The old Prince Charming in me and the ever-beautiful Cinderella in her were still very much the fairy tale couple we'd always been.

Long past the sunset, maybe.

But it was all still here.

I grabbed Sharon.

And I kissed her.

This Kiss

*H*ow many kisses in life are truly memorable? How many shake us, wake us up, make the world feel like a different place entirely?

They're first kisses, usually. Love is stumbled upon—revolutionary.

This kiss had to have been the ten thousandth between Michael and Sharon.

And yet, it was so powerful, it made the night sky explode with enough brilliant stars to light all the grand balls in progress across the globe.

A few blocks away, the fifty-year-old image of a first kiss, Sharon's masterpiece, was darkened by a shadow.

Because, quite simply, it had been eclipsed.

This new kiss—the one that had just taken place in Murio's—was, in fact, the powerful one promised in the more poetic passages of fairy tales.

A magical kiss. A transformative kiss.

A kiss that completely filled in their rut. Changed their landscape.

A kiss that reminded Michael and Sharon they were the complete twosome—and could still count on each other. Their magic was alive, even after having gone missing for so long. Resurrected, just like Sharon's busted old camera decades ago.

Yes, magic still breathed. It wasn't locked in some inanimate object. It was real. It was alive. It was theirs.

All those tiny little delicate pieces broken over the last fifty years were being swept up by the emotion of the moment. They were sliding back into place.

Not exactly as they'd been before. Nothing is. But there was also a chance that this time, the pieces would be stronger.

It was a kiss, in short, that had the ability to change everything.

Michael

With Sharon's lips on mine, I saw us the way Sharon must have always seen us: in snapshots.

Our whole lives, one image after another. Bleeker's, the square, Independence Day. The work—hers and mine. Upstairs, each night. The day in. The day out. Beginning and ending in a flash. Murio's. Her dad's house. His basement. Our portrait. *The Art of the Kiss.* Sunday dinner. Peter. The studio. Her classes. Mesmerized faces. Traffic jams. Time moving faster and faster, until the images mimicked the stills in an old flip book. My notebooks. Her portfolios. Faster, faster. Black and whites. Her Ugly Period. Sadness. Then sunrise. The carrying on. Yesterdays. Empty store aisles. My retirement.

The junk closet.

She was right. Life really is a series of seemingly disjointed snapshots. And it's not until you've sifted through the entire lot of them, all those short little slices of life, that you finally realize what it was all about. You see what it amounted to.

You see your story.

Sharon

A flash washed over my face.

It didn't feel like a flash, though. Not right then. It felt more like the explosion of a firecracker.

As I pulled away from Michael, I found Heather holding her camera chin-height and smiling slightly. She'd taken our picture, as I'd taken Ryan and Fayth's a moment ago.

Slowly, her smile fell and her face turned vivid shades of shock. Horror. Sadness. Not unlike the face she'd shown me when she'd witnessed Fayth and Ryan's kiss. She wasn't looking at me, though. Or Michael.

"Amanda?" Heather murmured.

I followed her gaze to find that Heather's friend was holding a camera toward me. An old one. With familiar dents and scrapes.

"That's—" I started, reaching for it.

"It's yours. Isn't it? You're Sharon." Amanda glanced fearfully at Heather. "I hid it in the back of the car. I was afraid the kids would find it. They like to tear up the closets. I—"

332

"You took it." Heather said it definitively. "You took it?"

"Heather," Amanda pleaded. "I—"

"What did you do?" Heather asked. "When?"

"I switched them when I brought you the clothes," Amanda admitted. As Heather backed away, Amanda scrambled after her, insisting, "I was scared. You were—you were taking off. My oldest friend. I couldn't stand the idea of losing you."

"You don't want me to succeed? You want me to stay the crummy friend. Is that it? The one who can't get it together. The one you love upping time and time again with your fancy life."

"That's not true. Don't you get it? I didn't want you to leave me behind. But I don't want to hurt you, either. Look, here it is. I'm bringing it to you. That should count for something, shouldn't it? I brought the camera back."

I watched Heather's face wrench with utter pain.

"Go away, 'Manda," she murmured. "You have to leave me alone. Now."

The crowd in the bar surged, nearly engulfing Heather.

Amanda attempted to follow, but with tears already rolling, she decided instead to edge closer to her confused husband.

I couldn't let Heather get away. I could feel the crushing tides of two heartaches trying to swallow her whole. Prince Charming had chosen someone else. And her best friend had shown her own villain's face.

Sure, Amanda had tried to make up for it. But sometimes, once you've seen the villain in a person, you stop being able to see anything else. It happens all at once, and irretrievably, like they've just snatched off their mask.

Was Heather crumbling? I couldn't let her.

I followed, calling her name. Finally grabbing her arm. "Scrimshaw!" I shouted.

She turned, eyes red, a long tear trailing down her cheek.

"Remember? Your grandfather's pipe."

"What?"

"The squiggle of a man. Dread Pirate Roberts. How tough he was."

"That was him. Not me."

"But he's in you. So is your mother. The one who promised good things would come if you were kind."

She sputtered, rubbing her forehead. "Good things," she muttered, like it was a lie, a sales pitch for snake oil. A scam she'd fallen for.

"You were good for me, Heather. More than you realize. Because you helped bring me back to everything I'd let drift out of my reach. My photography. My—my love. Myself. Without you, I'm not sure any of it would have happened. And now, I'm telling you, I'm here for you. The whole night, if you need me. But the thing is, you don't. You've grown so much. Working together down in my darkroom, I've seen it. I know all about how people can grow in basements."

I paused to smile, to wipe her tear.

"You can have this camera," I said, pushing the old dented, banged-in Nikon toward her. "But trust me when I say you don't need it. You're the one who made my camera work.

"I'm no fairy godmother. I can't snap my fingers and make it work out for you. It's in your hands. But I believe you can do this. With my old camera—or any other."

I cursed myself for not being as good with words as Michael. But maybe my words didn't matter. Maybe the most important words were Heather's.

"You made up a wild and lovely story about your grandfather," I shouted at her over the crowd. "But you made up an even

334

crazier story about my camera. Didn't you? All that stuff about the camera kicking your hand and showing you the way. Stories are important. Especially the ones we tell ourselves. So make up a new one about you. A wild legend about how this night will play out. Take a deep breath. And then get out there and make it come true."

My heart felt like it had swelled to the point that there was no longer enough room for it in my chest.

I squeezed the camera tighter. Pushed it a little closer to her. It wasn't so much that I even wanted her to take it. I was trying to edge her closer to a decision.

Just like Michael had done when he'd brought the camera down from the junk closet.

"I have to do it on my own," Heather finally muttered.

"You were, anyway," I told her. "In the park. The camera wasn't talking to you. You were talking to yourself.

"We don't ever think we're enough, do we?" I asked. "We assume we need help. We need magical wands. We need special gadgets. We do that all the time. We believe in forces outside us more than we believe in us. How could that be? We find strength in rabbits' feet and four-leaf clovers, but not ourselves?"

She shook her head in the same way you might when trying to shake off the pain of a finger that had been smashed in the door.

I watched her advance the film in the Nikon she'd shown up with, the replacement Amanda had admitted to switching out—the one that was still, for the most part, an unknown. She raised it to eye-level and began to search the crowd.

Michael slipped into place at my side.

Look, I know back at the beginning of all this, I discounted magic. Called it kid stuff. But right then, with Michael beside me and Heather forcing her way out onto the dance floor, I felt it. That tingle inside that can't be anything else *but* magic.

He squeezed my hand and nodded, knowing exactly what I had on my mind.

I gave him the old camera, the one that had started everything. With my newer DSLR in hand, I forced my way through the crowd and scrambled onto the stage. At the footlights, I had a view of everything, the whole bar. I could see Heather and the circle she was clearing so she could take her pictures. I was struck by how much she reminded me of the dancing woman clearing space for herself all those decades ago.

But I could also see Michael, and Amanda begging her husband to leave, and Fayth and Ryan slipping by Cody the Wolf as he held the entrance open for them. I could see Murio at the bar with his son. The whole big picture, all the moving parts, the past and the present.

I raised my own camera. And sent my flash to wash out across the entire scene.

From the Studio Walls
Hands, Then and Now

It hung in a new frame near the center of the store. Two hands—Sharon's and Michael's—fingers braided together. After a few seconds of staring, you realized you were actually seeing *four* hands—because you were looking at two pictures, one superimposed on the other.

Sharon had used a bit of that modern digital "trickery," as she had once so dismissively called it. The old image of their hands taken just after Sharon and Michael were married remained in its original black and white. The new shot, staged to perfectly mimic the old, had been taken in color—wrinkles, sunspots and all. She'd played with layers, played with levels of transparency. Until she came up with the right mix.

Finally, she'd found it, the image she'd been trying to nail down since hearing her husband's voice, still strong but somehow deeper and perhaps a bit more hesitant than she'd ever heard him,

337

on her favorite jazz station. Here it was: a single shot about nothing more than the simple passage of time.

According to Michael, one of the bests in a long line of career greats.

But no one was coming to stare. Not to the store. Not anymore.

No traffic jams outside.

"Now what?" Sharon asked out loud.

"Didn't you say you'd promised all those folks you caught kissing a print?" Michael asked.

"You think me sending out a few pictures will keep our front door flapping open?"

"All I know is, a promise is a promise," Michael told her. "Envelopes are where they've always been."

So she printed the kiss images, all of them. And she began to mail them out, one by one.

She expected nothing in return.

Until one afternoon a week later, when her door really did open. And the older couple from the square, who had jokingly accused her of being a spy, stepped in. "We've been here before," the wife said, her eyes bouncing across the images on Sharon's walls. "It's been so long. If I'd known it was you..."

The three of them dissolved into surprise and small talk and memories, appreciation for the old images on her walls and for the print she had remembered to send.

When the door opened again, a few days later, it ushered in the two boys from the high school.

Then the 5K runner.

The woman with the Schnauzer.

"Why did you expect anything different?" Heather asked in the basement as they developed her newest batch of shots, interrupt-

338

ing Sharon's uncharacteristically long-winded story of all her studio visitors. "If you're kind to the world, the world is kind back." Once again a firm believer in her mother's proclamation, it seemed.

Sharon had related this story too. Told Michael all about being schooled by the waif who just a short time ago hadn't been able to get so much as a sliver of her act together. She laughed as she spoke. Their apartment was frequently full of laughter now. Full of stories that started always with something like: "You'll never guess what I saw today," or "You'll get a kick out of this..." Even the forks clanking against dinner plates sounded like giggles.

"Kind to the world," Sharon repeated as she placed a serving of Michael's pot roast on her plate. Shaking her head like the idea was oversimplified and naïve. Little more than a superstition. Wishful thinking.

But Michael asked, "Why wouldn't they come by to thank you? Why wouldn't they want to be close to you, Shar? Best place in the world to be."

His words had warmed and encouraged her all at once.

Still. What did it all add up to? A few nice words from her husband. A few pings on her phone. A handful of visits. Was that it? The extent of everything? Or was it a sign? Could it be that the world really did have more for her than a cold shoulder?

She created a social media account and posted the image of her hand and Michael's, then and now.

And slammed her laptop shut, afraid she'd overestimated the photo's importance.

But while she wasn't looking, she got a few likes.

A few more.

A few shares.

A few more.

A kind of digital traffic jam formed—more likes, more

discussions, her name floating to the top like a bubble in a glass of champagne.

The ringing of the studio's phone shocked her.

"Is this Sharon Minyard?" the voice asked. Before she could answer, he continued, "I have a proposal for you. I've been a fan of yours since I was a little boy, and I was so excited to see new work coming from your talented eye. I'm sorry—I'm probably getting a little ahead of myself. I should start with an introduction. My name is Charles Liu."

This Story

This is the story of a man. And a woman.

And a dream.

Not an old dream tucked away on a shelf in a junk closet. Not a dream that has already come true, and is now relegated to being nothing more than a hazy memory.

A new dream.

It intersects with another dream, one that Charles Liu tells this man and this woman about during a meeting at his office in downtown Fairyland. A childhood dream, Charles says, one to make people feel the way his father had once felt looking at Sharon's *Art of the Kiss*. A dream to bring that kind of smile to as many people as possible. He's no artist himself, he insists, but he can be part of it. Provide his business and marketing knowledge. Everything he's learned about print media through advertising campaigns.

A book. That's what he's proposing. Michael's words, Sharon's images.

They could all three enter the publishing world. Hopefully,

this book could be the first of many.

"Just imagine what we can do," Charles exclaims, coming out from behind his desk to shake their hands.

A new goal. A new project. A new dream.

"Quick to press," Liu warns them. "We need to capitalize on some of the attention Sharon's been getting online."

To celebrate, where would they go? Why, Murio's, of course. Sharon and Michael order drinks. They toast their beginning.

They talk—one of those wonderful aimless conversations that meander, going nowhere specific and to the perfect places all at the same time.

On the other side of the bar, Fayth and Ryan are on the stage. The Tommies have become Murio's official house band. This weekly gig has become part of the new pattern in Fayth's and Ryan's lives, their own regular swinging back door, their own rhythmical comings and goings, the days in and out.

They, too, have found their satisfaction. It is the dresser drawer Ryan has in Fayth's place and his own favorite recipe for eggs with salsa on Saturday mornings. It's occasional long drives to the old cemetery, and songwriting sessions, and plans for the fall when Fayth will be back in front of a classroom again.

It doesn't have to mean that they've begun to dig themselves a nice little rut.

It could mean instead that they have discovered their favorite song. It could mean that every single time they bump into the same old melody, playing on the radio, it will be fate all over again. At once welcome and comforting. The opening riff will feel like coming home, whether they've heard it for the hundredth or the thousandth or the ten thousandth time.

Which way it turns out will be entirely up to Ryan and Fayth.

PHOTOGRAPHY FACT

Sharon Minyard's
Portrait Class

2018

Looking at a subject long enough—and deep enough—to take someone's portrait can be uncomfortable. Embarrassing. Especially at first. But in order to push yourself, get the best shots, you'll often wind up in uncomfortable situations. That's just the photographer's life.

You must always get permission from your subject. Sign the right forms, get the right signatures. When you take their picture, highlight their most unique feature, their strongest attributes, just like we've discussed.

Then I want you to get a second permission. One that doesn't require any form. No signature on any dotted line.

Ask them to allow you the pleasure of a story they would like to tell you about themselves. Don't settle for some simple surface anecdote. If they're hesitant, push them. Ask questions. If you tap down deep enough, you'll finally hit the well.

I want you to listen. Look right at them as they tell you the details. Don't interrupt once they get started. Just soak it all in.

Once they're finished, take a second picture. Be sure to take it while their story is still fresh, the words lingering in the air and in your mind.

I used to think people just wanted to be seen. Of course they do. I still think that's true. But as much as they want to be seen, they want to be heard.

So take that second picture. Compare the two. See what difference a single little story can make in your own work.

Excerpt from

Michael Minyard's
introduction to

The Art of the Kiss

A collection of photographs by Sharon Minyard,
printed by Liu Publishing Services

I am an old story man.

I don't care how the story is delivered—told by a friend, written down in a book, acted out on the big screen...

Or captured by a photograph.

I love it all.

I know firsthand there's one thing you can't go without when you're telling a story. It's not a main character or a bad guy. It's not a plot twist or a red herring.

It's a kiss.

I don't just mean the romantic kisses. That's what we auto-matically think of when we see the word, but we express so much with that simple gesture. We kiss inanimate objects (perhaps casino dice) for luck. We kiss crying children to reassure them. We kiss the foreheads of friends we have not seen in years, telling them without a single word, *I have missed you so much.*

Kisses speak. They are in no way one-size-fits-all. They depict all shades of love. Friendship. Or hope. Relief. Some are emotional, others habitual. Some sweet, others sensual. Some are perfunctory. Some are from your Great Aunt Edna, who smells like her three cats and pinches your cheeks before she's done.

Other kisses, though…They rock us to our core.

Cinematic storytellers love to save such soul-rocking kisses for their big finale, orchestra swelling in the background. It's an excla-mation point. Lips meet. Hearts melt. Everything the characters ever wanted is now within their grasp. Love has been found. The dream has been achieved.

Fade to black.

We leave the movie theater smiling, almost feeling in our hearts as though that final kiss, the one that we just saw, is still taking place.

It's as if those kisses never end.

But they do end. In real life, anyway.

With so many different shades and types out there in the world, so many different stories they tell, it's no wonder that my wife, Sharon, would have chosen to study kisses in this latest absorbing compilation of her work.

But to what end? Studying something has to lead to some new insight. Questions must be asked and answered.

So what has Sharon asked? What has she discovered?

Quite simply, she has asked if cinematic-style, soul-rattling kisses—those brief moments of sheer perfection—come just once in a lifetime.

While great storytellers love to use romantic kisses as their finale, in real life, they most often occur at the beginning of our love stories. In fact, the image that opens Sharon's collection (also titled *The Art of the Kiss*) was taken at the beginning of us.

It was our moment. Love has been found! It's all we dreamed it could be!

Sharon and I both know that in the aftermath of a life-changing kiss, we all face the same questions. We wonder: Is that it? Am I left with only the perfunctory? The Aunt Edna-style kisses? Now, am *I* the Aunt Edna, giving those kisses to my unwilling nieces and nephews?

Does a perfect kiss truly only happen once?

Sharon and I have been together—and *The Art of the Kiss* has hung on Sharon's studio walls—for more years than I care to admit. We were half a century removed from our perfect moment when Sharon embarked on her study of kisses. She aimed to capture them all—every one of their shades—in an exploratory way. After all, we don't understand the passionate without having also known the opposite, right? We have to have something to compare it to.

And by studying these kisses, all of them, the familial and the friendly and the superficial, Sharon asks: Is there a path here, in all these kisses? Some way back to the earth-shattering, the momentous, the life-altering?

Ultimately, though, while the photographs in this book took place during Sharon's search, they aren't entirely about us. Nor are they solely about the soldier returning home, or the mother and child at daycare, the teenage couple at the pool, or the older couple pictured on the Fairyland town square. Sharon's images are about you. Whoever you are, holding this book. Quite simply, we often best understand our own stories when we see them reflected in someone else. We get the kind of distance that allows us to see ourselves clearly.

You will see yourself in this book. You will remember your own Aunt Edna. Your first love. Your current love. Your highs. The comfort friends brought during your lows.

When you reach this book's end, you will see another image* that will tell you exactly what Sharon and I both think about whether perfect kisses come around a second time.

Hopefully, it will bring a smile. If, instead, it brings a tear, it is our wish that it is a happy one. That your heart is simply spilling over.

Trust what we have learned: perfect kisses exist. And they don't happen once. Another perfect kiss is waiting for you. It's right there on the opposite side of your own viewfinder, waiting to be developed.

*All images in this book were taken by Sharon Minyard, with the exception of the closing photo of myself and Sharon, titled "Kiss Revisited: 50 Years Gold," provided by Heather Scott, protégé and friend of Sharon Minyard.

Sharon

Heather races to the studio door as I'm locking up for the day.

"Am I too late?" she shouts through the glass.

"Too late for what?" I ask, letting her inside.

"I have another roll to develop," she says, still panting.

My eyes pivot to the shelf where I've placed my old camera—the original Nikon—on display. Heather has her own film cameras, an entire collection of them by now, late in the summer. Purchases funded, for the most part, by freelance work for Liu. "No way could I ever abandon digital completely, but there's something so special about the film cameras," she's been telling me repeatedly. "All the work that goes into getting one image down on paper. I like the slowness of it. It's almost like…" Her voice drifts off at this point, leaving me to fill in the blank. I choose: *It's almost like falling in love.*

Still no mention of her friend Amanda. There hasn't been, not since the night at Murio's. Not even when we'd developed a roll only to find a few shots of her old friend and her family, taken during what

349

appeared to be a backyard cookout. Instead, Heather'd worn a kind of sad faraway look.

Heather and Amanda might be broken beyond repair. I've come into her life, but I'm in no way a perfect replacement. Seems to me that that's how matters of the heart always go. Along with each happiness comes a harsh twist.

"Sorry, I was thinking you still had another class—"

"Not tonight," I say. The only night of the week I don't.

Traffic's coming back. Not like it had, not exactly, back when the store was new. A different kind of traffic now. A different sort of interest. Maybe even a different kind of respect.

But my name isn't the only one circulating through Fairyland. So is Heather's. Everyone agrees with me that no one's ever had timing like hers—an ability to snap photos at the perfect moment, whether that moment takes place during a small-town high school ball game, or as a flock of birds launch into flight, or when a smile just begins to form. She's getting work. Good work. The kind of work that generally leads to bigger and better jobs.

The kind of work that means she's also packing up the contents of her apartment. Getting ready for a big move.

The Creature would soon belong to someone else.

"I, ah," Heather shrugs. "I took some pictures of Darth Billy," she admits. "Figured his mom would like them. Kind of a parting gift, I guess."

I nod, attempting to fend off a knowing smile. "If you'd like to use the darkroom, you're more than welcome."

Which reminds me I have something to give her. I've just reached into the cash register when she asks, "Sharon?"

I turn to find that she's leaning against the front counter, eyes swollen with hope, face flushed slightly like she knows what she's about to ask might sound foolish. "Would you sit for me?"

350

I laugh. Some old lady. And it's not like she hasn't taken a picture of me already. But I understand what she's asking. She wants me to sit by myself. She wants me to know how she sees me. The woman who finally helped get her career off the ground. That single picture of hers in my *Art of the Kiss* collection is a big part of the reason her own phone is ringing.

"Only if you'll sit for me," I say. I have a few things to show her too. The girl who helped me find my own revival of sorts. The girl who was brave enough to insist that the photo I took of Fayth and Ryan made it into our book.

As far as I'm concerned, that took far more guts than any Cinderella-style waif has ever known.

"You'll have to do it fast," I warn, wagging my thumb over my shoulder, toward a travel trailer parked at the curb.

Heather realizes I'm telling her it belongs to me and Michael. "You guys are leaving?" she asks, worry splashing across her face.

"In spurts. Nothing permanent. I've got the new classes starting up at the shop, and Michael—well, he's got plenty he's working on. Mostly day trips, the occasional week, maybe. We're starting another book."

"What's the focus this time?"

"Rust."

Heather cocks her head slightly, her own laughter threatening to spill. Before she can ask if I'm teasing, I explain, "All kinds of rust. Most would probably say aging's a sort of rust. Taking time away from an activity can make you rusty. Or things rust when there's too much exposure to the elements. I figure we'll take portraits, landscapes, whatever strikes us. And for every single picture, Michael will include some sort of written passage. A character sketch. A story, a poem. But between my photos and his words, we'll get—"

"—the full picture," we both say in unison. And nod like we

do sometimes when we find ourselves using the exact same phrase.

"We'll be coming back between the individual trips," I assure Heather. "And for when we're gone…" I reach back into the register for the extra set of keys I'd had made.

She perks, relieved and happy, as she catches them. Gives me a quick half-shy kiss on the cheek.

The thing is, I know a lot of people would look at Heather's story and say, "Well, she didn't get her happy ending, did she?"

I say they haven't been paying attention.

All you have to see to know it's her happy ending is the way she lunges for the stairs. The way it all fuels her, thrills her—the dilated eyes, the flush on the cheeks. Work is love. When you're not punching a time clock. When it's work of the soul. It's love.

The rest of it? The romantic love? The right person comes along when you've made room alongside your dream. I believe that, every bit as fanatically as Michael.

Dreams come true.

Before I reach for the door, I let my eyes bounce across some of my newer work. Frames that have landed on the wall near the center of the shop. I do love the picture of my hands and Michael's, but I have so much left to say about where I'm going.

The future is a picture I haven't taken yet.

Which is why I left a giant space in the center of the studio wall. I'll hang it once I've snapped it.

In the meantime, it feels good to have a masterpiece to chase.

Michael

I see her coming up the sidewalk toward the radio station as soon as I settle into the DJ's chair. Here I am, ready to begin what has grown into a weekly show—all because of Fairyland listeners.

And there she is. Sharon. My partner. Who'd insisted Liu was right; I needed to write the introduction to her new photography book—her collection of kisses.

I'd loved banging that intro out on the keyboard. Loved that she'd enjoyed what I'd written even more.

I love, too, that we've bought a trailer—because there are stories out there beyond the city limits of Fairyland. Stories that need to be captured in both words and images.

I love that we've discovered a new life. And that this new life includes the best of the old times—playing off of each other, working together. Most of all, I love that we've rediscovered the magic we were afraid we'd lost.

In our story, the old camera was, of course, a metaphor. A symbol of the once-in-a-lifetime, magical love we had. But that's not some storytelling trick. In real life, we attach special meaning to so many things that surround us. An object is never *really* just an object. It's sentimental. Or it's a hindrance. Might be a reminder. A good luck charm.

Sharon and I told you the camera's story, going back and forth, as the two of us went about rediscovering the magic that was missing. Who was at fault? Who was to blame? We had once felt real, palpable *magic*—and what were we supposed to do when we didn't anymore?

Where had it gone? How did we get it back?

We all have our own brand of magic to try and keep alive, don't we? Even our no-longer-waif, Heather, who is becoming a better and better friend to Sharon as the days go by. Heather, who's realizing that she has to stand on her own two feet. No secret shortcuts to achieving anyone's dream. For her, Sharon's camera is also a metaphor. No one can simply give you tools that instantly make your dreams come true—not like Cinderella's fairy godmother.

But maybe (oh, I'm an old fairy tale man—I love this possibility) we do leave a little dust of ourselves behind. Maybe when someone like Heather comes along, there really is a piece of you left to guide the new girl. Maybe pieces of our dreams, Sharon's and mine, were still inside that camera. Maybe those dreams steered Heather toward her own.

I touched magic once, I imagine Heather often tells herself, thinking of the first images she created with Sharon's old Nikon. *Will I touch it again?*

Isn't that what everyone wants—to simply touch magic? Doesn't magic mean something different to everyone?

Sharon—and our past—certainly made a magical mark on me. A permanent one. A tattoo, but of emotion rather than ink.

I ramble. I'm an old man. That's what we do.

"Okay, Mr. Celebrity," Tony tells me. "I'm getting ready to

cue you up. You want me to tell everyone who you really are now?"

He's been asking me this every single time I show up at the station for another edition of my fairy tale vignettes.

"Not yet," I say, like always. If no one knows who I am, if I stay some shadowy mystery, isn't it easier to write to me? Don't they tell me more? I'd never keep this town from sharing their stories with me.

Tony follows my gaze outside, where Sharon's standing. He smiles and slaps my shoulder. "All right," he says. "Up to you."

Outside, on the sidewalk, Sharon raises her camera.

She takes my picture. Already, I know it will be a masterpiece.

But then again, as far as I'm concerned, they all are.

On Air

*H*appily ever after, dear listeners.

That's the question that comes to us this morning, courtesy of one Ms. Maryanne Whitaker, a fellow Fairyland resident. Do I believe, she asks, in happily ever afters?

What a lovely phrase. Doesn't it make you fill your lungs with a clean burst of air, then sigh with complete and utter satisfaction?

Your goal has been met, the beautiful princess rescued (if she so desired rescuing), all obstacles thwarted.

Love has won out in the end.

Isn't that what we really mean by this statement? *Happily ever after.* In the end, love has won.

We need to believe in that three-word phrase.

Better still: We *should* believe.

Why? Because if it's what we believe, don't we behave differently? Don't we lead with kindness and affection and good intentions? And in the end, isn't that what really makes our world a beautiful place?

356

Come to think of it, Maryanne, I don't think we can ever truly say that a story comes to an end with a happily ever after. After all, the characters do continue on their journey once the curtain falls. Fairy tales don't reward the main characters by killing them off.

Of course not. The tales send them off into the sunset. It's implied that their stories continued out of our sight, and the rest of their days were lived in glorious satisfaction.

But the thing is, the farther you get from a happily ever after, the more of a speck it becomes in your rearview mirror. The less it feels like a happy ending. It feels, instead, like a chapter square in the middle of a story. A momentary glimpse at perfection. A sample of what happiness tastes like…

Because the world isn't constant or predictable. Nor are the lives of those who inhabit it. Life throws one road block after another at us, even if the ring is on your finger and you've ridden your white horse straight into the bright red horizon, music soaring.

Sure, you can complain. You can rail against it, stomp your feet and insist the world is mucking up your satisfying ending.

But do you think the world actually cares?

You get the answer to that question when the world throws the next round of mud in your face. When you are forced to embark on a quest to restore that happily ever after of yours. Oh, I know. "Quest" is such a funny word. It's not the language of happiness. It's the language of struggle. Of fighting. Doing battle. It brings to mind the image of a medieval army in protective chain mail. Swords and armor blazing. But when the world does throw mud at us, don't we have to fight? For ourselves? Our love?

The world is not intrinsically beautiful. Our belief that the world *can* be beautiful makes it so. We insist mudslinging can't be the final word. We right the wrongs the world wants to dole out.

Yes, we make it beautiful.

Here's another thing I truly believe: the fictional law of there being a single happily ever after needs to stay between pages filled with Prince Charmings, princesses, and fairy godmothers.

Nobody really wants decades of a life that's nothing more than a beach chair and a bottomless margarita glass.

That would be boring. Overexposure can be the death of affection. Having nothing to eat but your favorite ice cream flavor begins to make you tongue burn, after a while.

I suppose, then, by ensuring that happy endings don't last forever, the world might actually be doing us a favor.

Oh, we love the idea of fairy godmothers and help arriving out of nowhere. I think, really, that's what we like more than anything about the tale of Cinderella. We like the idea of the universe coming to our aid simply because we are good. We have pure hearts and deserve rescue.

We know that for the most part, that kind of help never happens. Not unless we are out there interacting with the world. Not unless we make it happen. Wishes aren't exactly granted to us because we're sitting on the couch whimpering, right? We have to move beyond our front doors.

So maybe, just maybe, the world is acting as our fairy godmother by *not* allowing us to live out the remainder of our days floating along in a giant pool of bliss. Maybe the true happily ever after means being given the chance to make it across a race's finish line again and again. Reliving the thrill of success.

Send me your thoughts about this. I always love to hear from you. And thanks, Maryanne, for your thought-provoking question.

For now, dear listeners, in the spirit of this very broadcast, this is the old storyteller bidding you not goodbye, but *once upon a time...*

If you enjoyed
The Art of the Kiss,
you'll love
Miles Left Yet

It's Never the End of the Road

None of them really expected to wind up at the Granite Ridge Retirement Community for Active Seniors. And yet, here they are—Jim arriving after his wife's unexpected passing, Norma after selling her home to rescue her financially strapped daughter, and Mildred after her lifelong neighborhood becomes overrun by crime. It's an odd place to be, for sure—put out to pasture, some might phrase it. At the end of life's road.

And yet, inside, they all still feel as young as ever.

When a figure from Mildred's past emerges, a motley crew from the retirement community embarks on a road trip—in a vintage Mustang convertible, no less—which quickly turns into an adventure of second chances, fresh starts, and the discovery that love is never a landmark in the rearview mirror. No matter what the odometer reads, as long as there's gas in the tank, there are always still new roads to explore...plenty of miles left yet.

Check HollySchindler.com for availability.

Holly Schindler is a multi-award-winning and critically acclaimed author of books for readers of all ages. She holds a master's degree in English (creative emphasis), and has taught writing courses at the collegiate level. Schindler has also mentored extensively: honing students' creative and scholastic writing, and providing developmental edits to both published and unpublished writers for novels in a variety of genres. A firm believer that reading is as creative an activity as writing, she has worked one-on-one with students in grades K-12 to improve overall literacy skills.

Schindler insists that nothing is quite as magical as a good story or an exciting new "what-if." She is currently chasing down her next "what-if" as she writes her next book. She also loves hearing from her readers. If you'd like to get in touch or subscribe to her newsletters, please visit her online at:

HollySchindler.com

www.ingramcontent.com/pod-product-compliance
Lightning Source LLC
Chambersburg PA
CBHW021027120726
47905CB00009B/3221